'Emery!'

Her name was uttered with such anguish that it took her a moment to recognise the speaker as Lord de Burgh.

Emery's eyes flew open, relief swamping her at the knowledge that he had returned unharmed. For once she looked eagerly to his face, welcoming his gaze. But his dark head was bent over her body, and just as Emery would have spoken he put his hands upon her.

Stunned, Emery could do nothing except lie prone as she felt him check for injuries. Although she had performed the same service for Gerard, this man was not her brother. And the feel of his warm hands as they ran up and down her legs, gently probing for breaks, made Emery forget her aches and pains and all else.

Closing her eyes, she groaned as warmth filled her, along with a strange sort of yearning. Had she struck her head? That would account for her sudden inability to think clearly. Or was she dreaming? She knew only that she wanted him to continue, even though her very identity hung in the balance.

THE LAST DE BURGH

Deborah Simmons

MILLS & BOON

First published in Great Britain 2013
by Mills & Boon, an imprint of Harlequin (UK) Limited.
Harlequin (UK) Limited, Eton House, 18-24 Paradise Road,
Richmond, Surrey TW9 1SR

ISBN: 978 0 263 89808 8

Harlequin (UK) policy is to use papers that are natural, renewable and recyclable products and made from wood grown in sustainable forests. The logging and manufacturing process conform to the legal environmental regulations of the country of origin.

Printed and bound in Spain
by Blackprint CPI, Barcelona

A former journalist, **Deborah Simmons** turned to fiction after a love of historical romances spurred her to write her own, HEART'S MASQUERADE, which was published in 1989. She has since written more than twenty-five novels and novellas, among them a *USA TODAY* bestselling anthology and two finalists in the Romance Writers of America's annual RITA® competition. Her books have been published in 26 countries, including illustrated editions in Japan, and she's grateful for the support of her readers throughout the world.

Previous novels from this author:

THE DARK VISCOUNT
GLORY AND THE RAKE
REYNOLD DE BURGH: THE DARK KNIGHT
THE GENTLEMAN'S QUEST

**Did you know that some of these novels
are also available as eBooks?
Visit www.millsandboon.co.uk**

This book is dedicated to all the readers
who have come to love the de Burghs as much as I do,
to those who have waited patiently for more than
fifteen years after the publication of *Taming the Wolf* until
this final book in the series. Thank you for your letters
and e-mails and support, but most of all, thank you for
taking this journey with me, to Campion and back again.

Chapter One

Nicholas de Burgh kept one hand on the hilt of his sword and a wary eye on the company around him. He had been in worse places, but not many, and this inn might give even his brothers pause. Although the de Burghs were fearless, they weren't stupid, and Nicholas blamed a bout of recklessness for his presence here.

The stench of drink and vomit filled his nostrils, for these lodgings made no claim to cleanliness, a fact that seemed lost on the others who gathered in the dim common room. Indeed, those around him had the hardened air of men likely to do murder for a handful of coins.

Except for one.

It was the sight of that singular fellow that

caused Nicholas to linger. Barely more than a boy, the stranger wore the distinctive robe of the Hospitallers and probably had returned from a stint of fighting in the Holy Land. Although a knight, his limp and seeming lack of a squire made him vulnerable to the thieves, whores and gamblers who frequented these places.

The boy's eyes were bright with either too much wine or some kind of fever, which might account for his lack of judgement. Or maybe he was so glad to be back in England that he forgot there were plenty of dangers right here at home.

Whatever the reason, he appeared oblivious to the threats around him and Nicholas was determined to warn him. But as Nicholas stepped forwards, a Templar pushed ahead to capture the lad's attention. Although there were rumours of feuding between the military orders, these two were soon deep in conversation, leaving Nicholas free to go. Yet there was something about the Templar that made him hesitate…

Nicholas surged to his feet as the inevitable fight broke out beside him. Ducking when a cup of wine sailed by his head, he dodged the dark liquid that splattered against the wall and kept to the perimeter while making his way through the growing mêlée. When a bench overturned in his path with a loud thud, he leapt over it, avoiding a candle that fell to the floor with a hiss, its light extinguished.

Reaching the door, Nicholas turned to scan the room, but he could not find the Hospitaller or the Templar, even lying amongst the filthy rushes. There was no sign of the knights outside, either, but Nicholas did not remain, for he was eager to put some distance between himself and the inn before the brawlers spilled out.

Keeping an eye on the entrance, he took to the road, but he had only gone a short way before a figure emerged from the shadows to veer into his path. The slight young man would prove little threat to an armed knight and Nicholas did not halt, but fell into step beside him. 'Keeping watch, Guy?'

'I told you those lodgings stank of trouble,' his squire said.

'Which is why I quit the place,' Nicholas answered smoothly. 'Despite what you might think, I still value my neck.'

Guy shot him a chary glance and Nicholas held up a hand to forestall any further discussion. His squire frowned, but said nothing, and in the ensuing silence, a noise erupted nearby, too close to be the echoes from the inn. Halting his steps, Nicholas inclined his head towards a narrow lane, piled with refuse.

Ignoring Guy's protest, Nicholas crept forwards and heard the unmistakable sound of a fist connecting with flesh and bone. Inching around the corner of an abandoned cot, he peered into the darkness and saw the white robe of the Templar visible ahead. By the man's stance, Nicholas would guess he had someone by the throat, presumably the Hospitaller he had befriended earlier.

'Where is it?' demanded the Templar, if that's what he was. Although the order of the Poor Knights of the Temple of Solomon was not what it once had been, surely its members were not practising petty thievery. But whoever or whatever he might be, Nicholas had no intention of standing by while he assaulted a seemingly innocent fellow knight.

'Hold,' Nicholas called, drawing his sword. But the knave only thrust the Hospitaller towards him, forcing Nicholas to grab at the stumbling form or let the young man fall.

'Danger,' he whispered. 'Must help…Emery.'

Muttering an assurance, Nicholas shifted the injured man to Guy, so he could give chase. But the lane was so narrow and dark that he could not move quickly and soon he was faced with a stone wall. Since the Templar must have come this way, as well, Nicholas sheathed his sword and started climbing, hoping that an open drain or worse did not lie on the other side.

Although he could see little from the top, the drop was not a long one and Nicholas managed to land on his feet. But the Templar was waiting in the shadows, sword in hand. Dancing away from the blade, Nicholas narrowly avoided its bite while drawing his own weapon. Although the sound of metal upon metal rang out in the stillness, it did not rouse an audience. The area seemed deserted, and who would dare interfere with two knights? For whether a Templar or not, the man Nicholas was fighting was well trained.

'Who are you?' the Templar demanded, echoing Nicholas's thoughts.

'A knight who takes his oath seriously,' Nicholas answered. 'And where lies your allegiance, *brother*?'

The Templar laughed, as though amused or even relieved by Nicholas's outrage. 'No concern of yours, stranger,' the Templar said. 'You'd do better to mind your own business— and your back.'

The taunt had barely left the man's lips when Nicholas felt a blow. If he'd been himself, he might have heard the approach of another, even above the clang of the swords, or guessed that the knave spoke to distract him. In years past, he would never have been so easily ambushed, Nicholas thought, before falling to the ground.

Emery Montbard jerked awake, her heart pounding, and wondered what had roused her from sleep. She glanced around her small dwelling and saw nothing amiss in the darkness. And yet something had disturbed her slumber, so she lay still, alert to the slightest sound. And then she heard it: a thump outside, as though something was in her garden and no small animal, either. Had a cow wandered in to trample her neat rows?

Emery rose and hurried to the narrow window, ready to shout at the creature, only to swallow her cry. For it was no four-legged beast that lurched towards her shelter, but the hulking form of a man. The nearby Hospitaller commandery, an unwanted presence that loomed so large over her life now seemed too far away, should she need to summon aid.

Perhaps one of the workers there or even one of the brethren had helped himself to the wine and gone astray. Emery hesitated to believe that the intrusion was deliberate, but there was always the possibility that a stranger had learned of her solitary existence here. Just as the thought sent a chill running through her and she began to wonder how to defend herself, the man lifted his face, moonlight revealing features well known and beloved.

'Gerard!' Emery uttered her brother's name in astonishment. Although he did not answer and seemed unaware of her hail, Emery hesitated to call out. Instead, she rushed to the door and threw it open, only to find that he had collapsed upon the ground. Alarmed, Emery dropped down beside him.

'What is it? Are you hurt?' His lashes fluttered open and closed again, as though in confirmation. And though loath to leave him, Emery knew he would be better served by his order.

'Don't move. I will summon the brothers,' she said, but when she would have risen, his hand closed over her wrist with surprising strength.

'No,' Gerard muttered. 'Beware, Em. I've put you in danger. Trust…no one.'

'But you need help.'

At her protest, his grip grew tighter. 'Promise me,' he whispered. His eyes were bright even in the darkness, but was it intensity or fever that burned in them?

When Emery nodded her agreement, his hand dropped away and his eyes closed, his strength seemingly expended on his speech. *Trust no one.* The warning hung in the air, making the ensuing silence eerie, and suddenly the familiar landscape of the night took on an eerie cast, as though the shadows under the trees hid unknown threats.

A stray breeze fluttered the leaves above, and Emery held her breath, listening hard for the sound of pursuit—a soft footfall or the thud of a horse's hoof against the earth—but all she heard was the wind and the pounding of her own heart.

And if something was out there, watching in the darkness, there was little she could do from where she crouched by her brother, unprotected. The thought finally roused her to action, and Emery rose to her feet, dragging Gerard with her to the relative safety of her small dwelling.

Once inside, she barred the door and turned her attention back to her brother. Stoking the fire, she put some water on to heat and studied him by the light of the flames. He was bruised about the throat and face, including a cut lip, but the wound she found upon his thigh was most worrisome. 'Twas a gash that had not healed properly and she hurried to tend it. Was this what had brought him back from the Holy Land?

Having received no word from her brother for nearly a year, Emery had feared the worst. Yet her relief at seeing him was tempered by the circumstances of his appearance. Had he returned home without leave? Emery frowned, for those who disobeyed their superiors faced expulsion or even excommunication from the church itself.

But what else would cause him to shun the help of his fellow Hospitallers? Shaking her head, Emery told herself that Gerard might not be aware of what he was saying. Her first task was to heal him, so she cleaned out the gash, then brewed a tisane that settled him into a fitful sleep. Weary herself, Emery leaned against the side of her narrow bed, resting her head upon her brother's arm.

The warmth of the contact, after she had been isolated for so long, was comforting, but soon Gerard jerked against her cheek, crying out. Although Emery leaned close, she could make little sense of what he said except the words 'Saracen' and 'Templar', which were spoken in such dire tones that she looked over her shoulder, half-expecting to see another's presence.

When Gerard grew silent once more, Emery was relieved, but the bouts of muttering continued, including oft-repeated alarms about the Templar and the Saracen. Once he seemed to be lucid and awake, rousing Emery from her doze with his urgency. 'The parcel I sent you, where is it?' he asked, gripping her arm.

'Parcel? I know of no parcel,' Emery said.

Gerard released her with a groan. 'We are lost,' he whispered, turning his face away.

'Why? What has happened?' Emery asked.

But her brother closed his eyes again, and Emery wondered whether he was aware of his own speech. She worried that he needed the more skilled care of the brothers at the commandery, even though it was not a hospital. But his warning rang in her ears, and, selfishly, she was not ready to hand her sibling over to brethren who might remove him from her reach.

She'd wait until morn, and then see...

Emery came awake slowly, blinking in bafflement at her surroundings before she realised that she was lying on the floor. Had she fallen in her sleep? The question had barely flitted through her mind when the memory of the night's events came rushing back. She jerked upright to look at the bed, but it was empty, and she glanced about with uncertainty. Had it all been a dream? Her heart clenched at the thought that she had imagined her brother's appearance.

Maybe he had stepped outside, Emery thought, rising to her feet. But as she scanned the small area, she could find no signs of Gerard having been there at all. The cloth she had used to wash his wounds was gone, and the bowl that had held the water lay empty, as did the cup. Although the pot in which she had brewed the tisane hung over the dying fire, no herbs remained.

How could she have visualised his visit so

vividly? Emery raised her hands to her face in confusion, only to lower them again as something caught her eye. 'Twas a small detail, but one that could not be done away with while she slept. Under her fingernails lay proof of her brother's appearance, for they were stained with his blood.

But why would Gerard go to so much trouble to eliminate all evidence of his presence? For one startling moment, Emery wondered if unseen foes had carried him off, but she shook her head in denial. Surely no intruders could have entered without her knowledge. Her brother must have left on his own, without even a goodbye after they had been parted for so long. But why?

Trust no one.

Gerard's words came to mind abruptly, along with the cryptic warnings he had issued during the hours he had lain abed. But Emery had thought her brother raving, perhaps with some fever, which made his disappearance all the more alarming. The thought roused her to action and she went to the door, hoping to find him outside. But the pale light of the coming dawn revealed nothing and the small grove was silent except for the calls of birds.

What was she to do? Emery hesitated, leery of leaving the relative safety of her dwelling, yet Gerard might still be close by, too ill to travel, chased by demons of his own making. Or, worse, he could be fleeing some real threat. Emery shivered. Either way, it would be better for her brother if she found him, so she hurried back inside to dress properly.

Reaching for her plain kirtle, Emery once again glanced at the bed, only to spy something lying there, amongst the covers. Stretching out her hand, Emery fingered what looked to be a heavy piece of parchment, but 'twas like nothing she had ever seen before.

It was long—half a foot, she guessed—yet narrow, and was completely covered by a brightly coloured drawing such as those seen in manuscripts. In fact, at first she thought that it must have been cut from a book, yet the edges bore no trace of such abuse.

Eyeing the illustration itself, Emery realised that the pretty pattern surrounded a central figure that appeared to be a large black snake, curving ominously. Or was it a sword? Emery shivered at the vaguely threatening image. Had the object fallen from Gerard's things, or had he left it there deliberately as some kind of message?

She studied it more carefully, looking for anything else that might be hidden amongst the depictions of flowers and leaves, and soon she found it. A phrase had been written beneath the snake that anyone else might think the part of the illustration, but Emery knew her brother's hand and the words chilled her.

Trust no one.

Whether in his right mind or not, Gerard was in trouble and Emery sank down upon the bed, her hand shaking. Her first thought was to go to the Hospitallers, for they should take care of their own, but she could not ignore the warning held in her trembling fingers.

Who else could she turn to? She and Gerard had no relatives except their uncle and he could not be trusted to put the family's interest before his own. Who, then? Who had the wherewithal to stand against unknown enemies that might include the ecclesiastical authorities? Precious few in all of England, Emery thought, her heart sinking.

She could think of no one and Gerard's flight suggested that he intended she do—and say— nothing. But she could not ignore her brother's appearance and disappearance, especially when he was ill and in trouble. Emery shook her head, as if to deny the truth, yet she could come to no other conclusion.

She was the only person who could help him.

There was once a time when she would not have hesitated. Years ago, she had longed for adventure and excitement and thought herself well equipped to meet it, her twin's equal in nearly all respects. But experience had taught her otherwise and now she tried only to accept her lot, her dreams of another life long buried.

Yet, this was different. It was one thing to abandon her own hopes and quite another to leave Gerard to the mercy of whatever plagued him, real or imagined. He was alone and injured, and he needed her. Emery could not turn her back upon the only person she cared about in the world.

But she dared not leave this place. Both fear and loyalties warred within her until she was jolted from her thoughts by a noise outside. Visitors to this remote location were few, especially at such an early hour, so it was only natural to assume that Gerard had returned. But when Emery hurried to the window, it was not her brother she saw. The lone rider approaching the commandery wore the distinctive white robe of the Templars.

Emery shrank away from the window, her heart in her throat. The appearance of such a knight so soon after Gerard's warnings could be no coincidence and it forced her to act. Dropping to her knees, she pried at the loose tile in the floor until it came away, exposing a hole dug into the dirt. From it Emery removed the satchel she had managed to bury when she first took up residence here nearly a year ago.

Amongst the contents were some of her brother's former clothes, left over from the days when she used to switch places with her twin. It had been some time since she had last worn them, but she was relieved to find that they still fit. In their place, she put whatever food she could carry, her small store of herbs and the piece of parchment, lest it be found by others.

Had her brother left on foot? Emery thought longingly of the palfrey that had once belonged to her, but she could not appear at the stables in her boy's garb or take her old mount. She would have to look for Gerard by herself and swallowed against the apprehension that threatened to stay her. Instead, she forced herself to keep moving, tossing the satchel over her shoulder and throwing open the door.

In her haste, Emery had abandoned all caution, a mistake she realised only when she saw that she was not alone. Standing before her was a man and he was not Gerard. Neither was he the Templar she had seen on horseback, but he might well be a companion to the knight intent upon searching outlying buildings.

Emery took a step back, away from the figure who towered over her. Indeed, he was taller than anyone she'd ever seen, a good foot above Gerard, with wide shoulders and muscular arms that were hardly surprising, considering the short mail coat he wore and the heavy sword at his side. Obviously, he was a knight, though without the fierce visage of some.

While most certainly dangerous, he did not appear threatening. His nut-brown hair was thick and a bit shaggy, framing a face kissed by the sun. Emery would not call him beautiful, for his was not a feminine aspect, yet he was striking with eyes the colour of his hair, warm and compelling, and his gleaming white teeth…

Emery realised he was smiling at the same moment she caught herself staring. Drawing a shaky breath, she cleared her throat and managed to squeak out a question. 'What do you here?'

'I am Nicholas de Burgh,' he said, inclining his head. 'I am foresworn to help a Hospitaller knight I met upon the road and would make certain that he arrived safely. Would you happen to be Emery, young man?'

It took Emery a moment to understand that this knight thought her a youth—*a male youth*—and another moment for her to recognise the significance of his name. The de Burghs were a powerful family, known for their good looks as well as their fighting skills. If this one's visage was any indication, the rumours were true, but more important to Emery than a handsome face was the family's reputation for honour.

While knights were bound to protect the weak and defenceless, to honour women and to provide aid to those in need, not all held to those vows. But a de Burgh... Everything about this man, from his clothing to his bearing, bespoke wealth, power and privilege such as Emery had never known. Hadn't she just wished for a saviour with the might to stand up to anyone? Surely Nicholas de Burgh was one of those few. But what were the chances of such a famous personage suddenly appearing at her door?

Trust no one, Gerard had said. Gazing up at the great knight, Emery wondered whether her brother's warning included this man, who appeared both kind and trustworthy. But, then, so seemingly would a Templar or the Hospitaller brethren, all sworn to serve God, yet Gerard had cautioned against them.

Emery blinked, uncertain, and she might have remained so indefinitely if not for the arrival of another, a young man who stepped out of the trees to give her a jaundiced look. 'See here, you. My lord de Burgh was injured fighting a Templar who attacked this Hospitaller and you would do well to give him the courtesy of a reply. Are you Emery, or not?'

Emery blanched. The Templar! He would soon make his way to this place, whether directed so by the brethren at the commandery or not. And though Gerard hadn't spoken of a de Burgh, he had warned about the Templar. Emery swallowed hard.

'Yes, I am Emery. And Gerard was here, injured, but he was gone when I awoke,' she said. 'I was just going to search for him.'

'On foot?' the young man asked, his scepticism obvious.

'He's my brother,' Emery answered.

While the young man continued to eye her suspiciously, Nicholas de Burgh nodded his approval of her statement and Emery felt a sudden kinship with the great knight. Uncomfortable, she glanced away, for she had nothing in common with such an exalted personage. Yet she would rather trust him than the Templar and she had little chance of helping Gerard on her own.

Emery cleared her throat. 'Will you help me find him, my lord?' She held her breath as she waited for the man's answer, an eagerness that had nothing to do with Gerard seizing hold of her.

'You may ride with my squire, Guy,' he said and Emery loosed a low sigh of relief. Although Guy muttered a protest, after a quelling glance from his master he motioned for her to join him.

However, when Emery swung up behind the squire, she realised the problems inherent in joining the two males. Years ago when she had accompanied Gerard, he had been well aware of her disguise. Now she would be forced to hide the truth or forgo her place, for no man would condone such behaviour from a grown woman.

Despite these concerns, Emery felt her earlier fear and dread slip away, replaced by a certain anticipation. Uncomfortable once more, she reminded herself of Gerard's warning and resolved to trust no one, no matter how handsome and powerful. Yet, as Guy swung round towards the knight's great destrier, Emery had the strange sensation that she would follow Nicholas de Burgh to the ends of the earth.

If only she could.

Chapter Two

Nicholas gazed out over the endless moor and swore to himself. The few paths that cut through the heather were barely discernible and seemed to lead nowhere, twisting back upon themselves, while carpets of green moss disguised treacherous bogs. The bleak landscape was a far cry from the gentle hills around Campion, and Nicholas felt a sudden longing for his home. Would he ever see those golden towers again?

The thought made him glance towards Guy, who made no secret of his wish to return. Their simple journey had turned into something else entirely, and Nicholas felt a stab of guilt for keeping the boy away for so long. But he told himself that sooner or later Guy would go home—with or without his master.

Nicholas looked away, unwilling to meet his squire's gaze. Guy had been reluctant to take up the Hospitaller's cause, claiming that whatever happened between two strange knights was no one's business. But Nicholas was eager for the task, for it was an improvement over his recent recklessness. *Aimless* recklessness.

Even Nicholas had to admit to that truth. Their current search gave him a purpose which he sorely needed. And if he would like to prove himself after being bested by the Templar last night, who could blame him? Perhaps he could even banish the doubts that had assailed him these past months. But that possibility seemed slim now that he had lost Gerard's trail.

Scowling at the empty moor, Nicholas wondered where to look. Loath to disappoint the Hospitaller's brother, he glanced at the boy, only to find Emery's gaze upon him, startling in its intensity. The boy's eyes were blue and Nicholas felt an odd catch in his chest at their brightness. The sensation made him glance away, as though he had been caught ogling another man's wife, and he saw his squire's curious expression. Annoyed, Nicholas drew to a halt and dismounted, leading his horse to a narrow stream, but Guy, who soon joined him, was not fooled.

'What is it, my lord? Have you lost the trail?'

Nicholas frowned. Once he would never have heard such a question, couched in tones of concern, from anyone, let alone his squire. But that was when everything had come easily to him and he took for granted the skills and privileges that he'd always possessed.

Things were different now.

Nodding, Nicholas scanned the area once more, as though he might spy something previously missed. But he saw nothing and his gaze returned once more to Emery, who was stroking the neck of Guy's horse. For a long moment, Nicholas stared, transfixed by the gesture, before turning away to meet his squire's inquisitive look. 'Perhaps the boy can help,' Nicholas said.

Guy snorted. 'I think Emery is slow-witted, my lord. What's more, I'm fairly certain—'

Nicholas held up a hand to stop his squire's speech, having no patience for any further arguments. He had promised Emery's brother aid, and he intended to honour his word, no matter what Guy might prefer.

His squire sputtered, but Nicholas paid him no heed and motioned for Emery to come closer. He hoped that Guy was wrong about the boy's mental state. If the brother, Gerard, had left him near the Hospitaller commandery because he needed guidance, they had done ill by bringing him along.

'Do you know this country, Emery?' Nicholas asked, as gently as he could.

'A little, my lord,' the boy said, ducking as if afraid to meet Nicholas's gaze. He was a handsome youth, quite striking really, with long lashes that hid those startling eyes...

Nicholas drew in a sharp breath. 'Do you have any idea where your brother might have gone?'

The boy shook his head. He wore a snug-fitting hat that made it difficult to tell the colour of his hair, but his brows were nearly black and finely arched.

Nicholas glanced away, oddly uncomfortable. 'Where do these paths lead?'

'The moor is home to little except religious houses, the Hospitaller commandery, the Templar preceptory and—'

'The Templars? Where?' Nicholas asked. When Emery pointed towards a rise, Nicholas turned to Guy. 'Perhaps we should enquire about our blackguard there.'

Guy's frown made Nicholas swing back towards Emery. 'Do you know of any such knight who would have a dispute with your brother?'

Emery shook his head, then spoke haltingly. 'But last night Gerard warned me against a Templar, among others. I thought his ravings the product of fever until this morning, when a knight of the cross rode up to Clerkwell, the Hospitaller commandery that I...that is nearby.'

'This morning? You saw a Templar and said nothing?' Nicholas spoke more sharply than he intended, making Emery flinch. Immediately, Nicholas softened his expression, for the youth was just a stripling, slender and smooth-skinned. And he could not have known how eager Nicholas was to meet last night's foe.

'I was afraid and thought only of escaping, lest the Templar find me, my lord,' Emery said and Nicholas felt churlish.

He eyed the boy thoughtfully. 'You said the Templar went to the commandery, but if he was following your brother, he would have gone directly to your home. Perhaps the Templar simply went to the nearest Hospitaller commandery, hoping to find Gerard there.'

'Wouldn't these knights belong to the same house?' Guy asked, sounding confused.

'No,' Nicholas said. 'They are members of different religious orders, though, unlike most, both are military orders.'

When Guy blinked, Emery spoke. 'The Order of the Hospital of Saint John of Jerusalem was founded to provide medical care for pilgrims to the Holy Land, while the Poor Knights of the Temple of Solomon were founded to protect the pilgrims travelling there,' he said. 'The Hospitallers later became a military order, as well, so now both fight the infidels.'

'Dangerous monks,' Guy said, warily.

'The monks themselves do not fight,' Emery said. 'Only the knights, the young and able, are sent east. Those who remain here are pious men who tend to their properties, raise the horses and provide equipment that is needed, while seeking donations to the cause.'

A cause that was failing, Nicholas thought. By most accounts, the Holy Land was all but lost and some blamed the military orders, charging that the once-noble and selfless knights had become corrupt, arrogance and greed fuelling their decisions. But Nicholas knew that it was easy to pass judgement from the safety of England. And the privileges granted these orders, free from taxes and tithes, often drew resentment.

'I thought the Templars were already rich as Midas, the New Temple in London being filled with the king's gold,' Guy said, as if confirming his thoughts.

'At the king's pleasure,' Nicholas said. 'The Templars act as bankers, guarding wealth and arranging the transfer of it over distances, for they have long handled the monies used to fund their battles. I doubt that they have amassed much of their own, as they must continue to support the fighting in the east.'

'The rules of these orders do not allow for personal possessions and require selfless commitment,' Emery said.

Guy seemed unconvinced. 'If that is so, where did the phrase "drunk as a Templar" come from?' he asked. 'And I've heard worse about them, too, strange rumours of hidden hoards and secret meetings. Why, look at what that one did to you!'

Nicholas tried not to wince at the reminder. 'Perhaps not all are what they should be. Still, they could hardly condone the actions of the man we saw: attempted theft, intimidation and assault,' he said.

'Or maybe our man is not what he seems,' Guy said, with a sidelong glance towards Emery. 'He might not be a Templar at all, but simply garbed as one.'

'Well, there is only one way to find out,' Nicholas said. 'Let us go see what the good brothers have to say. And if Gwayne, as he called himself at the inn, makes his home there, he might well have returned already.'

Guy greeted the suggestion with alarm. 'If so, then he will be in his element, with a host of others at his beck and call.'

Nicholas frowned. The day had not yet come when he couldn't handle a houseful of monks, but he refused to be drawn into a discussion of his abilities. 'I doubt that the entire preceptory is full of villains,' he said, sending Guy back to his mount with a look.

However, his own steps were stayed by a light touch upon his arm. Emery, eyes downcast and slender face flushed, was standing at his elbow. Nicholas felt that odd hitch in his chest again, an unwanted sensation that made him speak more sharply than he ought. 'Yes?'

But this time Emery held his ground. 'Beware, my lord. This country is isolated and the religious houses even more so. They have little contact with the outside world and answer to none except the ecclesiastical authorities.'

Had no one faith in him? Nicholas wondered. They were not facing an army, but a monastery populated by men whose fighting days were long over. Yet the blue eyes gazing up at him were fraught with anxiety, making Nicholas glance away and choose his words carefully. Even if his abilities were suspect, the power of his family was not. 'Do you really think they would dare make enemies of the de Burghs?'

Yet Emery was not reassured. 'I don't know, my lord.' With a bow of his head, the boy headed towards the horses, leaving Nicholas to mull over his earnest warning.

Having done battle more than once, Nicholas had not been concerned with the prospect of facing a few elderly religious brethren, but he was not so arrogant as to dismiss Emery's words. Although it was unlikely that this remote preceptory was the home of violent men intent upon harming visitors, he could not deny that one Templar in particular was dangerous. Should there be more like him, Guy hadn't the strength or skills for much combat. And as for Emery...

Nicholas found himself watching the odd youth's graceful gait before turning abruptly away to find Guy eyeing him with an odd expression.

'See? He's not slow-witted,' Nicholas said, inclining his head towards Emery.

His squire snorted. 'That's not all he's not.'

Nicholas approached Temple Roode cautiously, but there was little that was forbidding about the sheep grazing in fields and the cluster of neat buildings: two barns, a church and a small house. The property was more a manorial farm than a fortress; there was no keep, no moat, no gate and no guards. In fact, there was no sign of life, not even of the lay people who presumably worked the land, yet all was in good condition.

The stillness was eerie, broken only by the sound of the wind moving through the spindly trees that surrounded the manor, and Nicholas saw the look of unease on Emery's face. He did not share it, fearing nothing any more except his own failure to protect Guy and the boy. In fact, his main concern was Emery because his squire seemed ill disposed towards their companion.

Guy did not seem to understand that, despite the events of the past year, Nicholas was still a knight, sworn to aid others. He had agreed to help Gerard, which meant that Emery was now his responsibility, and he refused to listen to his squire's arguments otherwise. He could only be grateful that, after several attempts at discussing the boy, Guy had lapsed into moody silence, for he had more important matters to consider than his squire's petty jealousies.

Dismounting, Nicholas glanced around and wondered whether the residents had been called away or if they were ill. He was reminded of his brother Reynold's experience with an abandoned village. However, if this place was abandoned, it had been only recently.

'Hello?' Nicholas's voice was loud in the stillness, but none answered his hail. The horses moved restlessly behind him and Nicholas motioned for Guy and Emery to remain mounted in case they needed to make a hurried escape. Striding forwards, he put his hand upon the hilt of his sword, sensing that something was not quite right.

As if to prove him wrong, a man appeared

at the manor entrance. Short, squat and balding, he wore a brown mantle that suggested he was more devout than dangerous. Still, he said nothing, forcing Nicholas to introduce himself.

'Good day, Brother, I am Nicholas de Burgh. I wonder if I might have a word with you and your brethren.'

'My brothers are in seclusion, fasting and praying. Are you lost?' the fellow asked. Although traditionally, monastic houses gave lodging to travellers, he tendered no such offer.

'My lord de Burgh, shall I tether the horses?' Guy said, as though to protest this treatment.

Nicholas shook his head, for he could not force his way into a man's confidence. Instead, he spoke calmly and plainly. 'We are seeking a Templar knight nearly as tall as I, but more slender and with light-coloured hair.'

'There are no knights residing here, my lord,' the brother said, his gaze shuttered, his speech short. Nicholas tried not to draw any conclusions from the man's manner, for he might have been isolated from the world for so long that he did not deal well with outsiders.

However, Nicholas made sure his own manner was cordial and encouraging. 'Although he does not reside here, perhaps the knight we seek is associated with this preceptory. He might have trained here or he could be returning home from the Holy Land.'

The brother shook his head, but did not elaborate, leaving Nicholas to guess at the monastery's usual inhabitants. He longed to talk to someone a bit more forthcoming. 'Perhaps a brother who has been at Temple Roode longer might recall?'

Again, the man shook his head. If not vowed to silence, he certainly spoke as little as possible. But perhaps that was the way of the Templars. Their secrecy had led to much speculation about them, little of it good, and Nicholas's opinion of the order was declining rapidly.

Although loath to distrust a holy man, he couldn't help feeling that the brother was hiding something. Nicholas could claim few dealings with those in religious houses, but he had sought shelter in such places and never received this sort of treatment. Were the Templars so different, or was his search responsible for this reception?

He decided to change tactics. 'Brother...?'

'Gilbert,' the man said, as though reluctant to part with that detail.

'Brother Gilbert.' Nicholas smiled. 'My father, the Earl of Campion, is a generous contributor to your cause and I'm sure he would be most grateful for any information you can provide me.'

But the monk was unmoved. It seemed that the claims of Templars having become greedy and worldly did not apply to this remote area, or at least this member of the order. And Nicholas could not press him further. He could only watch carefully as he posed his next question.

'You must have contact with other preceptories, so perhaps you have heard of this knight I seek,' Nicholas said. 'He gave his name as Gwayne.'

No flicker of recognition showed in Gilbert's dour expression. 'I know no Templar by that name.'

'He attacked a Hospitaller knight,' Nicholas said.

But even that news did not faze the man, who maintained his grim expression. 'Then perhaps you should look to Clerkwell, the Hospitaller commandery, which is not far from here.'

'Perhaps I will,' Nicholas said. Nodding graciously, he turned to mount his horse without a backward glance, gesturing for his squire to precede him as they rode away. Guy obeyed and did not slow until they were out of sight of the preceptory. In fact, he seemed unwilling to halt, doing so only after Nicholas had stopped well away from the track. Even then, he kept looking over his shoulder, as though expecting the Pope's armies to give chase.

''Tis just as I have heard, my lord,' he said, his eyes wide. 'The Templars zealously guard their secrets. Why, 'tis said they uncovered some hidden knowledge in the Holy Land that they now use to their own advantage.'

Nicholas gave his squire a wry glance. Guy had always been a superstitious sort and recent events had made him more so. Frequently, he tried to foist some talisman or charm upon Nicholas, claiming that the objects, whether a coloured stone or a splinter of bone belonging to some long-dead saint, bore special powers. Now, apparently, the Templars themselves were endowed with such.

'I thought you considered them sunk in dissipation, not keepers of some ancient wisdom,' Nicholas said drily.

But Guy was not to be dissuaded. ''Twas eerie, my lord, even you must admit to that,' he said, suppressing a shiver. ''Tis certain they did not want us there, with none to greet us except that surly fellow, who ought to be taught how to treat his betters.'

'Perhaps so, but I was loath to raise any suspicions with Brother Gilbert,' Nicholas said. 'Better he think himself well rid of us.'

'You don't mean to go back?' Guy asked in an incredulous tone.

'I would like to have a closer look at the place,' Nicholas admitted. 'Something didn't feel right.'

Guy groaned. 'Nothing felt right, my lord! Yet no good could come of probing into their mysteries. Who knows what goes on there? They obviously are hiding something.'

At his words, even quiet Emery glanced at him with an expression of alarm. 'You don't think they're holding Gerard in there, do you?'

Nicholas held up a hand to stop his squire's raving. While Templar preceptories in the east might have reason to keep prisoners, he could not conceive of the brethren locking up their own here at home.

'I do not suspect the Templars of capturing their fellows, no matter what dark tales are whispered about them,' he said, with a quelling glare at Guy. 'Nevertheless, I'd like to take another look at Temple Roode.'

Naturally, Guy did not agree. 'But if you do

not think Gerard is there, then we will only be wasting precious time in our search for him.'

While his squire had a point, Nicholas was not prepared to leave the Templar preceptory behind on the strength of one brother's dubious word. ''Tis possible that a return visit may yield nothing, for Brother Gilbert may be concealing little more than his larder from hungry visitors,' he said. 'However, I would make sure the man who left me for dead is not enjoying the hospitality of the house.'

The reminder of the attack finally silenced Guy and Nicholas looked out over the moors, assessing the possibilities. 'There's really no means of approaching the place without being seen unless we wait until nightfall, and even then the moon will prove both help and hindrance,' he said, remembering the stretch of open land that they would have to cross to reach the cluster of buildings. It was simply too barren, with few trees to provide shadows in which to hide.

'There might be another way.'

To Nicholas's surprise, 'twas Emery who spoke and the boy coloured, as though regretting his speech.

'Go on,' Nicholas said.

'It could be nothing but an old legend,' Emery said, hesitating.

'What old legend?'

Again Emery hesitated, but Nicholas urged him on with a nod.

The boy drew a deep breath, as though summoning his courage. 'There have always been rumours of tunnels beneath the Templar property, going back to when they first settled there.'

'Tunnels? What for?' Guy asked.

Emery shrugged. 'No one knows. Perhaps the Templars sought to travel from their preceptory to the village without notice. I can't imagine where else they would wish to go in secret.'

Guy muttered something and crossed himself, obviously leery of either the Templars, underground passages or both. But Nicholas knew the value of tunnels. He had gained access to his brother Dunstan's keep through just such means, foiling the enemies who held it. Castles, built for defence, often had escapes routes for use in times of siege.

But 'twas unlikely that a manorial farm, especially an ecclesiastical property like Temple Roode, could boast anything of the sort. Yet, what else had they to do until darkness fell?

'There's only one way to find out,' he said, eager for a challenge.

Guy groaned. 'And how are we going to discover in an afternoon what no one else has ever found, maybe for a hundred years?'

'As far as I know, no one has ever looked for them,' Emery said. 'Why would they?'

Guy shook his head, as if dismayed by the folly of both of his companions, and muttered to himself in dire tones, 'More likely, who would dare?'

Emery felt only dismay as they neared the village. What had she been thinking? While they wasted time hunting for tunnels that probably didn't exist, Gerard could be travelling in the opposite direction, putting miles between them. She should never have spoken.

But who would have thought her opinion would carry weight with any man, let alone Lord de Burgh? Emery had forgotten how differently she was treated when garbed as her twin. It had been too long ago and she had since learned to keep her silence. So what had possessed her to speak, especially in such exalted company?

Emery shook her head. Nicholas de Burgh

rode his huge destrier with ease, tall and proud, his gloved hands gripping the reins confidently. He was a noble, wielding the kind of power and influence that should strike fear into anyone pretending to be someone else. That, coupled with her brother's warning, ought to have kept her quiet and wary. And yet...

Emery glanced away from the handsome figure and told herself 'twas distrust of religious houses that had prompted the suggestion. She could not call it back now. But when they drew to a halt on the low rise that overlooked the village below, she was tempted. Where were they to find underground tunnels amongst the cluster of small homes, with people and animals roaming about?

Emery waited for some sign of scorn or rebuke from her companions, but Lord de Burgh appeared unperturbed as he looked out over the landscape. 'Now, if you were a Templar, where would you want to go?' he asked.

Blinking in surprise at the question, Emery turned to study the village she had not seen in some time. For a moment, the years fell away, and it seemed as though she were young and at liberty to explore the moors, Gerard at her side. And in that instant, the answer came to her.

'The church,' she said.

Lord de Burgh's smile of approval made Emery glance away, uncomfortable. She realised how long it had been since she'd felt pleasure or companionship, but this was not the time and place to seek such things. Nor was Nicholas de Burgh the one to provide them.

Emery was here for Gerard, not for anything else, yet she could not help but savour the first small taste of the freedom that she had known in years. She was riding again, seeing new places and experiencing new things, and her heart pounded with a combination of fear and excitement as they approached the distinctive round building.

'What kind of parish church is this?' Guy muttered, eyeing the place warily as he dismounted.

'I suspect it was built by the Templars, who favour that sort of construction,' Lord de Burgh said, heading towards the doors.

''Tis probably modelled after the Church of the Holy Sepulchre in Jerusalem,' Emery added, but her words did seem to comfort Guy, who appeared hesitant to enter.

Emboldened by her new freedom, Emery strode past the squire to follow Lord de Burgh inside, but her courage soon wavered. Plunging into the cool dimness, she was met with an interior unlike any other.

In fact, Emery took a step back in astonishment, running into Guy, who gulped and grabbed her by the arms, whether to steady her or himself, Emery wasn't sure. But for a long moment they stood together while gaping at the elaborate decorations. Although the number that crowded the small space was startling in itself, 'twas the strangeness of the designs that stunned Emery.

While she could not claim to be well travelled, she had never seen such carvings in any church, and, apparently, neither had Guy, for he resumed muttering in hushed tones, frozen in his position near the doors. But Emery finally moved forwards, peering in wonder at the images that appeared more heathen than Christian.

Heads that resembled pagan designs or some remnant of ancient legends were scattered amongst more traditional adornments. Emery blinked at the bulbous face of the Green Man, a symbol of fertility that some say had been worshipped in years past. And everywhere were horned figures that looked more like demons than saints.

'What kind of parish church is this?' Guy asked again, his voice cracking in the stillness.

'An unusual one, isn't it?' Lord de Burgh said, drawing Emery's attention. He, alone, seemed undismayed by the sights as he walked the perimeter, pausing only to knock on a wall or peer behind a decorative panel.

'What are you doing?' Emery asked, curiosity overcoming her unease.

'I've some experience in tunnels—and in hideaways, having played at seeking my brothers often enough in my youth,' Lord de Burgh said over his shoulder. 'And one of my brothers, Geoff, is fond of puzzles, so he taught me how to study a problem.'

Emery was startled to realise that the great knight really was searching for the rumoured tunnels. 'But wouldn't the floor—?'

'Too obvious,' Lord de Burgh said, stopping in front of a carving tucked under an arch. 'And unlikely because of the difficulty in concealing such an entrance. However, they would need to be able to access their passage without too much trouble, else why create such a massive work?'

When he turned towards her, Emery could only nod in agreement, struck dumb to be included in such a conversation. She knew her disguise was responsible, yet Lord de Burgh was being more than gracious to an unknown young man, and her wariness made her wonder whether he had an ulterior motive.

As Emery watched, he knelt before a grotesque image, running his hands over the surface and into the crevices along the edge as though searching for something, and soon he must have found it, for the massive piece moved slightly. Emery blinked in surprise, but even more amazing was the glance he shot her, one of triumph and shared success that stopped her breath.

Perhaps 'twas the way of men and their friendships, Emery thought, and held no special meaning. Yet she could do no more than look on while he shifted the heavy chunk of stone as if it weighed little, exposing a gaping hole beyond. Cool, damp air seeped from pitch blackness, hinting at lower depths and, stepping closer, Emery could see a set of worn stone steps leading downwards.

The discovery even lured Guy away from his

stance near the doors. He was soon standing beside Emery, muttering to himself. 'I don't believe it,' he said aloud. And then he turned towards her, his eyes narrowing. 'Did you know about this?'

'I knew only of the rumours of a tunnel,' Emery said. 'Lord de Burgh managed to find it.' And he had done so with seemingly little effort, which made Emery return Guy's suspicious glare with one of her own.

'How do we know that this doesn't lead into a bottomless pit?' the squire asked.

'We don't,' Lord de Burgh said. Apparently undisturbed by the prospect, he set about lighting a lantern he had found tucked away behind a screen.

'My lord, you cannot mean to enter there,' Guy protested. 'You don't know what lies below: foul air, rising water, precipitous drops. It may be an old cavern that has been blocked up, with no connection at all to the Templars or their property.'

'There's only one way to find out,' Lord de Burgh said. The mischievous grin that accompanied this sentiment made him look younger and dashing, perhaps even a bit wicked, and

Emery found it hard to ignore his excitement, which stimulated her own. Was that why her heart had picked up its pace?

'You can stay behind and watch the horses, if you don't care to explore the tunnel,' Lord de Burgh said, with a shrug, though it was obvious he had no intention of doing so himself.

Guy sputtered a protest, but was silenced by a look from his master, who then turned to Emery. Although he said nothing, expectation brightened his dark eyes, and Emery felt a sudden giddiness. Had Gerard ever offered her such a dare? Emery couldn't remember, but years of being stifled by duty and silence made her meet the unspoken challenge.

'I'll come with you.'

Lord de Burgh's answering grin did something to her that Emery could not explain, but she told herself 'twas wiser to keep an eye on the man rather than not. However, Guy had other ideas.

'My lord, you cannot think to take this—' the squire began, gesturing towards Emery. But Lord de Burgh held up his hand to stop any argument, leaving Guy to shake his head as his master ducked into the hole. 'Be careful, my lord,' he warned.

There was nothing for Emery to do except follow Lord de Burgh. But when she stepped on to the stone stairs, she drew in a sharp breath at the sudden change in her surroundings. The familiar figure of Guy standing in the dim recesses of the church was replaced by a blackness so total that she blinked several times before she could see anything at all. Finally, she spied the faint flicker of the lantern, barely visible ahead.

Having no time to regret her hasty decision, Emery hurried forwards, lest the pale talisman disappear from view. But she had not counted upon the shape in front of her and stumbled into the tall form of Lord de Burgh.

'Steady,' he said, turning his head towards her. 'Some people don't do well in tight quarters, especially below ground. My brother Simon, for all his courage, is one, and there is no shame in it.'

Emery wasn't about to argue, for she could not find her tongue. Lord de Burgh's face was so close that she could see the thick, dusky lashes of his eyes. The lantern cast a glow upon his cheek, a beacon of warmth in the cool darkness. And when his gaze met hers, Emery's heart began pounding so loudly that she was certain he could hear it.

Like an animal in the glare of a lamp, Emery was powerless to look away, her breath faltering, her pulse racing. Then something flared in his eyes, a question perhaps, but if so, it was one that Emery could not answer. Time stood still as their gazes held until, to her relief, he finally turned away.

Shuddering, Emery was glad of the shadows as she sought to control her clamouring senses. Thankfully, Lord de Burgh appeared little affected by what had seemed so momentous to her because he soon spoke over his shoulder.

'Watch your feet,' he said as he resumed walking. 'The Templars might have laid traps for unwanted visitors.'

Traps? Emery felt as though she had already fallen into one, as she belatedly realised the intimacy of the situation. Neither a past spent with her father and brother, nor her recent isolation, had prepared her for the experience of being alone in the dark with a man, let alone a man like Lord de Burgh. Panic stirred, and it was not the fear of being unmasked, now a very real possibility, or even the dangers of the tunnel that chilled her.

Something had just passed between them, something so powerful that Emery hoped he would never look her way again. Not like that. And especially not here in the darkness.

Chapter Three

Nicholas did not care to dwell on what had just occurred, though he had the feeling he could unravel the puzzle of his odd reaction if he put his mind to it. But now was not the time. Travelling underground in unknown passages required all of his attention, lest he fall or lose his way. And he had not undertaken this exploration recklessly, no matter what Guy might think.

Pausing to inspect the ground at his feet, Nicholas noted that it sloped slightly. But why go deeper under the earth? Perhaps the Templars had taken advantage of some natural formations, using and extending what already existed to suit their needs.

Although that would mean less chance of

the roof crashing down upon them, it posed other dangers. Having explored the caves near his brother Geoff's property, Nicholas knew that a mis-step could lead to disaster, especially when they had no rope. One slip into a crevasse would mean no escape, and though recently he might have courted such risks, he had no intention of losing his life—or Emery's.

The thought made him slant a glance behind him, just to make sure the boy was still following. The sight of the youth's bent head was a strange comfort, making Nicholas suddenly aware of home and family. Perhaps that explained his odd reaction. With six older brothers, he'd never had the opportunity to pass on his experience and knowledge to a younger sibling. Now he wondered whether he should share his skills with someone who might make use of them—before it was too late. And Emery seemed a more likely candidate than Guy.

'It doesn't look as though anyone has passed this way in a long time,' the youth whispered, as though confirming Nicholas's thoughts.

'Perhaps the way is blocked ahead, putting an end to its usage,' Nicholas said.

'Or maybe they no longer have need of a secret entrance to the church.'

'Yet if they still monitor the tunnels, we should keep quiet. Some of these places can produce echoes or amplify sound to warn those ahead.'

Emery fell silent then, and Nicholas knew a sense of loss. There was something soothing about the boy's speech, as though he were wise beyond his years. Or maybe Nicholas had just grown weary of his squire's company. Guy's constant fussing made him seem more like a nursery maid than a squire, and his harping to return home grew wearisome.

Frowning at the thought, Nicholas continued on, watching his steps even as he peered into the darkness ahead and studied the surrounding walls. It was slow going. Eventually, he began to wonder if the tunnel even led to Temple Roode. Perhaps they had passed some hidden niche that would have taken them to the preceptory or were caught in an endless loop, a vast maze below ground.

But then the light glinted upon something in front of them. Stretching out one arm, Nicholas gestured for Emery to stay behind while he inched forwards, keeping his body as close to the side of the tunnel as possible. Their path had remained level for some time, so they were probably well below any buildings above. Yet the narrow passage opened on to a wider space ahead, making Nicholas proceed with caution.

For long moments, he stood waiting and listening. When he heard nothing, he lifted the lantern closer to the opening. The light seemed to be swallowed up by the greater darkness, then it glittered upon shadowy surfaces. At first Nicholas thought they had stumbled upon a cavern of some sort, but it was not like any he had ever seen. Curious, he took a step and held the lantern higher, only to realise he was not looking at the exposed rock and ore of a catacomb, but something created by man.

Nicholas heard Emery's low intake of breath as the boy reached his side, and he could only marvel, as well. Whether originally an existing cave or something dug from the earth, the place in which they found themselves had been well worked by the Templars. In fact, it seemed that every inch of the surrounding walls was covered with carvings even more strange than those in the church: circles, swords, crosses, outlines of figures, arcane symbols and depictions of scenes, some of them holy, some wholly unrecognisable.

The carvings reached as far as the eye could see, or at least as far as could be illuminated. Stretching upwards to plunge into blackness, they must have taken years, perhaps decades or more, to complete. For long moments Nicholas simply stood staring, but when Emery would have stepped forwards, he stopped the boy with a gesture.

He had been looking up, rather than down, and Nicholas bent low to examine the ground before entering the chamber. Although it looked sturdy, he kept to the perimeter as he made his way inside, Emery at his heels. At first, he thought the surrounding walls formed a circle, much like the Templar church, but when he reached the halfway point, he realised he was standing within an octagon.

'What is this place?' Emery whispered.

Nicholas glanced towards a dark niche that might serve as an altar. 'Perhaps it is used for worship.'

'Surely not by the Templars,' Emery protested, sounding as unsure as Guy about the order.

Nicholas shrugged, for he knew little of what

went on in religious houses. Still, he suspected few harboured hidden rooms, especially an underground cavern like this one. 'Mayhap it has been here for centuries and the Templars simply turned it to their own needs.'

Although Emery looked sceptical, Nicholas wasn't concerned with the purpose of the place, only where it might lead. But a cursory glance revealed no exit, and he wondered whether they had walked all this way only to view a curious site, perhaps long forgotten. Were they below the preceptory or somewhere else, maybe even in a passage connecting two churches, one above and another below?

Wary of spending too much time in the tunnel, Nicholas gave the lantern to Emery, while he searched more carefully. He looked for the kind of stone they had found in the church, a carving of a Green Man, mouth wide open, as though in some sort of agony.

As he moved onwards, Emery followed, providing the light for his inspections. Although the boy could not be faulted, Nicholas felt distracted, for he was all too aware of his companion's nearness. He even had an unnerving urge to turn towards the boy, which he promptly quelled.

What the devil ailed him? The answer that

came only unnerved him more. Was it growing warm in here? Had the air become close? With a grunt, Nicholas forced himself to focus. All he had to do now was find the opening. But what if it lay above them? Without a ladder or rope, they could not hope to scale these walls. And the entrance might be unrecognisable, perhaps something he had already passed.

And as if he wasn't grappling with enough, his light dipped, casting wild shadows upon the very area he was trying to examine. With a low oath, Nicholas turned to rebuke the boy, but the reprimand died on his lips. Emery had gone pale and wide-eyed, as though staring at some unseen horror.

'What is it?' Nicholas whispered.

Emery raised a hand to point in the direction of other carvings, most notably one of a Templar over five feet in height. 'I thought...' the boy began, only to trail off, as though unable to continue.

'What?'

'I thought I saw something,' Emery whispered, haltingly. 'A pair of eyes watching us.'

Motioning the boy to silence, Nicholas put a hand to the hilt of his sword. Anything might be waiting in the blackness that lay outside their small circle of light. Bats were common enough in caves, but other, less friendly creatures might have wandered into the tunnel— or be kept there by the Templars to guard their secrets.

Nicholas rose slowly to his feet, though he saw nothing stirring and heard no scurrying or snarling. He turned to scan the rest of the chamber, but Emery stopped him with a gesture.

'No, they were there,' the boy insisted, pointing at the carving of the Templar. 'Its eyes… looked like…human eyes.'

Nicholas would have dismissed such a claim, but Emery did not seem given to whimsy, and the strangeness of their surroundings made anything seem possible. The boy had not declared that the stone came to life, just that it had human eyes, and he considered the answer to such a puzzle.

Approaching cautiously, Nicholas motioned for Emery to hold the lantern for closer inspection. One of the largest of the carvings, the Templar resembled those that graced the tombs of such knights, except the figure was standing upright, his huge sword in front of him, pointing downwards.

Moving closer, Nicholas reached towards the dark recesses of its features, touching a finger to the sightless orbs. He wouldn't have been surprised to find the sockets empty, but the surface was as solid and cold as any statue. Perhaps Emery had been fooled by a trick of the light. Still, Nicholas ran his hand over the figure's outline, attempting to move it as he had the stone in the church. It did not budge.

Reaching the bottom, he sat back on his haunches, eyeing the sword that pointed towards the earth at his feet. It was no different than any other of the outcroppings, yet its size and position made it more realistic than the others, as though it stood guard over something. Nicholas slid his fingers into the crevice below, and this time, he felt something give.

Tugging at the sword, Nicholas pulled the entire piece outwards and wondered if he had finally found the entrance to the preceptory. But Emery's gasp of alarm made him step back. Had he opened some kind of crypt, or was something very much alive hidden inside? He could only hope that Emery's brother was not entombed within.

Drawing his sword, Nicholas was prepared for anything, but when the makeshift door swung wide, no corpse was revealed, only the small figure of a man. He was no warrior, either, but wore the brown robes and serene expression of a monk. And unlike Brother Gilbert, he appeared unconcerned by the sight of the visitors, even in this underground sanctum.

However, he closed the portal before turning to face them, hands clasped before him calmly. 'You have no need of your weapon here, my lord,' he said in a soft voice. Old and wizened, he was hardly a threat, especially with the entrance shut behind him. None the less, he was an imposing figure and appeared to know more than he should.

Although Nicholas sheathed his sword, he vowed to keep his wits about him and nodded at Emery, glad to see the boy's hand steady upon the lantern.

'I am Father Faramond and I have been expecting you,' the priest said.

Nicholas heard Emery's indrawn breath at the words, but, unlike Guy, he did not think the Templars possessed of any unnatural powers. There was a more sensible explanation for this greeting and Faramond soon gave it.

'Knowing your sire, Nicholas de Burgh, I

feared you would not be easily dissuaded or dismissed,' he said.

'It was you behind the eyes of the carving, looking at us through some kind of slit,' Nicholas said.

The priest nodded. 'It is an old device, a precaution of our forebears, yet none in all these years have penetrated to this, our most private of places.'

'And what is the punishment for intrusion, Father?' Emery asked. By his tone, the boy expected the worst, though Nicholas had no intention of being killed for trespassing, no matter how ancient or sacred the site. His fingers tightened on the hilt of his sword, a nearly imperceptible movement, yet the priest must have noticed.

'Although we are a military order, we do not do murder, my lord.'

Nicholas was glad to hear it, but considering his earlier reception at Temple Roode, he was not prepared to trust any of the brethren, no matter how unassuming. At least not yet. So he kept his hand where it was, just in case the killing of enemies of the order extended to those who might reveal their secrets. And he tendered a warning. 'If you know my father, then I hope you would not rouse the wrath of the de Burghs.'

'And I hope that I might trust such a one not to betray us,' Faramond answered, his tone gentle but firm.

Lifting his brows, Nicholas nodded his agreement and a silent understanding passed between them before the priest turned towards Emery. 'As for you, child, you are bound by more than he to keep your silence.'

Emery paled and nodded, as though fearful, a circumstance that made Nicholas's fingers tighten around his weapon. 'If we are the first to penetrate this place, how did you know to look for us, or do you keep watch here at all times?'

'Oh, no,' Faramond said. 'We rarely gather here any more. I instructed one of the shepherds to report upon your whereabouts. When you went directly to the church, I took up my position here. The de Burghs are known to be tenacious, among their many admirable qualities.'

Faramond paused. 'However, my brethren may not be as untroubled as I by your incursion. Therefore, let us make this meeting as brief as possible. What is it you seek at Temple Roode, my lord?'

'As I told Brother Gilbert, who was less than helpful, I am looking for a Templar knight who gave his name as Gwayne. He assaulted me as well as this young man's brother, Gerard Montbard, a Hospitaller who is now missing.'

'I am sorry that you were made unwelcome and realise that is why you were driven to other means,' the priest said. He shook his head. 'I told the others not to deny a de Burgh, but they are afraid. Someone brought word to the preceptory that Gwayne had been seen not far from here and they cower, lest he return, although we no longer claim him as our own.'

'Why?' Nicholas asked.

Faramond glanced away. 'He was charged with an important task, which he did not fulfil.'

'What was that?'

The priest sighed and looked towards the empty niche. 'I can speak little of this, my lord. Know only that he possesses something that does not belong to him.' He shook his head. 'His appearance in the area is both unexpected and dismaying. But perhaps he has come to do penance for his wrongs—that is the outcome for which I will pray.'

Straightening, he faced them both again. 'Now, I fear that I must ask that you leave this place, never to speak of it to any other, even your own father, the great Campion himself.'

'What of my brother?' Emery asked.

Faramond eyed Emery sadly. 'I know nothing of the Hospitallers, nor why Gwayne would assault one of them. I know only that despite the robe he wears, he is not to be trusted.'

'So he stole something from this place?' Nicholas asked, gesturing towards the carved walls, steeped in Templar mysteries, that surrounded them.

'Oh, no,' the priest said, turning once again to Nicholas. 'He was given the mace.'

Emery followed closely after Lord de Burgh, eager to put the Templar cave behind her. She was aware of the power wielded by the religious orders, but nothing could have prepared her for the eerie chamber full of strange carvings with eyes that moved…

Emery shuddered at the memory. It had taken every ounce of her will not to flee in that instant. Only thoughts of Gerard had kept her where she was. Once it became clear that he had nothing to do with the place, she had been more than ready to go.

But Lord de Burgh had lingered, asking more questions about Gwayne and the object he was given, despite the fact that Father Faramond provided few answers and Emery did not want to hear them. Although she had given little credence to Guy's gossip about the order, she suspected that the less they knew about the Templars' secrets, the better their chance of escaping retribution.

What did she care about their relics? And why should Lord de Burgh? His interest made her wonder whether he had his own reasons for seeking the hidden tunnels. She reminded herself to trust no one, yet she inched ever nearer to the man as she peered over her shoulder, half-expecting to spy something hurtling towards them through the blackness.

Although she did not want to believe that holy men were capable of murder, she felt a growing unease. Perhaps no Templar knights would be sent to trap them in the narrow passage, but other mishaps could be easily arranged—boulders, fire or flood—that would entomb them here, ensuring their silence. The thought made her glance back again and, though she saw nothing, Emery felt a jolt as she slammed into Lord de Burgh's hard body.

'In a hurry?' he asked. His tone was one of amusement and, thankfully, he did not pause to look her way. But Emery was reminded that she had cause to be wary of everything, both in front and behind, here in the darkness.

'We shall arrive at the end soon enough, if we tread carefully,' he said.

And if they suffered no interference, Emery thought. But when they reached the church, what would they find there? 'Twould be an easy task for someone to overpower Guy and plug the hole from whence they had entered.

'The question is, where shall we go once we emerge?' he asked.

At the great knight's words, Emery's steps faltered and she struggled not to stumble with dismay. She had been so concerned about escaping the Templars that she had been distracted from her purpose. But now the passage's dangers receded, replaced by a new, greater fear.

'I do not know where to look for your brother,' Lord de Burgh said. 'And we might roam these moors for days without news of him or Gwayne.'

Emery's heart lurched, for she could not argue with the truth. And this man had done what he could to aid her; she could not expect him to dally with her for ever. As a de Burgh, he would have other commitments, perhaps even to the king himself. But if he gave up the hunt for Gerard, she would be left alone, with few resources and no mount, her quest doomed to failure and her future bleak.

'Have you no notion where your brother might go?' he asked.

Emery grunted a denial, unable to speak.

'His first thought was for you, but having assured himself of your safety, perhaps he travelled on to others who merited his concern,' he said. 'What of your parents?'

Was he asking idle questions, or did he intend to continue the search? Emery felt so dizzy with relief at that possibility that she nearly reached out a hand to steady herself against his broad back. Instead, she swallowed hard and found her voice.

'Our mother died in childbed and our father succumbed more than a year ago to a long illness.'

'I'm sorry for your loss,' he said, investing the simple phrase with such sincerity that

Emery could only murmur her thanks. Garbed as she was, she could hardly explain that she mourned not only the passing of her father, but the life she had once known.

'Have you any other siblings?'

'No,' Emery said. It had just been the three of them, their father choosing to raise his twins alone—and together. Instead of being sent away or shunted aside, Emery had run free with her brother, schooled along with him in the skills of men. It had been both a blessing and a curse, for although Emery could not regret one moment of the past, it made the present that much harder to bear.

'What of other relatives? Is there no one else with whom your brother might seek shelter?'

'There is only our uncle,' Emery said. 'But I doubt that Gerard would go to him.' Or would he? If her brother was desperate or feverish, he might head home, especially since he was not aware of the lengths to which Harold had gone to claim their heritage.

'Why would he not go to your uncle?'

Emery drew a deep breath. 'Harold convinced our ailing father to assign his property to the Order of the Hospital of Saint John of Jerusalem. Then he convinced Gerard to join

the order, conveniently giving up any claims
he might have to his legacy.'

''Tis not uncommon for men to provide for
their widows and children in such a manner,'
he said. 'Do you suspect your uncle of some
ulterior motive?'

'I suspect him of colluding with the master of the commandery to get what they both
wanted,' Emery said, her frustration spilling
forth. 'The brethren often had encroached upon
our land, causing disagreements over the years.
Now they have the disputed fields and my uncle
has the manor he always coveted.'

'And what of you?'

The simple question brought Emery back
to her senses, for there her candour must end.
Even if she trusted Lord de Burgh completely,
there were some things she could not share.
Thankful for the cloaking darkness, she drew
a deep breath and chose her answer carefully. 'I
live in the old gatehouse...through an arrangement with the Hospitallers.'

For a long moment, he was silent, as if considering her situation, and Emery regretted her
words. Although at one time she would have
welcomed a champion such as this great knight

to her cause, it was too late now, for both of the Montbard twins.

'Perhaps we should pay a visit to this uncle of yours,' Lord de Burgh said, 'just in case Gerard stopped there.'

Now Emery well and truly had cause to rue her speech, for she could hardly appear at her old home in her current garb. Harold would see through her disguise in an instant, putting an end to her efforts to find her brother and ensuring her banishment. Her future would be bleak, indeed, and Lord de Burgh... Well, he would not look upon her so kindly once he discovered her ruse, for men did not like to be fooled, especially by women.

Her heart heavy, Emery tried to think of some argument against his plan, to no avail. But perhaps she could lead him to the manor and then hang back, citing ill will between Harold and herself. That would keep her from immediate discovery, yet should Lord de Burgh speak of her as Gerard's brother, all would come undone.

'Your fears are baseless, young Emery,' he said, as though privy to her thoughts, and Emery glanced at him in alarm. It was only then that she saw the pale light of the church interior ahead, beckoning through the blackness.

'We have reached the end without mishap,' he added, and Emery realised he had been talking to her during their long, slow return in order to distract her. She blinked in surprise, uncertain whether Gerard would have done the same for his sister or if he even could. Somehow, she suspected only Lord de Burgh had the power to drive away dread and darkness with just the sound of his voice.

To her relief, when they exited the tunnel, no Templars awaited them, only an agitated Guy. 'Where have you been? I thought you'd been trapped in there,' he said. 'Are you all right, my lord?'

The question seemed ludicrous, tendered from a slight young man to a great knight armed with sword and mail and wits to spare. Yet Lord de Burgh nodded and Guy appeared reassured. Although he looked ready to bombard them with questions, Lord de Burgh prevented them by speaking first.

While the great knight returned the heavy entrance stone to its original position, he related the conversation with the priest. However, he made no mention of where it took place.

The omission not only proved that he was a man of his word, but Emery thought it just as well that Guy know nothing of the underground chamber.

The squire was leery enough of the Templars and their secrets, without hearing of a tomb-like effigy that sported real eyes and an eight-sided catacomb riddled with cryptic symbols. Yet, even without that information, Guy seemed eager for a mystery.

'What do you suppose this mace is?' he asked in hushed tones, as though somehow he might be overheard in the church.

Emery eyed him in confusion. A mace was a heavy club used to break armour in battle; surely a knight's squire should know that simple fact. But, apparently, Guy expected something more exotic from the order.

'Perhaps it is some sort of treasure,' he said. 'The Templars are rumoured to have vaults of gold and fleets of ships to ferry it across the sea.'

When Lord de Burgh made no comment, the squire continued. 'Or it could be one of the precious objects they are said to hoard, such as the Ark of the Covenant, a piece of the True

Cross, or even the Holy Grail itself,' he said in an awed whisper.

'I doubt they would refer to such things as a mace,' Lord de Burgh said, drily, and Emery had to suppress a smile.

''Tis said that they lost the True Cross to the infidels, and if they have any of those other things, why hide them away?' the great knight asked. 'They are more likely to put any relics on display and charge pilgrims for the privilege of seeing them.'

Although his words seemed harsh, Emery knew there was some truth to them, for the various orders squabbled over who could lay claim to the bones of the saints and such that drew veneration, donations and visitors.

But Guy would not be discouraged. 'They are rumoured to have learned some hidden lore in foreign lands. Perhaps this mace is a part of it, an object possessing special powers that they know how to manipulate.'

Emery frowned. The only special powers she had witnessed below were those Lord de Burgh wielded with just a single gaze that had affected her like no other and one she had never seen him share with his squire. Glancing at the knight, she flushed and turned away, only to find Guy eyeing her speculatively.

'Did anything else happen down there?' the squire asked.

Faced with the direct question, Emery could not find her voice, so she was thankful when Lord de Burgh answered.

'No,' he said. 'What do you mean?'

Had he felt what she felt? Emery dared not look towards the knight and Guy did not answer. Although she suspected the squire was not talking about Templar catacombs, if Emery had made any other discoveries in the darkness, she intended to keep those secrets close.

Chapter Four

Nicholas's steps slowed as he followed the narrow stairs upwards, and he bit back a grunt of weariness. He had pushed himself too hard today after the night hours spent on the road, though he would not admit as much to his squire. But he had been loath to quit the search, looking for any signs of Gerard in the area and asking amongst the villagers and at the outlying farms.

When the hunt had yielded nothing, Nicholas had turned his thoughts towards the uncle's home Emery mentioned. But by then the rainclouds were gathering and several anxious looks from his squire made him wary of punishing his body through a storm. And though he said nothing, Emery's exhaustion was obvious, so instead of pressing on, they sought shelter at the manor in Roode.

The owner, Odo of Walsing, was not in residence, but his steward, Kenrick, had provided them with a meal and the promise of a bed and Nicholas was glad of it. Although he'd slept outside in foul weather more than once, he hadn't the stomach for it these days and he was certain Emery was not accustomed to such accommodations.

At the top of the stairs, Nicholas took the opportunity to catch his breath while Kenrick presented them with a cosy room, complete with a fire in the hearth to chase away the dampness. Nicholas stepped inside, only to find himself alone, for his companions hung back as though reluctant to cross the threshold. In fact, Guy wore an expression of disapproval, although the accommodations were a marked improvement over the inn where Nicholas last sought lodging.

'Where are we to sleep?' Guy asked, frowning.

'The bed is big enough for all of us,' Nicholas said, nodding towards the heavy piece that took up most of the space. When his squire blanched, Nicholas shrugged. 'Or you can lay your pallet on the floor,' he said, removing his sword.

'But what about…Emery?' Guy asked.

'I'm sure Kenrick can find an extra pallet for him,' Nicholas said and the steward nodded.

Still Guy did not move. *'Here?'* he asked, in a shrill voice.

'Yes, here,' Nicholas said. Although most servants bedded down in the great hall, when travelling Nicholas kept his squire close at hand, and he intended to do the same with Emery. One of the reasons he had chosen not to make camp outside was because of the protection provided by the manor walls. Nicholas had no idea what was behind the attack upon Gerard, but Gwayne might not be the only threat to the Montbards, and he planned to keep both Emery and Guy safe from harm.

The thought made him glance towards where they lingered on the threshold, Guy poised as though to prevent the boy from entering. 'You want us both to stay with you? All of us? Together?' the squire asked, as though slow of wit.

What had got into him? 'Yes, you can put your pallets on the floor,' Nicholas said. 'I'm sure there is room enough around the bed.' The steward, hovering nearby, nodded again, but lingered. He was hanging on to every word of the unusual exchange, obviously eager to pass on any and all gossip relating to a de Burgh.

'But...' Guy began, only to trail off as he became aware of the steward's attention.

'But what?' Nicholas asked, impatiently. 'Would you rather sleep elsewhere? If some kitchen wench has invited you to join her, then just say so and be gone.'

Guy's mouth dropped open and he muttered to himself as he passed the gawking steward, Emery on his heels. Having no further excuse to stay, Kenrick finally took his leave with a low bow.

The matter seemingly settled, Nicholas turned away, shaking his head at his squire's latest foibles. He tried to make light of Guy's superstitions, but he was losing his patience. Then he felt a familiar stab of guilt, for how much of Guy's transformation was a result of what had befallen him?

Loosing a low sigh, Nicholas pushed the thought aside and concentrated on removing his mail. Although a shortened coat that he wore over his tunic, it was heavy, and after setting it aside he stretched, easing his sore muscles.

He paid little heed when a servant arrived with Emery's pallet, but was relieved to see another with a bowl of water and a sliver of soap. Nodding his thanks, Nicholas was eager to wash the road from some of his body, at least. But when he would have stepped forwards, Guy moved in front of him.

'Wouldn't you rather have a bath, my lord?' the squire said. 'I'll see if one can be prepared in the kitchens.'

Again, Nicholas wondered whether some serving maid from below had caught Guy's attention. It was not like the squire to seek fleeting female companionship, but Nicholas could not blame him. 'If you wish a bath, go seek one out,' he said. 'I am for bed.'

'Then let us all to bed,' Guy said. 'We had better sleep in our clothes in case of attack during the night hours and so as to leave quickly come the morning.'

Nicholas was still gaping at the suggestion there would be a midnight raid upon Roode's little manor when Guy blew out the candles that stood nearby, reducing the light to that of the fire.

'Do you know something I don't?' Nicholas asked, losing his patience. 'Has Emery confided something to you that I should know?'

The look on Guy's face was comical.

'Because unless you are aware of some scheme to assail us while we sleep, I hardly think we are in any danger inside these walls,' Nicholas said. Turning away in annoyance, he pulled his tunic over his head and tossed it aside. Let Guy sleep in his clothes, for he had not been wearing mail all day.

When Guy slunk away, suitably chastened, Nicholas moved to the bowl and splashed some water on his face. Then he dampened the soap and began working it over his arms and chest. The coolness on his skin felt so good, Nicholas tipped his head back and sighed.

He had learned to appreciate such small pleasures and the soothing ritual was bound to relax anyone, even his overwrought squire. In fact, Nicholas was about to urge his companions to partake of the water, too, but a glance in their direction gave him pause. While Guy was tending to their gear, young Emery was staring at Nicholas with something akin to shock.

Was the boy dismayed by his scars? Although Nicholas had his share, they were of no account and he opened his mouth to reassure the boy. But just then Emery's gaze met his own and Nicholas's response was both swift and inexplicable. Sudden heat rushed through him, along with a sharp awareness, and he felt the same strong connection he'd known when he looked at Emery in the darkness of the tunnel.

Just as it had before, Nicholas's surroundings fell away, the manor, his squire and all else, until there was only Emery, whose bright blue eyes were barely visible in the firelight. The moment might have lasted for ever or only for a heartbeat, but when the boy looked away the bond was broken.

'I—I must use the garderobe,' Emery stammered. Scrambling towards the doorway as if the devil himself gave chase, the boy pushed by Guy without a backward glance.

'Good idea,' the squire said as the fleeing figure passed him.

Nicholas turned away, unwilling to let his squire see his dismay. Was he feverish? Had he been stricken with some new malady? Nicholas finished his ablutions in silence, unease overcoming his earlier enjoyment.

Drying himself with a scrap of linen, he sat

down to remove his boots, but left on his braies. Although he suspected no attack from outside forces, such was his custom whenever staying in a strange place. He had learned from his brothers how to leave in a hurry and a naked man was vulnerable in a fight.

Lying back upon the bed, Nicholas heard Guy settle on to his pallet. The firelight lent a soft glow to the room, which should be enough to guide Emery's steps when he returned. Nicholas felt a stab of concern over the lengthy absence, but he doubted there were any threats within these walls. And he was not about to go after the boy.

With an effort, he turned his thoughts elsewhere, considering his plans for the morrow, when they would retrace their steps, heading back towards the Hospitaller commandery. For if Emery lived in the 'old gatehouse', then the uncle's residence must be nearby. And whether Gerard was there or not, their search for him likely would end since there was nowhere else to look. No matter what the outcome, Nicholas's quest would be over, as well as his association with Emery.

Nicholas shifted restlessly at the thought, balking at the approaching end of both. He had come to realise that he needed a task, something to be doing until he could do no more. And as for Emery... Nicholas shifted again as he acknowledged his odd kinship with the boy.

There was something about Emery that reminded him of home, which might explain the peculiar yearning that had struck him. Emery was obviously devoted to his brother, making Nicholas recall his own siblings with new affection. For a moment, he wondered about them and the changes these past months might have wrought, only to push such thoughts aside.

He also dismissed his plan to teach Emery some of his skills. He could not take on another squire, and he was not sure of his own abilities, considering the weariness, flashes of heat and strange giddiness that had come over him today. He would rather not start something he could not finish.

And Emery, like his family, would remember him as he should be, a knight and de Burgh, rather than what he had become.

Emery woke with a start, disoriented by the sight of unfamiliar walls. A pale glow entered through a narrow window above, where the sky showed the first hint of dawn, and beneath her was a hard mat that was not her bed. Then it all came rushing back: Gerard's appearance, her panicked flight and everything that had happened since, including her visit to the Templar catacombs. And yet, eclipsing all was what had occurred in this very room.

Lord de Burgh had taken off his clothes.

Although the morning air was cool, Emery felt a sudden flush at the memory. She knew better than to think of it, yet her mind returned to that moment when she had stumbled over the threshold, unsure as to why Guy was arguing over their sleeping arrangements. Perhaps the squire would rather bed down in the hall, but Emery felt safer near Lord de Burgh—at least until he removed his mail.

Then, Emery wasn't so sure. Transfixed by his casual movements and the flexing of his muscles, she had gaped at him, while her pulse picked up its pace. She still hadn't understood the implications of spending the night with the man, but then he took off his tunic, as well. And when he stood before her, bared to the waist, Emery felt as though her very heart had stopped.

She'd been unprepared for the huge expanse of sun-bronzed skin that was his back, the wide shoulders and torso tapering to a narrow waist where his braies hung low upon his hips. Heedless of Guy, she'd blinked, breathless, as the great knight bent over a bowl, dipping his large hands in the water. Then he'd taken the soap and slid it across his chest. Wet. Soapy. Gilded by firelight.

Emery had never seen anything like it.

Her heart had thundered, threatening to burst as he tipped back his head, baring his thick throat and loosing a guttural groan. And then, as if he was aware of what he'd wrought, he'd looked at her just as he had in the tunnel. It was lighter in the bedchamber and he wasn't as close to her, but what passed between them was even more powerful.

And frightening. Emery had need of a knight to help her find her brother, but she wanted nothing of the strange sensations that were stirring inside her. Hot, dizzy and uncomfortable, she finally wrested her gaze away. Afraid for herself—afraid *of* herself—she had fled to the garderobe, where she put shaking hands to her face and thought of fleeing even further. But where could she go on foot at night? It was a long walk back to the commandery, where her search for Gerard would end and her long penance begin.

Fear of more tangible threats than Lord de Burgh's dark eyes finally sent her back here and she had made her way to her pallet amid Guy's heavy snores. But it was not the squire who kept her awake well into the night. Long after she had become used to the sound, Emery remained aware of the man who lay in the bed, bare skin gleaming in the moonlight, his handsome face even more so in the shadows.

Now, as the memory seized hold, so did a terrible urge to look again. Quelling it firmly, Emery turned her face to the window, hoping that the morning air might bring her back to herself. And yet, yesterday, she had felt more alive than she had in years and far more like the self she used to be—except for her sudden interest in a man's state of undress.

The girl who had trained with her brother would never have felt this way. But that girl had been a child, not a woman. And she had never seen anyone like Lord de Burgh. Who could have predicted such a man?

Emery shook her head, dismissing such thoughts. For a while at least, she could be herself again and that did not include an unwelcome infatuation with one of the de Burgh brothers, no matter how comely they might be. Adjusting her boy's garb, she sat up and tucked her hair more tightly under her cap. Her twin would not be ogling the men in his company and she shouldn't, either. She needed to act more like a male and start thinking like one, too.

Yet, somehow, her gaze drifted to the occupant of the bed, where the first rays of sunlight kissed smooth flesh burnished golden. One strong arm was thrown across his wide chest in repose and his dark hair was tousled with sleep. Staring at him, Emery felt funny inside, as though she wanted to weep and smile at the same time, for a certain joy that came with looking upon him was mixed with the knowledge that she should not.

For an instant, Emery let herself imagine what it would be like to wake up beside Nicholas de Burgh and not on a pallet on the floor by his bed, to be acknowledged as a woman, not a passing youth. And her heart pounded with such yearning that she told herself 'twas just as well that she could do neither.

Nicholas nodded his approval of the little palfrey Kenrick offered him from the manor's stock and they concluded the transaction to their mutual benefit. Kenrick had assured him that he could return the animal later, but in the meantime Emery would have a mount. And as he led the sprightly creature towards where Guy and the boy waited, Nicholas felt absurdly pleased with his purchase.

It was a necessity, nothing more, but still he enjoyed presenting the gift. The boy's surprise and delight was a gift in return, reminding him of the bonds of brotherhood and friendship.

'Should our paths cross that of the Templar, we shall need speed and the ability to manoeuvre,' Nicholas said when Emery protested the expense. 'Guy cannot be worried about you hanging on behind while he rides.'

Emery nodded and Nicholas felt something constrict in his chest. He told himself this odd connection with the boy was brought on by yearning for his own family or perhaps even the son he would never have, yet he deliberately did not gaze directly into those bright blue eyes.

'I've a short sword for you, as well, should the need arise,' Nicholas said. Emery nodded again, but Guy sputtered in protest.

'Surely that is not necessary, my lord,' the squire said, with a shocked expression.

'Even a child can hack with a sword if cornered,' Nicholas said. While only knights and those attending them were trained in the use of such weapons, 'twas better to be armed rather than not, if they were waylaid by Gwayne or any of the brigands who preyed upon the roads.

'But 'tis dangerous! Emery might…get hurt,' Guy said.

'I hardly think the boy will cut himself,' Nicholas answered. And when Guy looked as though he might say more, Nicholas lifted his brows, effectively putting an end to the discussion.

Muttering to himself, as was his wont lately, Guy had kept shaking his head long after they had left Roode behind. And several times during the morning's ride, he seemed ready to broach some subject, only to fall silent. Nicholas wasn't sure whether his squire was worried about Emery or jealous of the boy, but either way, he did not want to be distracted by petty disputes.

After what the priest had said about Gwayne, Nicholas was more concerned with the Templar, who might still be roaming the area. But they saw no other travellers, only the occasional shepherd or freeman. Despite the stunning vistas, the moors were a lonely place and he would not mind leaving them behind.

Abruptly, Nicholas wondered what Emery thought and if he ever had a desire to journey away from his home. As usual, the young man was quiet, perhaps even more so today. Now that he had his own mount, Emery seemed to keep to himself, so when he approached, Nicholas felt absurdly pleased, an uncomfortable reaction at best. *What the devil ailed him?* Nicholas wondered again.

'Montbard Manor lies beyond these trees, my lord,' Emery said, gesturing towards the copse of elms ahead. 'If you please, I will wait for you within the wood. I have no love for my uncle and fear that my presence, indeed, the mere mention of me, might compromise the search for Gerard.'

Nicholas's eyes narrowed, for he did not see how a stranger would have more success than a relative in the hunt for a missing member of the family. 'Why would your uncle speak freely to me of Gerard's whereabouts?'

'Because you are a de Burgh,' Emery said, his mouth twisting wryly. 'And Harold is nothing if not ambitious, hungry to associate with the wealthy and powerful.'

Nicholas frowned. Personally, he was not wealthy or powerful, but his name was known and honoured, and if that would gain Harold's trust, then he would use it. 'Very well,' he said. 'I will make no mention of you, only that I am bound to help Gerard, which is true enough.'

Emery's relief was obvious and Nicholas sensed there was more to the story than the boy was telling. However, they could not linger here, else they be marked. With a nod, Nicholas urged them onwards into the trees.

Yet he found himself reluctant to leave the boy behind. He was struck by the notion that Emery might disappear in their absence, whether by his own accord or someone else's. While Nicholas and Guy could take care of themselves, Emery seemed ill experienced in the ways of the world and a short sword would do little against a determined foe. So Nicholas hesitated, his destrier growing restive, until Emery's blue gaze met his own.

'I'll be fine,' the boy said, as though reading his thoughts, and Nicholas looked away, feeling foolish. Setting his mouth into a firm line, he left the copse, with Guy not far behind.

But his uneasiness continued. Like Temple Roode, Montbard seemed unusually quiet. Of course, Harold could have gone travelling, taking most of the servants with him. 'Twould not be unusual, yet there was something about the silence that struck Nicholas with foreboding and he put his hand to the hilt of his sword.

'The place seems deserted,' Guy said, echoing his thoughts.

'You wait here,' Nicholas said. 'Should anything happen, make sure that you take Emery with you to my brother Geoffrey's home, as it is not too distant.'

'No, my lord!' Guy protested. 'I am bound to you.'

Nicholas shook his head. Guy's loyalty did him justice, but it surpassed his courage and they had Emery to consider now. Better that the two youths escape than endanger themselves for his sake, especially now.

'I would be assured of your safety, though I do not expect trouble nor do I seek it,' Nicholas said. And he spoke the truth. Normally, a manorial farm such as this one harboured no threats, but nothing since his encounter with Gerard Montbard had been normal. And there was always the possibility that Gwayne had followed up yesterday's visit to the Hospitaller commandery with a stop here.

When Guy gave his reluctant assent, Nicholas dismounted, yet still no one came out to greet him. The building appeared ill tended and Nicholas wondered about the arrangement Emery had mentioned. If the land itself belonged to the commandery, Harold might lack the resources to properly maintain the house he had gained.

Unheralded, Nicholas walked to the stone archway that had once held a large door, but now served as a portal to a smaller entrance. It was into this dim passage that he moved cautiously, only to watch the heavy wood swing inwards at his approach.

Nicholas stepped back, ready to draw his weapon, but it seemed that an empty hall greeted him. Scanning the dim recesses of the interior, he was at a loss, for he knew no errant breeze could have moved the heavy wood. He waited warily, but when the door wobbled, at last he spied a presence. A small boy, hardly old enough to manage the door, peeked around it to gaze up at Nicholas wide-eyed.

Moving inside, Nicholas kept a wary eye on his surroundings, but all he saw were the same subtle signs of neglect. Had Harold fallen upon hard times, or had his efforts won him a place to live and little else? Or was something more insidious responsible for Nicholas's lack of welcome?

With no one else in attendance, Nicholas was forced to address the boy, who might be serving as a page, despite his apparent youth. 'Please advise Master Montbard that Lord de Burgh seeks an audience.'

The child simply shook his head, forcing Nicholas to sink down on his haunches to face the lad directly. His manner had been formal, but now he spoke gently. 'Is Master Montbard here?'

Again, the boy shook his head. 'He's gone searching for the parcel,' the child said. 'The parcel Gerard wanted.'

It was all Nicholas could do not to seize the boy at the casual mention of the man he was seeking, but he kept his tone even. 'Gerard is here?'

The child shook his head again. 'He was here, but he ran away.'

Nicholas tried not to react to the boy's choice of words. 'Has Master Montbard gone to find him?'

Once more, the child shook his head. 'Master Montbard has gone to look for the parcel.'

'What parcel?' Nicholas asked.

'The one that Gerard sent to Emery,' the boy said. 'So the master went to where Emery lives now.'

Where Emery lives now? Had Gerard returned there, as well? If so, he might be dismayed to find Emery gone. And he might be even more dismayed to find his uncle at his heels, especially if he 'ran away' from the man. Nicholas rose to his feet, eager to give chase himself, lest Gerard slip through his fingers yet again.

But the sound of approaching footsteps stopped him and Nicholas put a hand to the hilt of his sword, just in case Harold had returned and would take exception to a stranger in his hall. But the new arrival was only a plump, older woman, who appeared none too happy to see an armed knight looming over what might be her child.

From her dress and bearing, Nicholas could not tell whether she was a valued servant or poor relation, but he inclined his head in greeting. 'I am Nicholas de Burgh and am seeking

Gerard Montbard, a Hospitaller knight I have sworn to aid.'

The woman paled, presumably at the mention of Gerard, who appeared to have left havoc in his wake, wherever he went.

'He has been here?' Nicholas asked, hoping for confirmation of what the boy had told him.

'Yes, but he's gone now,' she said, as if eager for Nicholas to leave, as well. Was she just reticent, with the wariness of isolated folk? Or did she hesitate to speak without Harold's approval? Nicholas wished that he had questioned Emery more fully about the household.

'Do you know where I can find him?' Nicholas asked. 'He was ill at last report and in need of protection against a Templar knight who would do him harm.'

'The Templar!'

Nicholas turned in surprise at the sound of the boy, who was quickly hushed by the woman. 'Was a Templar knight here, as well?' Nicholas asked.

The woman shook her head. 'We know only that Gerard spoke of such a man. He was…ill. But he went away. We know not where.'

She was telling the truth, of that Nicholas was certain. But she was afraid, most likely of

Harold, a man whom Nicholas was increasingly eager to question. Something or someone had sent Gerard fleeing from this place and that someone was probably Harold. Nicholas would take a grim pleasure in finding out.

'Master Montbard had gone to the old gate-house?' he asked.

The woman's eyes widened in surprise at his knowledge and Nicholas did not mention its source. 'I am not at liberty to speak of the master's whereabouts,' she said. 'Perhaps you will find him in residence at some later time.'

Obviously, Nicholas was not welcome to wait, which was just as well because his instincts were telling him the sooner he got to the gatehouse, the better. And if this Harold was so feared... Nicholas felt a sudden sharp concern for Emery and, with the barest of civilities, he left the manor, eager to assure himself of the boy's safety.

Outside, he was relieved to find Guy, but he did not waste time reporting upon his odd encounters. He was too intent upon retrieving Emery and heading on to the boy's home. Even if Gerard was not there, it appeared that Harold would be and Nicholas intended to find out why he was not searching for his ailing relative, but for a parcel that, by the page's account, did not even belong to him.

Too late, Nicholas realised why Emery had been reluctant to accompany him here and his uneasiness about leaving the boy behind increased. He approached the wood warily. When he did not immediately spy Emery, his heart tripped in panic. Frantically, he scanned the area where they had left the boy until Guy pointed towards a gap in the leaves. His squire's calm manner made Nicholas feel foolish and his jaw tightened as he peered into the foliage. Still, he felt giddy with relief when the nose of the palfrey appeared. He whistled softly and the animal nickered and moved towards them.

But its saddle was empty.

For a long moment, Nicholas stared, his emotions a mixture of dismay, anger and something unidentifiable. He was supposed to be one of the steadiest of the de Burghs and his brothers counted upon him to retain his reason in the midst of tumult. But right now he felt like howling his pain to the skies. And then, above the pounding of his heart, he heard a voice.

'Here I am, my lord.'

The sound of Emery's speech made Nicholas feel weak. Had the boy fallen? Nicholas looked at the ground only to realise that a rustling was coming from above. Lifting his head, Nicholas saw Emery nimbly swing from a limb to land upon his feet.

'What the devil?' The words burst from Nicholas as though the breath had been knocked from him.

'Gerard and I grew up climbing these old elms,' Emery said, flashing a smile.

Another time, Nicholas would have been glad to see a grin from the shy youth, but now his carelessness was not appreciated. Although this sort of prank smacked of his brothers' antics, Nicholas was not amused.

Emery must have seen his thunderous expression, for the boy hastened to explain. 'I—I feared discovery by...those at the manor and would hide myself, my lord, as well as watch the place from one of our old perches. All is quiet.'

Nicholas frowned, still displeased by the boy's actions—or perhaps his own response to them. 'That's because Harold is on his way to you.'

'What?' The boy paled so visibly that Nicholas regretted his taunt.

'It seems that your uncle has gone to your

home, so let us see if we can find him there,' Nicholas said, more gently.

But Emery shook his head. 'I can't, my lord. You go on and I shall wait here.'

Nicholas eyed the boy directly. 'I'm not leaving without you,' he said. Not again. He had no intention of reliving the past few moments any time soon.

Emery said nothing, as though afraid to argue, but unwilling to capitulate. Who would have guessed the youth's mild manner hid a stubborn streak?

'Think you that I cannot protect you from your uncle?' Nicholas asked. Unless Harold boasted a guard of armed men, he was no match for a de Burgh, even this one.

Emery's blue gaze met his, startling Nicholas with its intensity. 'I think, my lord, that there are some things that even you cannot control.'

Nicholas looked away, the words too close to the truth for his comfort, a truth that this boy could hardly comprehend.

'My lord—' Guy started to speak, but Nicholas cut him off with a gesture.

'We ride to the old gatehouse, as you referred to it,' Nicholas said to Emery. 'All of us. Once we near the place, you may hang back so that your uncle marks you not. Hell, you can even scale a tree, if it gives you comfort. But the three of us are not separating.'

Not now, Nicholas thought. Not yet.

Chapter Five

Emery had no choice but to go along, her new-found independence making her bristle at her companion's display of heavy-handedness. He was a de Burgh, so, of course, he was arrogant, imperious and accustomed to getting his own way, qualities that tempted Emery to disobey. After all, this man held no sway over her; she answered to a different authority.

But he did not know that. And thoughts of the secret she kept close reminded Emery of the danger she was in, even now. She could not afford to leave Lord de Burgh even if she would. And would she? Although she had dismissed her increasing interest in the man as some sort of unwelcome infatuation, she could not deny the power of his words.

I'm not leaving without you. It was something Emery had never heard before, nor had she ever expected to hear it. Her father, her brother and all that she had held dear were gone and she had spent the past months alone. So she could not help being affected by the declaration, spoken with such fierce determination.

Nicholas de Burgh was strong, honourable, loyal and generous, so perhaps he could be forgiven for being too domineering. No doubt the de Burghs were bred to command, Emery decided. And so she followed, ignoring the nagging suspicion that she would go wherever he led.

But she stayed low in the saddle, as if she could hide from all who might be watching: her uncle, the Hospitallers or any who worked these lands. The Templar knight did not concern her; she had no doubt that Lord de Burgh could protect her against any attack. But what could he do should she be recognised?

As they neared her home, Emery felt less like her old self and more like the frightened woman she had become, fear of discovery making her duck her head and pull her cap low. She realised that few here remembered the days when she had dressed as her brother and even fewer would expect her to be riding with strangers, yet she could not slow the frantic beat of her heart.

Only when they reached the familiar structure did Emery's anxiety ease, for there were no horses tethered nearby and she knew Harold would not have walked from Montbard. Nor would he have gone out without an attendant, for he liked to give the impression that he was a wealthy man. And perhaps he was. Emery knew few details of the arrangement he had made as her father lay dying.

The Hospitallers themselves would not ride, but she doubted that any would be waiting inside. Yet when they dismounted and walked closer, Emery saw the door standing open, which meant someone must have been here since her departure yesterday morning. Immediately, she thought of Gerard, who might have returned, perhaps even moments after she had gone or when the Templar had left the commandery.

With a low cry, she stepped forwards, but Lord de Burgh bid her stay back while he went ahead. Emery stood by Guy, impatient, but in the silence that followed, she realised that whoever had been here, whether Gerard or another, must have abandoned the place. Perhaps she had even left the door unlatched.

Her suspicions seemed confirmed when Lord de Burgh emerged alone, yet he motioned for her to join him while Guy kept watch. Emery hoped that he did not intend to question her as to the female clothing that she had left in plain sight and frantically tried to think of an explanation.

But when she entered, 'twas not a stray kirtle, but something far more dismaying that greeted her. Although the old gatehouse was not her choice of residence, it had been better than the alternative and Emery had done her best to make a home there. Now her efforts lay scattered and ruined at her feet.

Clothing, bedding and utensils were strewn everywhere, along with the straw that had once filled her bed. Even the loose tile that covered her hiding place had been pried up and broken, though the hole beneath was empty. Swallowing a cry of distress, Emery looked to Lord de Burgh, who was stepping carefully amongst the disarray. Stopping before a pile of bedding, he turned to eye her grimly.

'Is this your uncle?'

For an instant, Emery did not know what he was talking about. She stared blankly at the worn blanket, only to realise that something lay beneath it. And when she moved closer, she saw what it was: a man lying upon his stomach, seemingly lifeless. Swaying upon her feet, Emery blinked at Lord de Burgh, as if to draw from him the strength necessary to look down.

When she did, Emery caught her breath. The man's neck was twisted at an odd angle, but there was no mistaking Harold's features. His eyes were wide, as if in terror, and a trickle of blood dripped from his open mouth. With a shudder, Emery turned to lean against the great knight beside her, grateful for his solid form.

'Yes, that is my uncle,' she murmured, trying to act more like a young man and less like a frightened female. Still, she swallowed a gasp as Lord de Burgh bent low, reaching towards the body.

He must have removed his gloves earlier to search for signs of life, for he did not touch Harold now, but plucked away something that lay upon the dead man's back. Although Emery did not want to see, she forced herself to remain steady as he held out his prize to her: the same type of brightly coloured piece of parchment that Gerard had left behind in her bed.

With a groan, Emery swayed upon her feet, shutting her eyes, as though she might close out everything except the knight, her only anchor in a careening world. She longed to bury her face in the folds of his tunic, shutting out all ills, but she could hardly do so, for he was not her brother…

'Gerard!' Emery whispered, blinking suddenly. She eyed the knight in alarm. 'You don't think he…?' Emery could not finish the sentence. Their uncle had done the family ill and perhaps Gerard had finally seen that. But he was a knight and a member of a holy order. He must have fought valiantly in the Holy Land before returning home, injured…and raving. Yet, surely he would not do murder. Emery backed away, shaking her head, as though distance would aid her denial.

'No, I do not think that.'

The sound of Lord de Burgh's deep voice, low and gentle, steadied her, then his big hands cupped her face. Startled at the touch of his fingers, warm and calloused, Emery glanced up, only to realise her mistake. His dark gaze locked with hers, stealing her breath and making her heart pound.

Although she had always rejected the connection between them, now Emery embraced it, welcoming his warmth and strength as a source of comfort—and something else she could not name. Lord de Burgh seemed caught up in their mysterious communion, as well, and, when she leaned towards him, Emery thought he might lower his head.

She lifted hers in response, but suddenly, his hands fell away, as though her very skin had burned the pads of his fingers. His normally open visage closed, shutting her out, and he strode to the door. Only when he had reached the threshold did he turn back to her.

'We should not tarry here,' he said. 'If there is anything you would take, bring it with you.'

He stepped outside and Emery shivered, suddenly cold. Although she had spent the past months virtually alone, she had never felt so bereft as when this man turned away from her. Rubbing her arms, she watched him go, only to shiver again at the prospect of lingering here where her uncle lay dead.

Emery had known when she left yesterday morning that she would probably not be allowed to return, yet she still mourned the loss of her little home. She had been lonely here, but she had hung on to a small measure of independence that was not likely to be granted her in the future.

Standing amidst the ruins, not only of her possessions, but of the life she had made for herself, Emery said one last, bittersweet goodbye.

Nicholas's jaw tightened as he strode towards his destrier, for Harold's death upped the stakes. Theft and assault were bad enough, but murder was something else and would make their search for Gerard all the more difficult. Their presence in the area had been marked and to ask questions now would mean enforced delays, if not prosecution. Although the de Burgh name would stand him in good stead, Nicholas did not want to drag his family into this.

And he had Emery to consider.

Nicholas shook his head as he swung into the saddle. It seemed that he couldn't stop worrying about Emery. Or staring at Emery. Or feeling...odd about Emery. Again he wondered what ailed him and whether whatever it was would affect his ability to complete his task and protect Guy and the boy. That concern gave him a new sense of urgency.

'We must go,' Nicholas said, glancing towards where his companions stood, deep in conversation. 'Now.'

Both boys glanced up at him in alarm, and Nicholas noticed that Guy had a hand on Emery's shoulder as if in comfort. Already tense, Nicholas felt a stab of something akin to... No, it definitely was *not* jealousy, he told himself.

'Aren't we going to bury him?' Guy asked, apparently having been apprised of Harold's condition.

'No, we aren't going to bury him, unless you want to be tied up with the authorities for ever,' Nicholas said. 'And we still have Gerard to find, a task that is all the more important after discovering his uncle's death, though since Emery is missing, as well, they might lay the blame upon him.'

The boy blanched and Nicholas regretted his careless words.

'Even if I would do murder, I could hardly... snap his neck like that,' Emery said, with a shudder.

Nicholas shrugged. 'Sometimes, those in

charge seek the easiest explanation and he is lying dead in your house, having gone there seeking something, to which his household will attest.'

Nicholas could almost see the boy's mind work. 'But where are his men? Why would he come alone? And Harold would never have walked here. What of his horse?'

'I don't know,' Nicholas said. 'Perhaps he did not want anyone to see what he was about, or perhaps whoever he brought with him murdered him for the prize, once it was found. 'Twould be simple enough to take his horse or send it riderless across the moors.'

'What prize?' Emery asked, with a puzzled expression, but Nicholas stopped any further questions with a gesture.

'We cannot linger here within sight of the commandery,' Nicholas said. 'We need a sanctuary, somewhere we can discuss our next move away from prying eyes.'

'What of the church?' Emery said, taking Nicholas's words literally.

'Or the manor in Roode where we spent the night?' Guy said, obviously anxious to avoid any place related to the Templars.

Nicholas frowned. 'I hate to travel that far

away.' And yet, was Roode far enough? Their presence in the area was already noted. Sooner or later someone would wish to speak with them about the murder, if not the murderer himself...

'There's a ruin not far from Montbard Manor,' Emery said. ''Tis an old wooden fort that was here before the house was built. Little is left, but it would provide some shelter and seclusion.'

Nicholas nodded. He just wanted to get out of sight long enough to discuss what they knew, though that seemed to be precious little. His efforts to save an unwary Hospitaller had escalated into he knew not what and he felt as though he were groping in the dark with both hands tied behind his back.

Emery led the way as they retraced their steps, while Nicholas watched for any signs of Harold's men or a lone horse running free. But the area seemed desolate. It was almost too quiet, he thought, frowning. But silence was more welcome than sounds of pursuit, Nicholas admitted as they drew close to the copse where Emery had hidden. The boy had just headed into the cover of the trees when Nicholas saw horses standing at the front of the manor. And they were not riderless.

With a low word of warning, he urged Emery into the trees. 'Take to the heights, as you did before, and send your mount off, if need be.'

'But—'

Nicholas halted the boy's protest with a grunt and swung his mount around. Although he would have preferred to have his squire tucked safely away, as well, he had no choice. There were two riders ahead. One wore the distinctive white robes of the Templar and Nicholas suspected the other was responsible for the knot upon his head. And he did not care to be ambushed from behind again by Gwayne's henchman.

Taking advantage of whatever element of surprise he could, Nicholas drew his sword and charged. At the sound, Gwayne turned, the puzzlement on his face soon replaced by a flash of recognition and finally an evil glee at the opportunity to fight him again.

'You!' the Templar shouted, drawing his weapon. 'Why do you bedevil me?'

'Where is the Hospitaller?' Nicholas asked, as their blades met.

'And why does he concern you?'

'I am concerned for any victim of yours,' Nicholas said, refusing to give the villain any information.

'If I'd known you would trouble me again, I would have killed you,' Gwayne said, with a snarl. 'But this time I will make sure you don't return.'

'And how will you manage that without help, coward?' Nicholas asked. He nodded towards Gwayne's confederate, against whom Guy was faring poorly. But Nicholas could spare no thoughts for his squire, for his taunt made the Templar surge forwards in anger—and the knight was an opponent to be reckoned with.

A year ago, Nicholas would have had little trouble subduing the Templar, but he had lost too much of his strength and his reactions were not what they used to be. Only his blade and his wits were as sharp as ever and they served him well, for Gwayne honoured no knightly code. Unable to overcome Nicholas's defence, he swung his heavy weapon towards the destrier and only the animal's dance kept them from going down.

Although Nicholas had avoided a spill, his squire was not so lucky. Riding away to circle back, Nicholas saw Guy knocked to the ground, an easy target for either villain. With a bellow, Nicholas kicked at his horse to hasten towards the boy, but an echoing cry rang out, making him glance over his shoulder

Knowing Gwayne's methods, Nicholas had cause to be wary of some new menace, but 'twas no stranger who joined the fray. To Nicholas's shock, Emery burst from the woods, swinging the short sword above his head and charging towards the fallen squire with surprising skill. For an instant, Nicholas was paralysed with fear for the boy, but thankfully, his opponents were caught off guard, as well, perhaps leery of more riders emerging from the copse.

Seizing his opportunity, Nicholas bore down on the distracted Templar with a vengeance, slicing his arm. The Templar howled in pain and switched his sword to his other hand, but he began backing his mount away as if to flee. When Nicholas refused to give him quarter, Gwayne swung round to gallop away, his squire on his heels.

Roaring in outrage, Nicholas gave chase. He called to Guy to do the same, but when he glanced behind him, he saw that his squire was still on the ground, bent anxiously over Emery's prone form.

* * *

Emery drew a deep, shuddering breath and counted herself lucky that she wasn't dead. It had been far too long since she'd wielded a blade and she hadn't the strength to hold her own for long. In her younger years, her skills had equalled Gerard's, but eventually he outweighed her, outreached her and outfought her with muscles she could not hope to match. One day she had given up trying and their paths diverged, leading them to separate duties and different futures.

'Mistress Emery! Are you all right?'

Emery opened her eyes to see Guy's face swimming before her. He had pulled her under the trees, out of harm's way, it seemed, and she was grateful. But when she blinked up at him, the implication of his words sunk in. She drew another deep breath, flinching at its painful progress, before she could manage to speak.

'How long have you known?' she asked, not bothering with a denial.

'Nearly since the beginning.'

Emery closed her eyes against the hard truth. But it explained much, including Guy's wariness and resentment, along with his recent solicitousness. When she thought of his valiant protests over last night's sleeping arrangements, Emery nearly smiled. But the ramifications of her discovery gave her little amusement, and, though she ached all over, 'twas the pain in her heart that took precedence. Now what would she do?

'Why didn't you tell him?' she asked.

'I tried at the beginning, but he wouldn't listen,' Guy said. 'And, then, well, I realised that you…uh, your quest, that is…did him good.'

Emery might have questioned Guy more on that score, but the squire grinned. 'And if he's too dense to figure it out for himself, well, then it's not my place to enlighten him, is it?'

Emery frowned in confusion. She hardly dared hope that Guy would continue to keep her secret. Why should he?

'You saved my life,' he said, as if in answer to her unspoken query. 'I've never seen a braver act and I come from Campion, where the de Burghs are thought the most courageous in the land.'

Emery did smile then and tried to lift her head, but she felt too battered and bruised. She wasn't accustomed to taking spills any more, or had she been wounded?

'Are you hurt?' Guy asked, in an anxious tone.

Emery tried to tell him she was just winded, but she could produce only a wheezing sound that did little to reassure the squire before she fell back, gasping.

'I'm going to get help,' he said.

Emery shook her head, panic forcing her to speak. 'Lord de Burgh said—'

Guy cut her off. 'Lord de Burgh isn't here. And neither is your uncle. Surely, there must be someone in that house who can be trusted.'

Emery nodded. 'Gytha. Fetch Gytha from Montbard Manor.'

Gytha would not approve, but the servant would recognise her, even in this guise, and would provide care, if given the time. With some measure of relief, Emery let her lashes flutter shut once more. She heard Guy's footsteps as he hastened to the manor and then only the creak of the elms and the rustle of their leaves in the wind.

But it wasn't long before she heard something else: the unmistakable sound of a horse nearby. From her position on the ground, Emery could see little, so she could not judge her chances of escape. The limbs above hung tantalisingly out of reach and she did not think she could manage to scale them as she had ear-

lier. She might crawl further into the undergrowth, but the thud of boots upon the ground
told her it was too late.

All she could do was pretend to be dead already, which might convince the Templar, if not
her uncle's men. So Emery remained still, unflinching even when the footfalls approached.
Although she steeled herself against a kick in
the side, instead, the figure dropped down beside her. Would he take her sword? Her nearly
empty purse?

'Emery!' Her name was uttered with such
anguish that it took her a moment to recognise
the speaker as Lord de Burgh.

Emery's eyes flew open, relief swamping
her at the knowledge that he had returned unharmed. For once, she looked eagerly to his
face, welcoming his gaze. But his dark head
was bent over her body, and, just as Emery
would have spoken, he put his hands upon her.

Stunned, Emery could do nothing except lie
prone as she felt him check for injuries. Although she had performed the same service
for Gerard, this man was not her brother. And
the feel of his warm hands as they ran up and
down her legs, gently probing for breaks, made
Emery forget her aches and pains and all else.

Closing her eyes, she groaned as warmth filled her, along with a strange sort of yearning. Had she struck her head? That would account for her sudden inability to think clearly. Or was she dreaming? She knew only that she wanted him to continue, even though her very identity hung in the balance.

That alarming thought finally forced Emery to act, for she could not afford to lose the great knight's good will. She cleared her throat, but it was too late. His head lifted to reveal eyes wide with shock. And Emery's heart lurched, for she knew what would follow: anger, accusations, abandonment…

She wanted to apologise for her deceit, but the intensity of his gaze robbed her of her wits and all she could manage was what she had intended to say moments ago. 'I'm all right.'

'You're female!'

'I'm sorry.'

'I'm not.'

Emery was still blinking in surprise at his words when he lifted his hands. Would he strike her for her lies, as some men might? Emery braced herself for a blow, but his hands only cupped her face. Maybe he was searching for lumps, Emery thought, for she felt even giddier than before, a sure sign of head injury. Yet that did not explain why she yearned to lean into his touch, so featherlight it made her shiver. He bent nearer, perhaps for a better look. But then why was he closing his eyes?

The answer came as he placed his mouth to hers and Emery felt a jolt of astonishment. Surely, she was dreaming or deep in some fevered delusion, for that could be the only explanation for why he was kissing her. Yet never in her wildest fancies had Emery conjured the stroke of his fingers against her cheeks and the gentle brush of his lips.

The body that had been aching and stiff now was suffused with heat and urgency, as though he had breathed life into it. And for one startling moment Emery wondered if she had been dead, only to be revived by this man. He had done it before, though not literally and not like this.

In fact, Emery felt ill equipped to handle the sensations coursing through her, so heady and powerful that she gasped. But the sharp pain that followed put an end to them all, making him draw away even as she wanted to call him back.

'What is it? Where does it hurt?' he asked,

the expression on his face changing from intent to anxious in an instant.

When Emery shook her head in denial, he muttered several low oaths, apparently directed at himself. 'I'm sorry. I'm just so glad that you are female,' he said, his lips quirking ruefully. But there was a new glint in his dark eyes, hinting at things far beyond Emery's realm of experience.

What did she know of men? Or kisses? Or the wild yearning Lord de Burgh had roused inside her? Despite her youthful freedoms, or perhaps because of them, Emery had little dealings with males outside of her family. When other girls might have been making arranged marriages, she had been trying to keep up with her twin. And once her father became ill, Emery rarely left his side until he passed away. How could she understand the subtleties of a man like this one? Or her own reaction to him?

Uncertain, Emery was grateful for the arrival of Guy, dragging a wary Gytha behind him. After one look at her former mistress, the servant insisted they return to the manor. But before Emery could try to rise, she was lifted into the air, tucked against Lord de Burgh's broad chest as though she weighed nothing.

A day ago or even an hour ago, Emery might have protested, but after all that had happened, she welcomed the warmth and safety to be found in the great knight's arms. 'Twas only for a few moments, after all, and provided a balm against the shocking changes wrought in her absence. For Emery soon discovered that most of the furnishings in her old home were gone and her chamber seemed a shadow of itself, lifeless and empty but for the bed where Lord de Burgh laid her.

Her bleak surroundings served as a reminder not to linger here, in a dead man's domain, and Emery was impatient to get up. 'I'm all right,' she insisted, trying to sit.

But Gytha pressed her back down and turned towards Lord de Burgh and Guy. 'Please leave us,' the servant said, making it plain that she did not care to tend to her mistress in the presence of two strange men. Guy immediately started towards the door, but Lord de Burgh leaned his tall form against the wall and crossed his arms over his chest.

'I'm not leaving him,' he said. 'Or her, as the case may be.'

Emery felt a funny flutter inside at his speech, so reminiscent of his earlier words:

I'm not leaving without you. And she dared not look at Gytha, who was the only one privy to her circumstances.

But Gytha only instructed the males to turn around. And when they did, she set to work, poking and prodding. She was less gentle than Lord de Burgh, but more thorough, and found a ripening bruise below Emery's breast.

'There, now, I'll wrap your chest and it should aid your breathing, as well as your manner of dressing as your brother,' Gytha said, eyeing her askance.

'We must find Gerard,' Emery said as Gytha set to work. 'He was here?'

Gytha glanced at the two men, as though reluctant to speak.

'Harold can do no more,' Emery said, suspecting that Gytha's reluctance stemmed from her uncle's ill treatment. No doubt he had insisted upon silence about all his doings from his servants, but there would be no further retribution from the man.

Gytha loosed a low sigh and nodded. 'Gerard was here, but Harold vowed to summon the brethren and turn him out—until he began asking about the parcel,' Gytha said. 'Then

Harold became interested, but it was too late. Gerard made his escape.'

'To where?'

Gytha shook her head.

'What is this parcel?' Guy asked, as the men turned to face them once more.

'I don't know,' Gytha said. 'But from Gerard's ravings, Harold imagined it was something of value, perhaps from the Holy Land. And he was determined to have it, as he has taken all else.'

She gestured towards the bare chamber. 'As you can see, he felt the grip of the devil's bargain he made, taking the manor that was rightfully Gerard's, only to find himself with little else.' She paused. 'And now the devil has claimed his due.'

'So Harold went to…the old gatehouse looking for this parcel, only to be killed there,' Emery said, with a shudder. If not for Lord de Burgh, she might well have been the one to fall prey to the murderer, her corpse lying undiscovered in the small structure where she had lived.

'But neither he nor Gwayne could have found it,' Guy said. 'Else why would the Templar follow Harold's trail back here?'

At the squire's words, Lord de Burgh stirred

and Emery realised that, despite his casual pose, he had been watching out the window, alert for anyone's approach, while following their conversation. He turned to Gytha.

'What did the Templar want here?' he asked.

'The parcel,' the servant said.

Emery loosed a low breath of exasperation at the continual mention of this mysterious object. 'I doubt there is such a thing,' she said.

'There is a parcel,' Gytha said.

'Then what is it?' Guy asked. 'And *where* is it?'

Gytha looked to Emery, as though seeking approval. At her nod, the servant took a deep breath before answering, ''Tis here.'

Chapter Six

Emery eyed the worn leather pouch warily, as one might something dangerous. And well she should, for it had caused terror and bloodshed and disruption of lives. She wondered what would have happened if Gytha had given the thing to any of those, including Gerard, who sought it out.

But with unyielding devotion, the servant had hidden the delivery away from Harold's notice, refusing to acknowledge its existence to any except the intended recipient. Now, her duty done, she slipped away, leaving Emery to stare at the parcel that had finally found its way to her.

A superstitious Guy had argued against opening the bundle at all, but now that Harold was dead, the manor and its contents belonged to the Hospitallers, so Emery could not leave this behind. Yet, faced with the prospect of discovering the contents, Emery hesitated so long that Lord de Burgh finally stepped forwards, taking the pouch in his capable hands.

'Wait!' Guy's anxious shout made Emery flinch, but he only pointed to the flap that Lord de Burgh had lifted. 'There's some writing there. Perhaps it's a warning.'

The squire's tone made the simple leather container seem even more threatening. Did he expect some admonition not to open it upon pain of death or promise of a curse?

Emery shuddered, but Lord de Burgh seemed unconcerned. '"Robert Blanchefort, Knight Templar",' he read aloud. ''Tis the name of the owner of the pouch, if not now, then at some point since its making.'

With a wry glance at his squire, Lord de Burgh reached inside and pulled out an object wrapped in old linen. From Guy's dire predictions, Emery half-expected the great knight to be stricken with some malady and fall to the floor. She even took a tentative step forwards, as though she might provide some aid should that occur.

But he remained standing, tall and strong, while he carefully lifted away the cloth to reveal what lay inside. A hush fell over the chamber then as they all leaned forwards and Emery glimpsed the smooth sheen of a curved surface, caught by the light from the window.

Guy whistled and Emery took a step back, shocked at the sight of a small figure. Perhaps six inches in height, it gleamed with a richness that could only come from one source. No wonder Harold had coveted it, Emery thought. But why would Gerard have a golden statue? Surely it couldn't be real. Emery shook her head, as if to deny its very existence, a reaction encouraged by its strangeness.

Although Emery had seen sculptures and carvings and religious icons before, this bore no resemblance to any of them, not even to the Templars' work. It appeared to be the representation of a man, garbed only in a tall hat and something that hung like a towel around his waist, as well as jewellery such as no man would ever wear. Even the few depictions of the ancients that Emery had seen were nothing like this.

'What is it?' she asked.

Lord de Burgh did not immediately answer.

He hefted the object in his hand and ran his fingers over it in a way that made Emery remember his light touch against her cheek. She shivered, despite a rush of heat, and looked away.

''Tis a gold statue, presumably from foreign lands, perhaps of some god and perhaps taken from some larger piece, for it appears to have been broken off at the bottom.'

''Tis probably some Templar relic,' Guy said. 'Be careful! It might possess powers that we don't know about.'

Emery eyed the squire in alarm. Although she could not countenance such claims, he might be right about the item's ownership. Was this a treasure from the depths of a Templar catacomb, perhaps the very one where she had stood with Lord de Burgh? A glance towards the great knight told her his thoughts were the same.

'Perhaps we should take it to Temple Roode,' Emery suggested.

With a subtle shake of his head, Lord de Burgh warned her not to speak too freely of what they had seen there. 'I think we have used up our welcome at Temple Roode,' he said. 'And while I would not keep something that rightfully belongs to the Templars, I hesitate to dispose of this too quickly—when we may have need for it.'

'What do you mean?' Guy asked, obviously wary. 'Such things are better left alone, my lord, rather than trying to turn them to our purposes.'

'I hardly think this statue possesses mystical capabilities, heathen or Christian,' Lord de Burgh said. 'But it might come in handy should we need to bargain with those who seek it, perhaps for information about Gerard.'

Or Gerard's life.

Although the knight did not say the words aloud, Emery knew from his shuttered expression what he was thinking and her mouth went dry. Thus far, her brother had managed to evade his pursuers, whether the Templar, his own uncle or some unknown villain. But where was he now? And how were they to find him? Emery stared numbly at the statue that provided no answers, only more questions.

'Even if we could find Gwayne, I don't think he's the type to bargain fairly for information or anything else,' Guy said, looking anxious at the prospect of another meeting with the Templar.

'I doubt that Gwayne knows anything, else

he would not be going over the same ground, looking for Gerard and the parcel and killing those in his way,' Lord de Burgh said.

'Who, then?' Guy asked.

Lord de Burgh did not answer and Emery could think of no one else to ask, except the Hospitallers, and Gerard had warned her against trusting them. At the reminder, her gaze drifted again to the contents of Gerard's parcel and she frowned. Had her brother cause to fear the brethren because of something they had done—or something he had done?

Such thoughts led down a path that Emery was not prepared to travel. If her companions wondered why a Hospitaller knight, sworn to poverty, had come by such a valuable object, they did not say so and Emery was grateful. But with nowhere else to go and her uncle's murder making it unwise to stay here, their quest seemed hopeless. How much longer would Lord de Burgh and his squire keep to it?

Just as Emery began to fear the worst, the knight broke the silence. 'Perhaps we should ask Robert Blanchefort,' he said, inclining his head towards the name on the pouch.

'And how do you propose to do that?' Guy asked.

Lord de Burgh lifted his dark brows. 'Where else to find a Templar, but in a preceptory?'

'But you said we shouldn't return to Temple Roode,' Guy said, frowning.

Lord de Burgh grinned and Emery felt a sudden giddiness at the sight of those lips curving upwards. 'There are plenty of other Templar properties whose residents might prove more welcoming to passing travellers. In fact, didn't we pass one on the eastern road?'

For a moment, Emery thought Guy would not answer, but he nodded grudgingly.

''Tis only a few days' ride from here, but should be far enough away to escape any connection with Gwayne,' Lord de Burgh said.

'My lord, 'tis courting trouble to walk right into their lair,' Guy protested. 'We are already being chased by one of them, perhaps more.'

The knight paid his squire no heed. Moving quickly now that he had a plan, he wrapped the dubious treasure and put it back in the pouch. But when he reached out to give it to Emery, she shook her head.

'You keep it safe,' she said, swallowing an odd lump in her throat. The excitement of armed combat, her injury and the discovery of the parcel had kept more mundane concerns at bay, but now they came rushing back. She was grateful that the great knight had not abandoned Gerard. But what of his sister?

Emery steeled herself for what she knew must come, for surely none would willingly travel with a woman garbed as a man. Her heart felt heavy and something pressed against her eyes, but 'twas not just the thought of her future that caused her grief. Her gaze lingered on Lord de Burgh and she was startled at the sharp ache that came at the thought of their parting. But she could only watch as he took up the bundle with a casual nod, oblivious to the turmoil that roiled through her.

'Then, let's be off,' he said, moving towards the door. And when Emery remained where she was, blinking in his wake, he paused to wait for her, so that Guy could bring up the rear.

There was no argument about her joining them, no talk of her staying behind or being deposited somewhere while they continued on, and no lecture on the morality, let alone the danger, of her garb. All the objections Emery had been preparing died upon her lips and the pain that had gripped her was forgotten.

For now, at least, she would follow Lord de Burgh.

* * *

Nicholas watched her from a distance with a kind of wonder reserved for thunderstorms and conjurer's tricks. 'Twas as though the cup he had thought empty was suddenly full of fine wine or the caterpillar he'd caught had turned into a butterfly before his very eyes. He shook his head as he thought back over their brief association and the odd connection with her that he'd felt from the very beginning.

Perhaps now it was explained, but as what? The answer that came made him only slightly less uncomfortable than the one he had imagined before his recent discovery. At least now he knew what ailed him. Or what didn't ail him. Whatever it was, he had no time for it, especially when he needed all his wits about him.

Nicholas shook his head as he approached the horses. He put little faith in hunting down the name on the pouch, for Robert Blanchefort likely knew nothing about this business, his satchel having been lost or stolen or even passed on after his death. But Nicholas could think of nothing else to do and they needed to act.

He should have chased down the Templar, he thought grimly. He'd set off in pursuit of the two armed riders, but he had been loath to leave behind his fallen companions, and the sight of Emery on the ground had immediately made him turn back.

Nicholas tried not to think of those first moments when he'd found her lying amongst the undergrowth, still and silent, and assumed the worst. He'd seen his brothers react violently to a perceived loss, but had never experienced it himself. It had shaken him, stripping him of pretence and all the normal boundaries of correct behaviour.

Which explained what happened next, Nicholas told himself, though he was unwilling to think too closely about the kiss, either. But who would have imagined that the person riding hard to Guy's rescue was a mere girl? Nicholas shook his head again, though he knew better than to underestimate any female. Some of his brothers' wives were as fierce as their men.

The realisation gave him an odd feeling deep inside, a sense of recognition that he'd never known. And for a moment, he simply stood there, stunned, unwilling to admit to a possibility that hadn't occurred to him before. But just as quickly he told himself it didn't matter if Emery was like those women: a beauty who could hold her own, a partner, a fitting addition to the de Burghs...

Nicholas lifted a hand to his head, as if to stop his very thoughts, for there was no point in telling himself it didn't matter when the truth was far more painful: it was too late.

Drawing in a harsh breath, he glanced towards Emery, who was taking her final farewell of her former servant and the family home, head held high. He had to admire her strength, her intelligence and her courage. And he could not ignore the connection that had been forged with what he'd thought was a boy.

But it was too late.

Shaking his head, Nicholas turned away only to find Guy eyeing him with a smug expression. His eyes narrowed. 'Watch yourself with Emery,' Nicholas said, with sudden resentment. 'I'll not have you bothering the girl.'

Guy snorted. 'Me? I've known her gender almost from the beginning.'

Although Nicholas gave his squire a dubious look, he knew Guy wouldn't lie. But if Emery's sex was so obvious, why hadn't Nicholas known it? Even the most thick-headed of his siblings wouldn't have been fooled, so why had he been taken in? It was tempting to blame his current condition, to add decreased powers of observation to his problems.

But Nicholas suspected the answer was far simpler: he hadn't wanted to know. He had dismissed what he felt for the boy Emery as longing for family or a son or the desire to train a successor. And he had ignored all the signs pointing to it being something else.

Because it was too late.

'What do you plan to do with her?'

Guy's thoughtless words made Nicholas swing towards his squire. He could do nothing with her and Guy knew that full well. Yet the squire appeared oblivious to his poorly chosen speech, eyeing Nicholas with a dogged expression.

'Are we taking her along?'

Nicholas stared stupidly as he realised what Guy was saying, yet no other possibility had crossed his mind. 'Of course we're taking her along. What else would you have me do, with her uncle dead and the Templar on the loose?'

Nicholas's show of annoyance masked another, more violent reaction to his squire's question. If he had been attached to Emery, the boy, he felt…much more strongly about Emery, the woman, and he was not prepared to part with her just yet. He'd given up so much already, his family and his future, and then Emery had appeared, with her quiet strength and her captivating gaze. He had so little and she had nowhere else to go, and he had sworn to her brother...

But Guy hastened to object. 'There are safer places than riding along with us.'

Shaking his head, Nicholas turned towards his mount. Guy had resented Emery from the beginning, so, of course, he would want to be rid of her. But Nicholas wasn't going to leave her at a nunnery or anywhere else where he couldn't be assured of her protection. Perhaps he wasn't at the best of his abilities, but he trusted no one else to—

'What about your brother Geoffrey's manor?'

Nicholas's hands, poised over his saddle, stilled, as did the rest of him, arrested by Guy's words. He could not so easily deny this suggestion, for there was no safer place than with the de Burghs, any of them, yet he couldn't do it. He refused to let her go, not before her brother had been found, not before the quest was complete and not one moment before he must.

His back to Guy, Nicholas shook his head again and mounted his destrier. He told himself he was right to dismiss his squire's proposal. Setting aside his own reluctance to see his family, there would be assumptions made should he deliver a woman to them, misconceptions that would lead to further difficulties. He would not have Emery subjected to them.

He had already taken more liberties than he should, Nicholas thought, ruefully. Although he had warned his squire away from the young woman, Nicholas knew he would do well to heed his own words. More than once, he had seen a reflection of his own burgeoning feelings in Emery's bright blue eyes and he would do well not to foster them.

Because it was too late.

Emery turned away from her family's manor without a second look, for she had bid goodbye months ago to the house and the life she had led there. Instead of lingering, she hurried towards where Lord de Burgh and Guy were waiting. And when she mounted her palfrey, Emery realised that she felt no sense of loss, only an eagerness to rejoin her companions, free from the constraints that had bound her.

Perhaps now she truly was herself, no longer forced to act a boy, nor yet under the restrictions of a woman. It was as though the past few years had disappeared, leaving the Emery Montbard who had once joined in her brother's adventures. Of course, her guise was partially responsible, for it gave her a freedom unknown by most females. And travelling played a part, for certain duties were always left behind upon the road, while new experiences lay ahead.

But more important than anything else was the approval of her fellows. Not since the days she'd spent riding with Gerard had anyone accepted her as she was, recognising her wits and competence. For this moment at least, Emery felt a resurgence of her old confidence and an anticipation she had not known in years.

She told herself that the anticipation had nothing to do with Lord de Burgh, yet her gaze drifted unerringly to him, so at ease astride his war horse, his dark hair caught by the breeze. Had he grown more handsome or did he simply seem so because she had come to know and like him? Or was it because of the kiss they had shared? Flushing, Emery knew she must put that memory from her mind for ever, as well as her increasing admiration for her companion. She wrenched her gaze away from the great knight, only to find Guy eyeing her speculatively.

'His hair needs cutting,' Emery said, inclining her head towards Lord de Burgh, as though that small fact explained her breathless scrutiny of the man.

Guy grinned at her knowingly and called to his master. 'My lord, Emery would cut our hair for us.'

'No, no,' Emery said, dismayed at the suggestion. While she had trimmed her brother's hair, touching Lord de Burgh in so intimate a fashion would be too unnerving. Too tempting. *Too dangerous.* She cleared her throat with difficulty. 'I have no shears,' she said, hoping to put an end to the discussion.

But Guy appeared to be enjoying her discomfort. 'Perhaps a knife would do?' he asked, with an air of amusement.

'Can you handle a knife?' Lord de Burgh asked, gallantly rescuing her from Guy's teasing.

Emery nodded, grateful for the change of topic.

'Where did you learn to wield a sword so well?' he asked, his dark brows lifted in query.

Emery felt a surge of pride at the compliment. 'My father taught me,' she said. 'He trained us both, for Gerard and I are twins, and 'twas easier for him to include me since he knew naught of female tasks.'

Few had looked kindly upon her instruction and, from Guy's shocked expression, Emery expected to hear the usual outcry. But when the squire spoke, 'twas not about her skills with weapons.

'Twins!' he said, his eyes wide. 'If you are a twin, you should be able to sense where your brother might be. Can't you communicate silently with him?'

Emery shook her head. Since she and Gerard looked no more alike than the usual siblings, she rarely was subjected to the rumours surrounding twins, and she was glad of it.

Guy's disappointment was obvious. 'But you must try!'

Emery shook her head. 'Twould be far easier if she could locate her brother through some mystic connection, but the bond they had shared in younger years had frayed as they took their separate paths. Now their worlds were vastly different, Gerard taking up arms in the Holy Land, while Emery laid hers down.

Yet, surely, she would know if something… happened to him.

As if aware of her unease, Lord de Burgh again came to her rescue. 'You may have noticed that Guy has steeped himself in superstitions and lore,' he said, with a wry glance at his squire.

'Twins are rare, my lord,' Guy said. 'I simply thought—'

Lord de Burgh stopped Guy's words with a subtle glance, perhaps to prevent him from mentioning other legends associated with twins, and Emery was grateful. She did not care to hear that if one twin should die, the other not only grew stronger, but might be able to heal the sick or injured.

'Perhaps every bit of lore is not based in truth, but you can't dismiss all of it, either,' Guy protested. 'Why, look at your family's gifts. You can't deny that you are wasting your own abilities.'

'I? I have no abilities,' Lord de Burgh said flatly.

Although Emery did not understand what Guy was talking about, there was something in the great knight's tone that belied his words.

Or perhaps he simply had grown impatient with his squire's banter.

Guy did not argue with his master, but turned to Emery. 'All the de Burghs have abilities,' he said. ''Tis an open secret that the Earl of Campion is possessed of a certain...prescience.'

Emery glanced at Lord de Burgh in surprise, but instead of disputing the claim, he simply rode ahead, refusing to listen to his squire's chatter. Emery was tempted to follow rather than engage in gossip, yet she was curious and would learn more about the renowned family.

And so she let Guy extol the virtues of the clan, from the venerable Campion and his third wife to his seven sons by the wives who had gone before her. Guy described the famous castle with its golden towers and Emery felt a sudden longing to see it with her own eyes. She could not imagine living in such a grandiose home, though Guy claimed it was full of warmth and laughter.

'The family must make it so,' Emery said, a bit wistfully, for she'd had no one except Gerard and her father. What would it be like to live amongst a bustling brood, with a loved one always at hand to share a conversation or

a meal or an outing—or even the more oner-
ous duties of life?

'The earl makes it so,' Guy said. 'He rules
the household with kindness and wisdom and
generosity. And while his children and grandchildren visit often, none actually live at Campion these days, for they have homes elsewhere,
throughout the land. All are married now, most
with children of their own, except Nicholas.'

Nicholas. The great knight had introduced
himself at their first meeting, but Emery savoured the reminder. *Nicholas de Burgh.* The
news that he, alone, of the brood was not wed
made her feel funny inside and 'twas only
through great force of will that she did not
glance towards the man's broad back.

'Simon's wife, Bethia, was trained in the battle arts, just as you were,' Guy said. 'In fact,
when Simon met her, she was an outlaw who
waylaid him upon the road. And he is probably
the most able knight, except perhaps for Dunstan, the eldest.'

Emery blinked in surprise, for she found it
hard to reconcile such a figure with a member
of the august family. Surely Guy was exagger-
ating, yet Emery wished she could meet this
woman and find out for herself.

'Geoffrey's wife, Elene, also had a reputation for being quite fierce, though she is long settled these days. And Brighid, who married Stephen, comes from the ancient Welsh family l'Estrange, some say with powers of their own,' Guy said.

Emery was puzzled by Guy's recitation, for she thought the sons of an earl would seek advantageous marriages to gain political influence, land or titles. Yet it sounded as though the handsome de Burgh brothers had made love matches. 'Twas too bad that her own family had never encouraged such possibilities, she thought. But who could she have loved? All too quickly she glanced at Lord de Burgh, only to flush and turn her attention more firmly back to Guy.

'All the de Burgh women are strong, able to hold their own with the knights,' the squire said, giving Emery a look that she couldn't decipher. Then he leaned closer to speak in a low voice. 'You would fit right in, mistress.'

With a grin, the squire rode on, leaving Emery blinking in his wake. Apparently, he had not finished teasing her.

Chapter Seven

Nicholas looked over the neat chamber with its white painted walls and realised it was not that different from the one in which they had slept the night before.

Yet everything was different.

Now that he knew Emery was no boy, his perspective on the sleeping arrangements had changed, and the walls closed in as if to make the space more intimate, especially at this hour. The sight of the bed made him feel warm and he drew in a sharp breath, suddenly uncomfortable. As though sharing his unease, Emery withdrew, muttering about the garderobe.

In her absence, Nicholas walked to the small window and looked out into the darkening sky, both to feel a cooling breeze and to search the growing shadows one last time for any signs of pursuit. He had been unwilling to dare the main roads, where they would be more visible and their enemies less so. Instead, Nicholas had kept to the narrower pathways between manors, hoping to avoid notice while finding safe shelter.

If he had been reluctant to sleep out of doors or in the crowded accommodations of most inns because of Emery, now he refused even to consider such possibilities. His concern for his companion, already heightened, had increased tenfold with the discovery of her gender. Unfortunately, so had his awareness of her.

The interest Nicholas had dismissed or excused when he'd thought her a youth had become so pronounced that at one point he'd ridden ahead, lest his attention wander to her slender form in its boy's guise. Even that garb failed to deter him, for he wanted to remove it, piece by piece, slowly revealing her woman's body to his gaze, his hands, his lips... Nicholas blew out a shaky breath and tried not to think of the bed that stood behind him.

When he heard soft footfalls approaching, he tensed, waiting for the gentle brush of a slender hand, eager for something he knew he had no business wanting. *Touch me*, he longed to say, and when the silence stretched out too long, he turned, impatient, only to face Guy watching him with a knowing expression.

''Tis just me, my lord,' Guy said. 'Emery is still in the garderobe, though I can call her back to witness your ablutions, if you intend to bathe.'

Nicholas winced as he realised how he had stripped to the waist the night before while Emery looked on, wide-eyed. No wonder the girl had fled the room.

Nicholas frowned at his squire. 'Very amusing,' he muttered. He turned towards the bed, only to turn away, flustered. He would sleep on the floor tonight—and in his clothes.

'She's probably not so bad when she cleans up,' Guy said. 'Perhaps she's the one who should be having the bath.'

Nicholas's mouth went dry at the thought before he realised just what his squire had said. 'What do you mean *not bad*?' he asked, his eyes narrowing.

Guy shrugged. 'Well, she has been able to pass as a boy, which doesn't say much about her beauty.'

'She doesn't look one bit like a boy,' Nicholas answered sharply. Her thick, dark lashes and smooth skin would give Emery away to anyone except the most slow-witted, which apparently included himself.

But Guy appeared unmoved. 'Still, she manages to wear the clothes convincingly, easily hiding her feminine shape.'

Nicholas nearly sputtered in outrage. Emery was slender, strong and lithe, and infinitely more desirable than those who boasted more rounded bodies. 'Surely you cannot prefer a fleshy form to one such as hers,' he protested.

'Ah, but 'tis not what I prefer, now is it?' Guy asked, with a sly grin.

Suddenly Nicholas realised that the youth was taunting him, a jest for which he had little use, but scolding his squire would only make things worse. Instead, he effected a shrug. ''Tis of no matter to me,' Nicholas said, lying through his teeth.

Guy snorted, but did not answer. And how could he? He knew full well why Nicholas could not form an attachment to any woman and why they did not return home, but moved amongst strangers, marking time... Sucking in a harsh breath, Nicholas snatched up Emery's pallet and rolled it out for himself.

He removed his mail and his sword and lay down, fully clothed, listening as Guy settled down for the night, too. No fire had been laid, making the chamber nearly black, but Nicholas was glad for the privacy. Although he owed a debt of gratitude to his squire, sometimes he grew weary of Guy's company and the eyes that saw more than he might want.

When long moments passed without Emery's return, Nicholas felt a twinge of concern and wondered whether to send Guy to check on her—or go himself. But searching for Emery in the darkness might prove too tempting a task for him to undertake. And then he remembered how long she had remained away last night, perhaps to avoid the sight of him bathing, Nicholas now realised. Heat washed over him and he shifted uncomfortably.

At the sound of her soft footsteps, he closed his eyes, pretending sleep, rather than watch her as she slipped into bed. But the footsteps stopped before him, then he felt the gentle touch he had been craving, warm and tentative, upon his shoulder. Nicholas couldn't help himself. He reached for the fingers even as they slipped away.

'My lord!' Even when tinged with surprise,

Emery's voice was so smooth that Nicholas wondered how he had ever thought it belonged to a boy. And in that instant, he wanted nothing more than to pull her down beside him.

'What do you here?' she whispered.

'I intended to sleep,' Nicholas said, though now other opportunities rose to tease him. Indeed, the very air seemed to hum with possibility, as if he was looking into that bright blue gaze that had so often arrested his own. But all he could make out was the shape of her head. Nicholas had never seen her without that awful cap and he was tempted to fling it aside and let her hair flow loose across them both.

'But what of the bed?' she asked.

What of the bed? Nicholas found he could not answer.

'Why aren't you sleeping there?' The suspicion in Emery's tone was belied by a certain breathlessness and Nicholas wondered what she would do should he pull her to him. His heart pounded and he grew warm, yet 'twas no fever that gripped him. He felt whole and eager, his world alight with promise in the darkness. If he reached upwards, could he touch her cheek?

'The bed is for you,' he said, so softly that she was forced to lean close. She was near enough now for him to take her face in his hands and steal a kiss. The memory of his mouth on hers returned, making him hungry for more. That kiss had been born of the moment, a celebration that she was alive—and female. But it had been only a taste and Nicholas yearned for a long, slow exploration…one that might take all night.

'No, my lord,' Emery said.

Had she divined his thoughts? Nicholas hesitated.

'The bed is for you,' she said, with insistence, yet her voice cracked.

If he put a finger to her lips, would it stop her protests? Nicholas lifted a hand to find the gentle curve of her cheek and let his thumb caress the softness. He felt her quiver in response, but she did not pull away.

'The bed is for you,' Nicholas whispered, 'unless you wish to share it.' The words were out before he could call them back and he heard the swift intake of her breath, whether in alarm or delight, he didn't know. The silence and the heat gathered around them, the connection between them growing and building until the tension seemed unbearable, and Nicholas leaned upwards, ready to leap recklessly into the darkness.

But then a loud snore erupted within the confines of the chamber, reminding them that despite the cover of the night, they were not alone. Guy lay close by, privy to all that occurred between them, a realisation that cooled Nicholas's blood and sent Emery scurrying away. The great bed creaked and he was left clutching at the air, as if trying to hold on to a dream.

Emery stared at the crumbling remains in dismay, as though, if she looked long enough, they might transform into a proper manor. But Lord de Burgh had not taken this route before and the path had led them to a place long abandoned. This evening there would be no welcoming hall, bustling with residents and servants, and no gates or guards to protect them. And a glance towards the setting sun told her they had no time to retrace their steps and look for shelter elsewhere.

Emery shivered. It seemed her adventure had gone from bad to worse. Her behaviour last night had been bad enough, making her reluctant to face her companions this morn. Thankfully, Guy must have slept through it all, for she was spared any odd glances or teasing. And, to her relief, Lord de Burgh did not appear intent upon pursuing her during daylight hours. In fact, he seemed rather distant, as though he, too, regretted his behaviour.

Perhaps the darkness and the close quarters had conspired to affect his judgement, too. Emery could only guess, for she had never been in such a situation. And she hoped never again to find herself there, balancing upon the edge of a knife, where one slip could mean a fall into ruin. Unnerved anew by the memory, Emery stared unseeing at the blackened remains of walls open to the sky until a call from Guy made her urge her palfrey forwards, to follow Lord de Burgh.

Surely he did not intend for them to travel at night? Even Emery was aware of those who preyed upon the roads, stealing purses or worse, and though they had seen no further sign of the Templar, that did not mean they had left him behind. But she forged on, through tall thickets that fell away to reveal another building, half-hidden by undergrowth and small trees. Presumably a barn, it seemed to have fared somewhat better than the manor house, perhaps having escaped some past fire.

'We'll bed down in there,' Lord de Burgh said. Emery blinked at the bleak structure, with its door askew and half its roof missing. Although it would serve as some kind of shelter, the place seemed lost to the elements, wild and unwelcoming. Once inside, Emery shivered again, for much of the space already lay in shadow.

A sense of gloom seemed to settle over the company as they set up a camp, of sorts, under the portion of the roof that remained. There they lay their pallets and ate in silence, sharing wine given to them by last night's host. Emery would have liked a fire, if only for comfort, but Lord de Burgh did not want to draw any attention.

'Who would see it inside these walls?' Guy asked, echoing Emery's thoughts.

'Someone who is looking closely,' Lord de Burgh said, offering no further explanation. The good-natured knight seemed out of sorts, and Emery wondered if she were responsible. But she dared not ask, for she had no wish to discuss what had happened last night.

Had she worried about following Lord de Burgh anywhere? She had nearly followed him into bed, unable to resist the lure of his deep voice, the brush of his fingers, and his large shadowy form radiating heat and strength and mystery.

Loosing a sigh, Emery settled upon her pallet, but she was too tense to sleep. And, even though her companions were close by, she felt more alone than ever. She shivered, chill upon the ground compared with the cosy chamber where she had spent last night, tucked into the big bed, the only threat to her that of Lord de Burgh's appeal.

The stillness was broken by a rustling and Emery flinched, unnerved by the sound. More than likely 'twas some animal moving around the barn, for the horses stirred, only to soon quiet. She heard the men settle down to sleep on either side of her, easing her fears, yet she knew an urge to move towards Lord de Burgh. She told herself she sought the warmth and comfort of his big body, but there were other desires that she could not risk rousing. And so she lay awake long after Guy began to snore.

At last she must have dozed, for when something startled her, Emery blinked in alarm, before remembering where she was. Thankfully, the moon had risen, sending its faint glow through the broken roof. Beside her Guy was a black shape, curiously silent, and she wondered whether it was the cessation of his snoring that had woken her from a restless sleep.

Turning her head, Emery sought the larger shape lying to her right, but she could not find it. Heart thundering, she told herself that Lord de Burgh had probably gone to relieve himself, but she rose up on her elbows, searching the darkness, anxiety putting a knot in her throat.

When she saw something by the door, Emery swallowed hard, ready to reach for her sword. But 'twas no white-robed Templar slipping through the opening. The wide shoulders and casual stance of the figure told her Lord de Burgh was standing there, looking out, keeping watch. Had he slept at all?

Wide awake now, Emery rose to her feet and walked to his side. He had positioned the door to hide as much as possible of the barn's interior, while giving himself a good view of the land that sloped down to the manor's ruins.

'I'll stand guard,' Emery said, but a stray breeze snatched at her words and made her shiver.

To her surprise, Lord de Burgh drew her close, putting an arm around her shoulders and enclosing her in his cloak. They stood in

companionable silence for a long moment and
Emery felt a heady relief that the events of the
night before had not destroyed their budding
friendship. Indeed, for the first time since then
she felt a sense of peace and contentment en-
velop her. She slid her arm around his waist,
as though he were Gerard.

But this man was not her brother. And the
seemingly innocent gesture stirred up other
emotions beyond camaraderie. Abruptly, Emery
was aware of the heady scent of him that clung
to the cloak and the heat of his body, far too
close to her own. And before she knew what
had happened, he was turning, as was she. They
faced each other in the welcome cocoon of his
cloak, and he lowered his head.

His lips met hers, soft, sweet and seductive,
and pleasure surged through her right down to
the tip of her toes. Emery had only a few moments to wonder how such a strong man could
be so gentle, before his tongue brushed against
her teeth, sweeping inside, and the kiss took a
different turn, so dark and delicious that she
swayed upon her feet.

Lord de Burgh caught her close, pressing
his hard body against her, and Emery slipped
her hands around his neck, her fingers weav-

ing through the hair that needed cutting. It was just as thick and silky as she had imagined and she never wanted to let go. Nor did she want his hands to stop roving over her back beneath the cloak, spreading warmth with each motion, and she strained against him.

He groaned, sending a jolt through her, and Emery gasped as his lips left hers to move along her cheek and throat. She was free to breathe and speak, at last, but could form no words, for she felt witless and bereft of will, as though she had been drugged, such was his power over her. Yet some small part of reason remained, struggling to assert itself.

'My lord, I—' she began.

'Nicholas,' he whispered. 'My name is Nicholas.'

Emery's heart lurched, sending her good sense skittering in its wake. Guy was asleep inside the barn. Who was to see them? Who would know? But the answer came all too swiftly, chilling her to the bone.

Or perhaps it was the loss of Lord de Burgh's warmth that cooled her. One moment, Emery was in his embrace, clutching him tightly to her, and the next, she was set behind him, the edge of his cloak thrown aside as he put his hand to the hilt of his sword.

Startled at his abrupt change from lover to warrior, Emery blinked into the night. She had heard nothing, seen nothing, but how could she when all of her senses had been engulfed by Lord de Burgh, by *Nicholas*?

'What is it?' Emery whispered when she found her voice.

'I think someone is out there.'

His answer, low and serious, made Emery shiver and she remembered Guy's talk of the de Burghs with their so-called abilities. Had Nicholas some of his father's prescience, or was he simply more alert than most, as befitting a great knight?

'Shall I wake Guy?' Emery asked, even as she wondered what kind of stand they could make in the old barn in the dead of night. Her heart was pounding apace, but now with dread, rather than desire.

'No.'

'But what if they should both come at you?' Emery asked, remembering the last fight they had waged against Gwayne and his man.

'It's not the Templar.'

Although Emery should have been relieved,

something in his tone chilled her, as though
the white-robed knight and his squire would
be preferable to whoever was out there in the
darkness, watching and waiting.

Rothston loomed out of the mist, its grey
stone a welcome sight, for they were all eager
for respite from the rain. Nicholas had forged
on through the drizzle, despite Guy's protests. Although he understood far better than
his squire the risks of pushing his weary body
through foul weather, he was wary of stopping.
Even now, with the Templar preceptory ahead,
he took a moment to scan the area, his gaze
lingering behind them and beyond, to a stand
of woods that stood well back from the road.

Had he seen something moving amongst the
trees? Nicholas's eyes narrowed, for it might
well have been a trick of the rain. And yet ever
since yesterday afternoon, he'd felt a presence,
as though someone was following them. But he
had no proof, just glimpses of a movement here,
a shadow there. Indeed, if given to whimsy, he
might have thought a shadow or ghost pursued
them, which was why he had said nothing to
his superstitious squire. The Templar, with his

crude methods, would not be capable of such stealth. So who was it? Or was it anyone at all?

Nicholas turned away, fighting back a wave of weariness, and caught Guy eyeing him a little too closely. He would have assured his squire of his condition, but for the presence of Emery. He was not about to talk of such things in front of her, or invite Guy's warnings about his so-called recklessness.

Nicholas frowned. He had been reckless, but not with his health and in a manner he hoped had escaped his squire's notice. He did not need to add Guy's rebuke to his own—or the one he imagined his father giving him. Nicholas shifted uncomfortably in the saddle, knowing full well what Campion would think of his youngest son's behaviour.

To pursue a dalliance with a woman who was under his protection was bad enough, but to do so when Nicholas could not give her a future was unconscionable. Yet he had not thought twice when Emery had come upon him in the darkness. She approached him innocently enough, but he soon turned the situation to his advantage, despite her reluctance. Had he become that careless, that selfish?

Nicholas shook his head. He knew better and

Emery deserved better. Although she spoke little of her situation, he suspected she was alone in the world except for her missing brother, a man he had vowed to help. Nicholas grunted in disgust, for Gerard had not had seducing his twin in mind when he asked for aid. And if they found the Hospitaller, how would Nicholas face the man, should he act ignobly with his sister?

Yet somehow he could not regret those moments in the darkness, Emery acting as a spark to stir him to life, as well as a balm to his weary soul. 'Twas more than desire that united them, for she seemed to fill the great void inside of him, standing as sibling, friend and companion in all things and providing solace in the black hours of the night. Was it wrong for him to want to take what he might, while he could, to claim something special for himself, just this once?

Nicholas knew the answer, though it was not to his liking. The de Burghs held to a strict code of honour that he could not abandon at his convenience, no matter what the circumstances. And as they entered Rothston, Nicholas decided a monastery was as good a place as any to vow to keep his distance from the young woman under his protection.

As if to prove him right, they received a warm welcome upon their arrival. One brown-robed figure waved them inside while another attended to their horses and Nicholas felt some of the tension ease from his shoulders. For now, at least, the walls of the monastery would provide some protection from both the rain and any who might be following.

But Guy did not appear to share his relief. 'Do you consider it wise to let them take the horses, my lord?' the squire asked, looking over his shoulder nervously. Apparently, he did not care to linger, despite the weather.

Nicholas ignored the question, for Emery had already disappeared inside, eager to be out of the elements, and he hastened to follow. And he could not share Guy's unease about these Templars, who seemed like members of other religious houses he had visited. Their hall was small and simply furnished, and boasted none of the bizarre carvings of the church at Roode. And if any tunnels lay below, Nicholas had no interest in them.

He sank on to a bench as one of the brethren set out a meal for them, and when they offered a room for the night, he accepted gratefully. While he had once been able to go without sleep and feel little effects, these days his endurance was limited and his body lodged its protest.

'I don't like it,' Guy said.

Nicholas almost responded in kind before realising that Guy was referring to their hosts. He shook his head to clear it. 'What?'

'I don't like the idea of sleeping here, amongst them,' Guy whispered. 'Remember that one of their own has attacked us twice.'

'Would you rather bed down in the rain?' Nicholas asked, only to snort when Guy actually appeared to consider the choice.

The squire even looked upon the food with suspicion, as though the good brethren might have dosed it with a sleeping draught or some kind of poison, though how or why was beyond Nicholas's comprehension. When it came to danger, he had long ago learned to listen to his gut—and his gut told him to eat his fill. He intended to stay here, as well. The day had turned oppressive, and he was eager to be rid of his mail and rest.

Still, he had not forgotten their purpose, and when an elderly brother paused to greet them, Nicholas engaged him in conversation. Eventually, Nicholas asked about the man they were looking for, but, as he had feared, the brother shook his head.

'There are only a handful of us here at Rothston, my lord, for ours is but a small preceptory,' the brother said. 'And I know no Robert Blanchefort, though I never served as a knight of our order.'

Nicholas's disappointment must have been obvious, for the man smiled encouragingly. 'But you must not give up hope, my lord. There are dozens of Templar properties throughout England. The knight you seek might well be here, rather than in the Holy Land, especially if his fighting days are over.'

Nicholas heard Guy's low groan at the news. No doubt the squire feared a visit to every preceptory in the land was imminent, but they hadn't the resources to travel the length and breadth of the country and back. Nor had they the time. Although Nicholas hated to admit it, sooner or later he wouldn't be able to continue. And he intended for Emery to be long gone by then.

Again, the brother gave them a gentle smile. 'But there are few knights at most of our preceptories,' he said. 'Perhaps you should look at one of the retirement communities, at Penwaite or Oxley. There you are more liable to find the old warriors, resting after their battles.'

Oxley was only a day's ride away and seemed a likely enough destination, for where else had they to go? Guy would not like it, but Nicholas wanted to keep moving, and if their travels confused any pursuers, all the better. He thanked the brother, who bid them goodnight as another brown-robed man appeared to lead them from the hall.

'We recently lost one of our brothers, so there are two rooms empty at present, if you would care to take both,' he said.

The innocent question made Nicholas pause in his steps, as the thought of sharing a room with Emery struck him with dizzying force. The privacy that had eluded them the past two nights was suddenly within reach, along with a bed, and he could well imagine what might occur should he answer in the affirmative. But Guy was eyeing him anxiously, obviously fearful of being left alone in a Templar cell, and Emery... Well, she soon took the decision out of his hands.

'My lord de Burgh keeps us at hand at all times,' she mumbled, 'even in this holy place.'

The reminder of their whereabouts recalled

to Nicholas his vow and he realised just how close he had come to breaking it already. Resuming his steps, he felt too warm for comfort, the air thick with something. Were they burning incense, or was it the closeness of Emery that affected him so?

Keep your distance, Nicholas told himself. Yet that would be difficult, he realised, as he stared at the tiny cell, barren except for a small window and a bed. He nearly turned on his heel and left, taking Guy with him. But he did not want to leave Emery alone. Hell, he did not want to leave her at all.

Oblivious to his tortured thoughts, Emery walked to the window and turned around, surveying the space that would be crowded with the three of them. But when she spoke, she did not make mention of the other room or even scold him for his hesitation over the offer.

'This is how they live,' she said, in an odd tone. 'This is your life when you have committed to a religious house.'

'I'm sure Gerard is not so confined,' Nicholas said, since she seemed dismayed at the prospect of such an existence.

'And Gerard's not a Templar,' Guy said. ''Tis only the Templars who are shrouded in mystery. Why, according to their own Rule, a brother may be expelled from the order for revealing its secrets, so they must have something to hide.'

Guy shook his head. 'I don't like staying here, my lord, right in their midst,' he said. 'Who knows what kind of strange rituals they practise? And what if our reputation has preceded us? There might be secret tunnels leading from one preceptory to another and a prohibition against any who discover them. Why, there could be a hidden entrance leading right into this room.'

Nicholas doubted such a thing would fit in their tiny chamber, and he was growing weary of his squire's nonsense. Rothston was a small property, with a few residents who did not pose a threat to a knight and armed companions. And no underground passageway could lead from here to Roode, some seventy miles away. Yes, there was nothing to stop Gwayne from entering this place, unless there was some proscription against him. But Nicholas did not think 'twas the Templar who followed them.

'We are safe within these walls and it is late, so let us seek our rest,' Emery said. Nicholas glanced at her in surprise, for she spoke to Guy in a gentle tone that, nevertheless, brooked no argument. 'Lord de Burgh needs his sleep, for he did not get any last night.'

Guy's uneasy expression changed to one of alarm as he swung towards Nicholas. 'My lord, you must take care of yourself—' he began.

But Nicholas stopped any further speech with a sharp glance, for he had no intention of engaging in this discussion in front of Emery.

The squire sputtered, as though he would say more, then his brows furrowed. 'And just why did you get no rest last night?' he asked, eyeing them both with suspicion.

Nicholas felt a moment's dismay, as though he had been caught out by his father, before regaining his composure. 'I was keeping watch,' he said. 'Since we were out in the open, I was wary of being seen, should we be followed.'

Guy paled, but this time he kept his worries and his theories about the Templars to himself. 'Twas a small mercy for which Nicholas was thankful and he looked to Emery in gratitude, but she had turned away. He eyed her thoughtfully, arrested by her slim figure and the quiet strength and authority she exuded.

He and Guy had been alone so long that Nicholas had forgotten what it was like to have someone take care of him, or rather someone *else* take care of him. Oftentimes, his squire seemed overly concerned for Nicholas's welfare, his behaviour more annoying than helpful. But Nicholas reacted differently to Emery's steady manner.

Perhaps it was her gender. Nicholas had known precious few females in his life until his brothers began to wed and those women hadn't remained at Campion. By the time his father remarried, Nicholas was full grown and eager for adventure, not coddling. Now, suddenly, he longed for a woman's touch, a woman's comfort, a woman's solace.

But it was too late.

Chapter Eight

Emery blinked into the darkness, unable to relax, even though the men had given her the bed. Lord de Burgh had pushed it against the door to placate Guy, who was certain that they might be rousted in the night by evil monks, and now she found herself staring at the worn wood at her feet as though it might suddenly burst open.

She told herself the notion was ludicrous, yet she remained tense, while the squire's low snoring indicated he had found some rest, despite his worries about hidden passageways and powerful cabals.

Emery shivered, though the small cell was oppressive. As always, there was just enough truth in Guy's wild claims to make her anx-

ious. The religious houses *were* influential and
nearly autonomous, and she *had* seen a secret
chamber riddled with bizarre carvings that
even Guy could not imagine.

As for the rest of his theories, they were
easier to dismiss, especially since he spoke of
little else. But Lord de Burgh had been com-
parably silent on the subject, making what he
did say more alarming. Even if he possessed
no special abilities beyond a warrior's honed
senses, when he said he thought someone was
out there, Emery believed him.

But if the Templar and his squire were not
in pursuit, then who? Was another member of
the order, besides Gwayne, seeking them out,
as Guy so often suggested? What of Gerard's
own brethren? Her brother had warned Emery
not to trust anyone, which included the Hospitallers. What part did they play, if any?

That thought led to another, more insidious
one that Emery had long avoided, but could not
any longer. Now, in the darkness, she finally
faced the fact that Gwayne and Harold and her
brother all seemed to be intent upon one thing:
the parcel. With her uncle dead and Gwayne
rousted for the time being, at least, that left
only one person likely to be seeking the prize.

Emery loosed a shaky breath. Although she didn't like to consider such a possibility, she was forced to wonder whether the shadowy figure on their heels was Gerard. But how did he know they had recovered his pouch? And why wouldn't he simply come forwards? Surely he recognised her, even in her male guise, for she was wearing his old clothes.

Perhaps he was wary of Lord de Burgh. Yet, supposedly, he had asked the great knight for aid. Did her brother fail to recognise him, as well? By all accounts, Gerard had not seemed to be thinking clearly, so Emery wanted to dismiss most of his behaviour as the product of injury and fever.

Yet, whatever the cause, there was no denying the importance he'd placed upon retrieving the parcel that had once been in his possession. And although Lord de Burgh had spoken no more about the statue, Emery could guess what he had been thinking—what they all had been thinking—what was a Hospitaller knight doing with such a precious object?

Had he got into some kind of trouble, not of his own devising, or had he forgone his duty, armed with a stolen valuable with which he intended to start a new life? 'Twas not unheard of. Men deserted their families only to be discovered in another village, with a second wife and children.

Still, Emery did not want to believe Gerard capable of such perfidy, for it would mean he intended to abandon her, as well as his vows. Although he had already left her to their uncle's machinations, this would be far more deliberate—and painful. Emery closed her eyes against the possibility, only to open them abruptly.

Had she heard a noise beyond the door? Stiffening, she held her breath, listening intently in between Guy's low snores. Now there was no mistaking the sound of footsteps outside the room and Emery looked to Lord de Burgh in panic.

'Twas too dark to see whether he was alert, so Emery reached for her own small sword, wary of raising an alarm. She waited for one long moment, her heart pounding, her arm stiff with tension. But just as she expected the door to rattle, the footsteps continued on past the chamber, to be joined by others. And Emery released her grip upon the weapon in relief.

If Guy were awake, he might have suspected that a host of Templars were preparing to attack them in their sleep, but Emery knew bet-

ter. The brethren were being called to prayer,
not combat. Shaking her head at her own foolishness, she settled back upon the bed. But still
she found herself listening to the night noises
and wondering if any of those footsteps might
belong to her brother.

Oxley was a long, weary day's ride from
Rothston, and Nicholas was glad to reach it,
though Guy looked ill pleased at the sight of a
preceptory far larger than those they had visited before. While Nicholas did not share his
squire's distrust of the Templars, he was wary
of the marshy land they had drained here, over
which a damp, unhealthy air lingered.

It seemed an odd place for a hospital, or perhaps a likely location, Nicholas thought, with
a frown. For whatever reason, this was one of
the few Templar properties that provided care
for the aged and ill members of the order, including those who had fought in the Holy Land.

As such, 'twas the most likely spot to learn
of Robert Blanchefort. Still, Nicholas was not
prepared when the good brother who welcomed
them not only recognised the name, but told
them Blanchefort lived at Oxley. That was the
good news.

The bad news was that he was insane.

'Or so they say,' Guy whispered, ever suspicious. 'Perhaps they don't want us talking to him.'

However, after conferring with his superior, the brother led them towards a massive oak, lit by the last of the sunlight. He pointed to where a bench under the dappled leaves was occupied by a lone figure. The Templar's hair was nearly as white as his robe and his hands rested upon his chest as though he slept. Although Guy might claim his pose was that of the tomb, he seemed harmless enough and the brothers would hardly allow a dangerous man to roam the grounds at will.

Still Guy hung back. 'How do we know that it really is him?' he whispered.

'There's only one way to find out,' Nicholas said. Leaving Guy and Emery behind, he approached the sleeper. 'Robert Blanchefort?'

At the sound of his name, the Templar roused himself and greeted them as though he were wide awake and knew them well. Perhaps the man's madness was only the result of battle and old age, Nicholas thought. After introducing himself, he joined the knight on the bench, while Guy and Emery seated themselves on the grass, just out of reach.

'Ah, you have a sword for me!' Blanchefort said, eyeing Nicholas's weapon. 'And mail, as well, though I cannot use that short coat. I would be covered when I face the Saracen. 'Tis far too dangerous to be unprepared.'

Nicholas wondered if the old knight thought himself still at war, which, while sad, hardly made him a lunatic. But then Blanchefort leaned forwards, his pale eyes shining a bit too intently. 'He's coming for me, you know. He's been here.'

Was he speaking of an enemy long vanquished? Nicholas did not know, but he tried to wrest control of the conversation. 'I've found your pouch,' Nicholas said gently. 'Did it go missing?'

But the elderly knight, seemingly lost in his own world, ignored the question. 'He haunts me!' he said suddenly and with such anguish that Nicholas flinched. 'I told them he was here, but they didn't believe me. He slips in and out of the shadows like a wraith, accusing me, though I told him I don't have it. I gave it up long ago.'

Nicholas felt the hairs on the back of his

neck rise at the mention of a shadowy pursuer, but far too many years had passed for the same person to be harrying them both, unless Blanchefort was talking about recent events.

'When?' Nicholas asked.

Blanchefort looked off into the distance, as though he might spy someone lying in wait even now. 'Ever he has haunted me since that night.' He swung back towards Nicholas. 'You don't know what he is capable of. Others have come asking about him, as you have, but they don't understand. There's no stopping him.'

'Who?' Nicholas finally asked.

'The Saracen.' Blanchefort practically spat out the words. His expression was bitter, as though he suffered a fool in speaking with Nicholas. 'And you are no match for him.'

Was Blanchefort talking about the infidels he had fought in the Holy Land or a specific person from those foreign climes? More than likely his mind had been broken by what he had seen and done in battle, but Nicholas knew there might be some grain of truth in his ramblings, so he listened as the man continued.

'The spoils of war, that's what William called it. He said others had amassed plenty in the sacking of heathen cities, so what was to stop us? He found out soon enough when the Saracen came after us. He paid with his life,' Blanchefort said.

''Twas not for William, who saw only riches for himself and would have renounced his vows for them. 'Twas not for any of us, and so I told them,' Blanchefort said, shaking his head. 'But they thought 'twould assure victory to any who possessed it.'

At first Nicholas thought the old warrior might be talking about the very thing that lay hidden in his pack. But a gold statue possessed no powers, certainly not to sway the outcome of battles, and he realised 'twas foolish to seek enlightenment in the ravings of a madman.

As if aware he was losing his attention, Blanchefort suddenly reached out and grasped Nicholas's arm with surprising strength. 'He will not rest until he has it.'

'What?' Nicholas asked, with no little impatience. 'What is it?'

The question was a mistake, for the Templar's hand dropped away and his expression hardened. 'Would you trick me?' he asked. 'Others have tried. They have come here, seeking what we found, but I don't know what they did with it. I don't know where it is—'

Blanchefort broke off in a sob, as though wretched beyond bearing. And, if Nicholas hadn't feared a worse reaction, he might have produced the knight's old pouch to see whether the answer lay inside. Instead, he retrieved something else and stretched out his hand.

'Have you ever seen anything like this?' he asked.

Blanchefort reared back in horror. 'Where did you get it?' he whispered, shaking as he stared down at the piece of parchment with its strange markings. Nicholas didn't reveal that he had found it on a dead man; he didn't have to.

The Templar lifted his head, his face pale. 'Yes, I have seen his mark before,' he said, sounding remarkably lucid. ''Tis the Saracen's. 'Tis the sign of his handiwork. 'Tis the sign of death.'

At the sight of the brightly coloured piece of parchment, Emery's heart had lodged in her throat, making her aware of little else. She was so alarmed that, when a brother approached, for one wild moment she believed all of Guy's warnings. Would they be seized by the Templars? Put to death? But the smiling figure did not appear intent upon doing them harm, only in helping Robert Blanchefort back to his room for the night.

The elderly knight had been struck silent, completely undone by the odd paper, and, for once, Guy, too, was quiet, staring wide-eyed at what Lord de Burgh held in his hand. Only the arriving brother seemed unaffected, for he greeted Lord de Burgh with a smile.

'Do you play?' he asked, inclining his head towards the strange item.

'What?'

'The Moorish Game,' the brother said. 'What you have there is called a card, though there are other names and many other designs. Most have depictions of different numbers of coins, cups, swords, or such, though some carry only foreign words for rulers. Where did you come by it? I have never seen one outside the Holy Land.'

Whatever Lord de Burgh answered, Emery did not hear it. She stared unblinking at the 'card' even as the smiling brother led Blanchefort away, leaving the three of them alone under the great oak. Only then did she manage to look up at Lord de Burgh, tearing her gaze away from the thing that had graced her uncle's corpse.

'You kept it,' she said, uncertainly.

'I thought it was important,' he said. ''Twas obviously left as a message of some sort, perhaps as a warning.'

''Tis probably in some secret language known only to the Templars,' Guy whispered, armed with new fodder for his theories.

But Lord de Burgh shook his head. ''Tis more likely just what the monk said: part of a betting game learned from those in foreign climes.'

Guy snorted. 'Or that is what they would like us to believe,' he said. 'If such a game is well known in the Holy Land, then why is this the only one of these so-called cards in all of England?'

'Actually, there is another,' Emery said in a low voice. She flushed guiltily, for she had never spoken of the parchment Gerard had left behind. But she had kept it close and produced it now, wrinkled and creased, to present to Lord de Burgh.

'I found it after Gerard stayed with me,' she said. 'I had forgotten about it until I saw the one…on my uncle, but there was no time to speak of it.' And in the days that followed, Emery had faced more pressing concerns.

Taking the card, Lord de Burgh examined it carefully alongside the other. At first Emery thought the two were identical, but then she noticed subtle differences.

'This has two swords and yours only one,' Lord de Burgh said.

'With curved blades,' Guy muttered.

'I thought it was a snake,' Emery said. No matter what its meaning, she found the image repulsive and threatening, perhaps deliberately so.

Turning the card, Lord de Burgh narrowed his eyes at the words Gerard had written. '"Trust no one",' he read aloud. His dark brows lifted. 'I wonder if that includes your brother?'

Although Emery had her doubts about Gerard, she was reluctant to share them. She told herself that her brother could not have changed that much, but it had been years since they'd been close. And Gerard had always been easily swayed, which made it simple for their uncle and perhaps others, far worse, to prey upon him. Still, he had a good heart. Else how had Harold convinced him to join the Hospitallers?

Emery shook her head. 'I would not have thought so before Gerard left for the Holy Land,' she said. But she could not imagine what might have happened to him there, for such an experience had broken Robert Blanchefort. Had it broken Gerard, as well? Had he been ill when he stumbled upon her doorstep, or was he more permanently...damaged? Emery eyed Lord de Burgh bleakly, yearning for some words of comfort from the great knight.

But 'twas Guy who spoke. 'Do you think you ought to be brandishing those things about so freely for all to see?' the squire asked, his expression wary.

Emery felt a sudden rush of affection for the young man who seemed to harbour no suspicions about Gerard, only the Templars. And, as if to prove her right, he leaned forwards intently.

'Did you ever consider that the kind of men who adopt the pastimes of the infidels might adopt other of their habits, as well?' he asked. 'I, for one, wonder whether this Moorish Game isn't the only foreign practice the Templars have embraced.'

The squire paused to look around, though no one was near as the sun sank behind him. 'Could it be that what we carry is not a simple statue, but a golden idol they have taken to worshipping?'

Emery blinked. Although Guy had suggested that the Templars might covet or revere the parcel as some kind of icon, this was the first time he'd accused them of heresy. Emery glanced at Lord de Burgh, who lifted his brows in a sceptical fashion that nearly made her laugh.

Guy must have seen her lips twitch, because he scowled. "Tis no matter for amusement,' he said. 'We hold something precious to them, with unknown powers. How do we know it's not calling to them right now, making them aware of its presence here?'

Guy's words were sobering, for the simple reason that it was easy to forget the statue's existence when it was out of sight. However, Lord de Burgh dismissed his squire's latest theory with a shake of his head.

'We can speculate all we want, but we have not established that the statue has anything to do with the Templar order or that it possesses any powers beyond the usual lure of gold,' he said. 'The only thing of which we can be certain is that what we carry is valuable enough to tempt even the most saintly of men.'

He paused to hand the piece of parchment to Emery. 'And whether a harmless part of a game, the symbol of a bet gone awry or something else entirely, these cards appear to be linked with it somehow.'

Emery looked down at the paper in dismay, tempted to refuse its return, but she took a deep breath and tucked it away again. 'Twas enough that the great knight bore the burden of the statue itself, as well as the card that had graced a dead man. She should keep the one with Gerard's message and, perhaps, some day she might make use of it.

Slipping the other card from sight, Lord de Burgh frowned. 'We need more information,' he said. 'I had hoped to gain it from Robert Blanchefort, but if he had anything useful to impart, 'twas difficult to decipher.'

He looked off into the distance, as though mulling over what little they had learned from the elderly Templar, and Emery's old fears threatened to return. Just how long could she expect these two to aid her and Gerard, especially when her brother might be a thief—or worse?

But Lord de Burgh showed no signs of indecision or defeat, only calm deliberation. 'Since no man will tell us what we wish to know, then perhaps we must seek what we need from another source,' he said.

'Where?' Guy asked, warily.

'Where my brother Geoff would have sent us long ago,' the great knight said. 'If what we possess holds some significance, to the Templars or anyone else, then 'tis likely to be mentioned somewhere, perhaps in some Greek or Latin text or a foreign manuscript that has been translated over the years.'

Guy snorted. 'The Templars aren't going to share their secrets with us.'

'Secret or not, I doubt they have many manuscripts, for they are a military order,' Emery said. ''Tis the responsibility of other monks to copy and preserve written knowledge.'

Guy groaned. 'You can't mean for us to go to another monastery.'

Lord de Burgh frowned, as though taking Guy's reluctance under consideration. 'If not a monastery, then a castle with a large collection.'

The squire cheered up considerably. 'Campion,' he said, breathing the word as though it were holy.

But Lord de Burgh shook his head. 'Stokebrough is close and will do well enough,' he said. 'If our golden man is important, perhaps he has left his mark upon the pages of history.'

Nicholas had been to Stokebrough before, but as he entered the great hall, he was gripped with a certain tension, for this was the first time in nearly a year that he had approached a place where he was known. And he was sharply aware that his brother Geoffrey's manor was not far away.

'Twas a gamble, but he thought it unlikely that Geoff would be visiting Stokebrough. In fact, he doubted that the Strongs, who had held this land for generations, were even in residence. Fiercely ambitious, they usually travelled with the king. Yet the castle was a large one, and Nicholas hoped to disappear amongst the Strong relatives, attendants, servants and villeins who made up the household.

In fact, he hoped to disappear from the notice of anyone, including those on their trail. Although Nicholas had seen no sign of pursuit since they'd left Oxley, Blanchefort's description of the Saracen was too familiar for his liking. And rather than continue to travel from one manor or preceptory to another, he thought it best to make a stop elsewhere. A busy and populated place might throw any followers off the scent, while allowing them to keep out of sight for a while.

And there would be other advantages, as well. Although Nicholas and his squire had made the road their home, snatching some rest wherever they could, they could hardly expect Emery to continue sharing such an existence. Despite her seeming comfort with her guise, she was a gently reared young woman who had been travelling for days with two men and never once had she complained of the heat, let alone her own difficulties. She deserved a respite. And better accommodations. And a bath.

The thought of Emery washing away the sweat and grime of their journeys led Nicholas's thoughts in a direction he did not trust himself to go. For two nights now he had kept to his vow, maintaining his distance from the woman under his protection. But he could not congratulate himself when her every innocent glance stirred a longing that would never be assuaged.

And 'twas not only desire that gnawed at him, but a yearning to simply take Emery in his arms and hold her, as though her very presence might drive away all ills. Frowning, he dismissed such nonsense and wondered at this new weakness, that he should crave comforting, like a child. Yet 'twas not mothering he wanted, but something that came from those close to him, who were all far away.

As if to remind him of that fact, the Strongs' steward asked after his family and Nicholas was forced to answer as generally as possible, for he had no recent news. His brothers' wives might be expecting, babies could have been born and milestones celebrated without his knowledge.

Suddenly, Nicholas wondered about his father. The earl seemed invincible, having survived two wives and taken another. Yet as the son who had lived at Campion most recently, Nicholas knew that his joints pained him, especially in winter. Had the season past been kinder or harsher to him?

Nicholas told himself that had anything bad happened, he would have heard of it. Indeed, the Strongs' steward would be speaking of it right now. But the man asked no pointed questions and Nicholas felt a stab of relief. He was also pleased to learn that Earl Strong was at court and that he was welcome to stay as long as he liked.

'I had hoped to look through the manuscripts,' Nicholas said. 'I'm searching out a bit of history.'

The steward appeared surprised, perhaps by Nicholas's sudden turn towards intellectual pursuits or the fact that he sought information here, rather than his own family's well-stocked cupboards.

''Tis an errand for my brother Geoffrey,' Nicholas said, and the man's face cleared. Geoff's reputation as a scholar was well known and no cause for comment. Again, Nicholas felt a measure of relief and thanked the steward before heading off to fetch his companions. He had told them to hang back, for he did not want anyone studying Emery too closely.

She was standing by Guy, her head ducked low, but Nicholas saw her furtive glances of awe and amazement and realised that she had never been to such a place as Stokebrough. Selfishly, he wished her first sight of a castle would have been the golden towers of Campion, set amongst beech-covered heights and lush vales.

Suddenly he wanted nothing more than to show Emery his home: the bailey where he and his brothers had honed their skills and got up to mischief, the pond where they skated in winter and the vast hall where his father ruled, beloved by all. 'Twas a fool's wish, he knew, for he could no more take her there than he could go alone.

Instead, he would make sure she enjoyed her stay at Stokebrough, he decided as a servant led them to a bedchamber. He had occupied the room during his previous visit, paying little heed to it. But now he watched Emery turn around in wonder as she eyed the bright tapestries, the tall chest, the settle lined with ornamented pillows and the enormous bed.

And when she reached out to test its softness, Nicholas sucked in a harsh breath. Desire rose up in him so strong he could taste it, and not just at the thought of joining her in that bed. He wished he could give her everything: elegant furnishings, precious jewels, fine clothes, a home, a family and all she might desire.

But he could not and the bitterness of that admission nearly choked him. Turning away, he told himself that most of those things did not matter to Emery, who seemed content with little, though she deserved far more. Still, he wondered if there wasn't something he could do to give her pleasure and the answer came to him quickly.

He called for a bath.

Chapter Nine

Emery leaned her head back and sighed with enjoyment, though she had already spent too much time in the bath. But it had been so long since she'd had a proper tub, or the firewood necessary to heat such an amount of water, that she lingered. The fine soap felt smooth against her skin, and her hair, deliciously clean, hung outside the rim.

Emery eyed her hat with distaste and wished that she could wash it, as well. For a moment, she longed to let her locks fall free. As much freedom as her guise gave her, there were some advantages to dressing as a woman—and being a woman. Her thoughts immediately drifted to Lord de Burgh, and she shivered, despite the warmth of the bath.

Would he follow her here? Emery flushed at the notion of the great knight stepping into this water after her departure. Or would he insist upon replenishment or replacement? Either way, he was likely to occupy this tub, and suddenly, Emery found it difficult to think of little else.

Her breath caught as she remembered when he had been naked to the waist, his strong body gleaming golden in the firelight, his braies hanging low on his hips, past the flat stomach so different from her own. His skin had glistened with moisture, his big hands gliding over the slick surface with a sureness that made her swallow stiffly.

She tried to imagine the rest of him, long, muscular legs, hard from days in the saddle, and the bare feet she had glimpsed. But soon her heart was pounding so wildly that she feared it might burst from her chest. Indeed, it seemed so loud that she sat up to listen, only to realise someone was knocking on the door.

Heat swamped her as she envisioned Lord de Burgh outside, eager for his turn to wash—or be washed. Rumour had it that in some castles, ladies bathed important visitors like Lord de Burgh and Emery felt the keen bite of jealousy.

Even though she could not do such a thing, she did not want anyone else to, either.

Leaving the tub, Emery wrapped herself in a sheet of linen and stepped forwards, only to stop and wrap her hair in another, though that would do little to disguise her gender. Still, she was glad of her efforts when a female voice answered her query. Unbolting the door to peer out, she saw a young serving girl waiting.

'Mistress Montbard?' the girl said. 'I've some clothes for you.'

Emery was too stunned to answer, fear making her pulse race. Had she heard the girl aright?

'Lord de Burgh sent me, mistress.'

Emery could do nothing except admit the girl, who bustled past her, arms piled high, to spread her burdens out upon the bed. Blinking in astonishment, Emery approached the array like someone in a dream, for here were no tunic and braies, no castoffs from a page or squire. Laid before her was a surfeit of kirtles in brilliant blues and yellows and crimsons, fine silks and delicate linens, and fur-trimmed mantles. Emery had to sink upon the settle, for she had never seen the like.

'I brought quite a few, for I wasn't sure what

might fit you best, though Lord de Burgh said you were tall and slender.' She turned to peek at Emery and smiled. 'I've some shifts, as well, lovely ones with elegant edging that the earl's daughter used to wear in her younger days. We've kept all of her old things should she have use of them, but she's been blessed with several children already, so I don't think that will happen.'

Emery simply stared, dumbfounded, at the chattering girl and her bounty. 'Twas as if Lord de Burgh had snapped his fingers to magically conjure a wardrobe for her. She only hoped he had not spent good coin on things for which she would have no use in the future. The thought, tangled up with foolish longing, made her feel melancholy.

'If you wish, I can help you dress and arrange your hair,' the girl said as she sorted through the clothes, choosing the most likely pieces. 'I am to attend you while you are staying here in my lady's room.'

Emery blinked uncertainly at the news that this spacious chamber was hers alone. Somehow, spending the night in luxury and privacy was more daunting than sharing a narrow cell with her travelling companions. The space suddenly felt too large and empty and unprotected, without Lord de Burgh within reach.

And Guy's presence, though often unwelcome, had served her well, far better than her own conscience. Without him nearby, what was to stop her from succumbing to temptation? Or was that Lord de Burgh's intention? Emery drew in a sharp breath and flushed, glad that the servant's back was turned.

'Lord de Burgh explained how you were separated from your attendants and trunks, so he's bid me stay here with you until they arrive,' the girl said over her shoulder.

Emery's wild imaginings, so abruptly loosed, were firmly quelled and she released a low sigh of relief. Of course, Lord de Burgh didn't expect anything in return for this generosity and thoughtfulness, and Emery was grateful. If she felt a small twinge of disappointment, as well, she refused to admit it, even to herself.

Emery knew a certain nervousness as she waited to be joined by her companions. Having dressed her in finery, the girl, Alda, had left and, without the servant's chattering to distract her, Emery was acutely aware of the fact that

Lord de Burgh had never seen her garbed as a woman. Although she had no business wanting his attention or approval, no matter what her guise, she could think of little else.

Only when Lord de Burgh strode into her chamber did her anxiety disappear and that was because she could do nothing except stare at him. Freshly washed and clothed, he was more handsome than ever, at ease in a magnificent castle like his own. Emery had known him as a knight errant, a tracker and a warrior, but here was a lord, who moved comfortably within a world of wealth and power and privilege.

'Twas a reminder of the differences between them, and yet, for tonight, Emery was garbed and perfumed as a lady, befitting her surroundings. She wore a shimmering blue kirtle, with her feet tucked into the most delicate of slippers. And even if she felt just as much a fraud as when she was dressed as a boy, there was no denying the admiration in Lord de Burgh's dark eyes.

Indeed, when his gaze met her own, she felt the familiar pull, along with a new yearning, sharp and insistent. 'Twas so tempting that she might have taken a step towards him, if not for the arrival of Guy, who stalked by her with a frown, then turned towards his master.

'Where's Emery?' he asked.

The long, charged moment was broken, and if Emery felt a twinge of disappointment, it was replaced by amusement and delight at Guy's reaction. Whirling towards him, she spread out her hands, as if to prove her existence, and enjoyed his stunned expression. She suspected 'twas the first time in their association that the talkative squire was struck dumb. But he soon recovered his voice and both of her companions were fulsome in their compliments.

'Twas the beginning of an enchanted evening. Although her fortunes would change soon enough, tonight she was served her meal in her chamber, just like the lord and lady when they wished to withdraw from the hall. And Emery had never tasted such fine fare as that laid before them. Fat capons, meat balls in aspic, fruit compote, and cheese tarts were followed by almonds and sugared dates.

The company was fine, as well. Instead of harping upon the Templars, Guy related amusing gossip he had heard below. And when they had eaten their fill and the tall tapers were lit, the servants filed out, leaving them alone with the last of the wine and sweetmeats.

They were able to speak freely then, but all seemed loath to broach the topics that had consumed them for days. And, for a time, murder and mayhem and madness were forgotten as Lord de Burgh began recalling a previous visit to Stokebrough. The various members of the Strong family were considered, and then, somehow, the conversation turned towards Emery.

Although the transition seemed natural enough, Emery was wary of the interest she saw in Lord de Burgh's dark gaze, and after a brief mention of her father, she deflected the questions back to him. At first he seemed no more comfortable than she at being the subject of discussion, but when she asked him to compare Stokebrough to Campion, he stirred to life.

Emery saw Guy's look of surprise, quickly masked, as the knight started to talk about his home. Then, 'twas as if a well had been tapped, setting pent-up memories to flow as he introduced Emery to his brothers.

Dunstan, thirteen years his senior, was old enough to be his father and, thus, a rather distant figure, though much revered as a tracker and a warrior. The next in line, Simon, was also skilled in battle, but more volatile than the first-born. And Stephen, well, even Emery had heard of his reputation with women, though Nicholas claimed that now he was devoted to his Welsh wife.

'Twas the siblings closer to his age of whom Nicholas spoke most warmly: Reynold only a few years his elder, Robin, the jester of the family, and Geoffrey, the scholar, with his sharp intellect and steady temperament.

'I bet he would know what you've got in the pouch,' Guy said, breaking the mood of reflection with the stark reminder of their situation.

Although Lord de Burgh nodded briefly in agreement, he returned to the stories of his youth, enthralling Emery with tales of Geoffrey's experiments, Robin's tricks and Stephen's efforts to dupe the unwary. As expected, a household of seven boys was known for mischief, injuries, misbehaviour and staunch loyalty.

The de Burgh name stood for something, but it also engendered deep devotion amongst those privileged to bear it. In fact, Lord de Burgh spoke so lovingly of his home that Emery wondered why he was travelling. Had she interrupted his return? she wondered, with a pang.

'How long have you been gone?' she asked.

As if a cloud passed over his handsome face, Lord de Burgh dropped his gaze, his long fingers fiddling with the silver spoon that still lay upon the table. When the silence lengthened without a response, Guy spoke.

'We set out last spring to visit Reynold,' he said. 'We left his manor house in summer and have been on the road since.'

Emery glanced from one man to the other, confused by the sudden tension between them. 'Have you been visiting your other brothers since then?' she asked, for it seemed that all the de Burghs except Nicholas lived elsewhere, with demesnes of their own.

'No,' Guy said.

Lord de Burgh glared at his squire, as if bidding him to silence, and Guy said no more.

'Why?' Emery asked. 'You obviously miss your home and love your family. What keeps you from them?'

Lord de Burgh did not answer; he would not even look at her. And for the first time since meeting him, Emery began to wonder about the man she thought she knew. She had been so focused on her own problems, on Gerard and the consequences of her decision to search for him, that she had not even considered the possibility that all was not well with the man who would aid her.

And why should she? The son of a powerful earl, Nicholas de Burgh had been raised by a loving family in luxury that only now could Emery begin to imagine. In truth, he seemed to have so many advantages that Emery found it hard to believe that anything was wrong.

Had he suffered a rift with his siblings? Disobeyed his parent? Fallen from favour? Emery was forced to hazard guesses, for he obviously had no intention of enlightening her. In fact, without giving her an answer, he rose to his feet.

''Tis late, and we should seek our beds,' he said. 'I'll send the girl in to stay with you.'

Emery could only gape as he strode to the door, without a glance backward, an uneasy Guy at his heels. In the quiet that followed, she was shocked to realise that this man who had seemed so open and good-natured might be hiding something from her. The very notion was painful, for she thought they shared something more profound than a few kisses and lingering gazes.

Yet how could she blame him for keeping secrets when she so zealously guarded her own?

* * *

The next morning Emery faced the arrival of her companions with concern, but the strain and awkwardness of the night before seemed to have been forgotten. Guy was in fine spirits and even Lord de Burgh had regained his usual temperament. Yet Emery wondered how much of it was genuine. He had seemed so easygoing and imperturbable, but now she wasn't so sure. Had she been blind, or had he buried his problems so deep that none could see them? And what could she do to help him?

Apparently, she was to cut his hair.

Grinning like an idiot, Guy brandished a pair of shears, which he presented to Emery with a flourish. ''Tis time to take you at your word, mistress.'

Emery might have argued that she had given no such promise, but she was grateful for the light-hearted mood, so she accepted the shears with a nod.

It appeared that Guy had not warned his master of what he was about, for Lord de Burgh looked startled. 'I'm sure we can find a barber,' he said, perhaps leery of her skills.

'You are long past a barber, my lord,' Emery said, as Guy urged him towards the settle. 'I hope you are not one of those knights who fears a trim will rob you of your strength, like Samson himself.'

Guy laughed. He was acting positively giddy and Emery wondered whether this was his normal behaviour when he wasn't looking over his shoulder for Templars. She shook her head at his antics while Lord de Burgh took his seat. But when she moved to stand behind the great knight, her own fine humour dissipated.

The nearness of his dark head made Emery regret her hasty assent. All too easily she recalled the feel of his thick locks when she revelled in his embrace, his mouth upon her own. Frowning, Emery tried to dismiss the memory, but all she wanted to do was repeat it.

'I'll be back later for my turn,' Guy said. He headed towards the door, jerking Emery's attention from the past to the present.

'Where do you think you're going?' Lord de Burgh's normally smooth voice sounded as strained as Emery felt. Was he, too, recalling the last time he had held her? Emery shivered.

'I told the groom that I would check on our horses this morn,' Guy said, reaching for the latch.

'No.' Lord de Burgh's single word rang out rather sharply, stopping Guy in his tracks.

'But, my lord, I—'

The knight must have ended his protests with a look, for the squire scowled and dropped his hand.

While the argument had provided Emery with a brief respite from her task, now she was aware of the slow passage of minutes while she stood, immobile, staring at Lord de Burgh's wide shoulders and the back of his head.

She took a deep breath, but that only filled her nostrils with his scent, deep and rich and inviting. She nearly sagged against him then, but instead she forced her hands upwards, only to realise they were shaking. Flushing, she glanced around guiltily, but Guy was not watching. He seemed intent upon the tiles at his feet. And Lord de Burgh was not facing her, though her long hesitation and trembling fingers might soon draw his scrutiny. They certainly could not instil confidence in her abilities.

Steeling herself against the urge to slip her arms over his shoulders and hold him close, Emery finally touched his hair. It was just as she remembered and she felt her nervousness disappear, replaced by a warmth that spread and settled low in her belly. She took a long lock between her fingers, rubbing it back and forth between them, as though she might commit the smell and feel to her memory for ever.

In front of her Lord de Burgh remained still, seemingly frozen in place, but beyond him, Emery saw Guy head towards the door again.

'I'll be right back,' he muttered. 'I need to visit the—'

Again, Lord de Burgh cut him off. 'You. Stay. Right. Here.' He spoke through gritted teeth, as though he were caught in the grip of some great emotion. Did he feel what she felt, or did he only want to prevent Guy from avoiding a trim?

And then Emery realised Lord de Burgh might simply dread the shears and, if so, she was discomfiting him with her long delay. The suspicion set her to work and she managed to cut the ends, at least, making them more even, though her heart was pounding wildly. And whenever her knuckles brushed against his neck, she shivered, awash with a heat and want that she could not acknowledge.

When she was finished, Emery loosed a low sigh filled with both relief and regret. She might be dressed as a woman, in finery fit for a great lady, but she was still Emery Montbard. Her circumstances had not changed with her clothing and neither had the future that awaited her.

Setting aside the shears, she reached out to brush the stray hairs off his wide shoulders, stealing one last touch before stepping back and away.

In comparison, cutting Guy's thin, ginger-coloured hair took only moments and left Emery undismayed, although the squire's mood seemed to have soured. Perhaps he had hoped to escape from his duties while she was busy with Lord de Burgh, but his master had not allowed it. And once she finished, Guy no longer was in a hurry to go anywhere, lagging behind as he accompanied them to the solar.

If Emery thought she had become accustomed to Stokebrough Castle's beautiful appointments, she was soon disabused of that notion. The solar was even larger than her bedchamber and boasted a thick, colourful carpet and a large round window that filled the room with light. On either side, two massive cupboards, burnished until they practically glowed, were filled with written works, so well kept that Emery stared in amazement.

She and Gerard had been well educated, but the family had owned few books and Emery suspected Harold had sold those, rather than donate them to the Hospitallers. She could not imagine possessing the large number collected here, which included works in English, French and Latin.

Although most were religious volumes, there were romances and histories, as well, and it was upon these last that they focused. Unfortunately, most concerned their own country and were unlikely to contain any mention of a statue of foreign origin. Their choices were winnowed to a precious few that they divided amongst themselves.

Having seen such a small number of books, Emery was enthralled by the illustrations, so intricate and bright that they seemed to leap off the page. And even though the tales of events long past in places far away were just as compelling, she forced herself to concentrate on the search. But she had barely settled into reading when Guy interrupted with more talk of checking upon the horses, an errand Lord de Burgh again dismissed as unnecessary.

Silence fell over the group then, but it wasn't long before the squire claimed he needed to use the garderobe. Without waiting for a nod from his master, he made his exit swiftly, shutting the door behind him. And suddenly Emery was aware that she was alone with Lord de Burgh, at ease in a patch of sunlight that gilded his dark hair.

Oblivious to her scrutiny, he frowned at the door that cut them off from the rest of the castle's inhabitants and finally rose to his feet to swing it wide once more. When he muttered something about Guy, Emery bit back a smile.

'Your squire seems restless this morn,' she said. 'I begin to suspect he longs to shirk his duties on such a fine day.'

'I begin to suspect some castle maid has caught his eye,' he countered drily.

Indeed, Guy was gone for such a length of time that Lord de Burgh finally hailed a passing servant, asking the young man to look for the squire.

'Shall I bring you dinner, as well, my lord?' the servant asked. ''Tis no longer warm, but your squire told all and sundry that you were not to be disturbed.'

Something flickered on Lord de Burgh's

face, though he was most gracious when answering the servant. 'I'm sure he was concerned that we be able to read quietly, but you may disregard any such cautions.'

When the man had gone to fetch their meal, Lord de Burgh returned to his chair, shaking his head.

'Perhaps you were right about the maid,' Emery said, her lips twitching with amusement.

'I wonder,' he said. But he kept his thoughts on the matter to himself.

When Guy reappeared, along with the cold dinner, he seemed oblivious to Lord de Burgh's displeasure. Giving some vague explanation for his absence, he set about enjoying the meal, especially the ale, with gusto. 'Twas obvious the squire did not fear his master's wrath, and as Emery thought the infraction minor she took delight in his high spirits.

But Lord de Burgh eyed Guy suspiciously and when they had finished eating, he insisted they return to their search, much to the squire's dismay. 'Reading is for nobles,' Guy said, grumbling. 'And those born to the manor,' he added, when Emery raised her brows at such a claim.

'I am not needed, for you two are well versed in all these languages. The solar is peaceful and sunny. Make yourselves a cosy berth amongst the pillows to read at your leisure,' Guy said, motioning towards the large cushions that were scattered upon the two chairs and the carpet itself.

Emery swallowed hard at the suggestion, which reminded her of an illustration she had seen of a knight reclining upon a grassy slope, his lady's head resting upon his stomach. But such things were the stuff of romances, not her experience. And she flushed at the thought of lying with Lord de Burgh in an improper pose, no matter what her circumstances.

Apparently, the knight agreed. 'What are you up to, Guy?' he asked, his eyes narrowed.

'I am up to nothing, my lord,' the squire protested, assuming a look of such innocence that Emery had to bite back a smile. But Lord de Burgh gave his squire a speculative look and Guy suddenly took an interest in the manuscript he had earlier abandoned.

Did the squire want to enjoy the day out of doors or visit with a comely young maid or snatch a game of dice with the other young men who served? Emery didn't know, but she blamed herself for his restlessness. 'Twas her fault Guy was cooped up inside, spending long hours searching for mention of a statue that had nothing to do with him.

By the time a servant appeared to ask them about supper, Emery felt as discouraged as Guy appeared to be. Unlike Guy, she enjoyed reading, but that had not helped her discover anything useful. None of them had, after a whole day of study. And more pages lay ahead tomorrow, making her aware of the enormity of their task.

If they went to an abbey where scribes devoted themselves to copying manuscripts, they could spend weeks or months looking through a collection and still, they might find nothing about Gerard's parcel, while he remained missing, perhaps growing more ill or more vulnerable to enemies.

Emery set aside her work and eyed the others bleakly, but Guy seemed cheered, now that he could put down his manuscript. 'Shall we sup in the great hall this evening, my lord?' he asked, rubbing his hands in anticipation. ''Tis said we shall have the entertainments of a travelling troop that arrived earlier.'

Already feeling guilty, Emery did not want to deprive the squire of his pleasure. 'You should go, my lord,' she said. 'I am content to enjoy my meal in my chamber.'

'If you two wish to eat in your chamber, my lord, I would beg leave to go below,' Guy said, looking like an eager pup at the prospect.

Lord de Burgh frowned, his eyes narrowing as he gave his squire another speculative glance. 'Perhaps we should all eat in the hall and enjoy a few moments of well-deserved distraction from our quest.'

Emery felt a rush of excitement at the promise of a fête, however small, at the grand castle. This was her only chance to experience, however vicariously, the world that was so familiar to Lord de Burgh. Yet she hesitated, unsure.

'Twas one thing for her to stay hidden away in the private rooms and quite another to boldly appear amongst others, where questions might arise. Emery was certain that none would know her or know *of* her in any of her guises, but she was here under false pretences and even her companions were not aware of her real circumstances.

Emery swallowed hard. 'Perhaps it isn't wise for me to join you,' she said. 'Won't people wonder who I am?'

Lord de Burgh shrugged. 'There are always guests at Stokebrough and the steward knows you are under my protection,' he said. 'Just stay close to me.'

Emery nodded, though she needed no urging to do so, no matter where they might be. Indeed, 'twould be easier than staying away from the man. And that realisation was more worrisome to her than facing a hall full of strangers.

Chapter Ten

When they reached the great hall, Emery's nervousness disappeared, swallowed up by her wonder at the size and splendour of the place, the arches above seeming to reach to the very heavens. They sat near the head of the table, amongst a few knights and even fewer ladies, yet Lord de Burgh managed to deflect any conversation about Emery. As a son of the Earl of Campion, he attracted nearly all of the attention anyway, though Emery suspected he did not relish it.

Once the meal was over, they drew away to sit upon a bench by themselves, though Guy soon appeared to ply them with more wine. He took a place at their feet, ready to fetch them sweetmeats and fill their cups, his mood giddy. The three of them settled back to watch and listen.

Although Emery had seen minstrels perform, few travelled to the isolated area where she had made her home, so 'twas a rare treat. This group was small, but well skilled, demonstrating feats of juggling before singing and dancing with a little dog while one of them played the lute.

Emery clapped with delight at the spectacle, made even better by the man at her side. His broad back leaning against the wall behind them, Lord de Burgh seemed more interested in her reaction than the entertainment itself and Emery felt absurdly aware of herself.

Had she ever been a woman? Or known such leisure? She had learned a man's skills alongside her twin and then taken care of her father during his long illness, never once wishing to be anywhere else. But now she realised what she had missed—not the luxuries of a noble household like this one, but the opportunity to look her best and enjoy the company of a handsome man.

Yet the time for such things had passed and, even through her euphoria, Emery knew that she had no business engaging in them now. She shook her head, feeling a bit dizzy, especially since Guy kept replenishing her cup. He hovered nearby, and if he had his eye on a maid, 'twas not apparent.

It wasn't long before the listeners were urged to join in the singing and some rose to dance, as well. They clasped hands to form a circle about the minstrel and stepped in unison to a sprightly tune. When Guy leapt to his feet, Emery laughed aloud, certain he intended to prance and jape, but 'twas only to turn to his master with some urgency.

'My lord, you must lead Emery out upon the tiles,' he said, his face flushed as though he, too, had had his fill of wine.

Emery refused even before Lord de Burgh could comply, for she had no experience with dancing and feared her head might spin should she attempt it. Just how much wine had she drunk? She had forgotten how little she had been provided this past year. Perhaps tonight's supply had gone to her head?

'Hoodman's Bluff, then,' Guy said. 'Let us call for a game!'

'Isn't that for children?' Emery asked. If she was thinking correctly, a boy or girl wearing a hood tried to catch hold of someone, which

could make for some roughness. She had never
seen it played by adults, but she suspected the
game took on quite a different tone should a
maid or a man use their hands to blindly seek
out another.

''Tis not so restricted at Campion,' Guy protested. 'Why, the earl himself has been known
to play during Christmas celebrations.'

Lord de Burgh seemed ill pleased by the reminder. 'We are not playing Hoodman's Bluff.'

'Then you must dance,' Guy said.

Emery saw wariness flash in the great
knight's dark eyes, but before she could protest, Guy had pulled her to her feet. The sudden
motion was unexpected and she swayed precariously, steadied only when Lord de Burgh
came to her side.

Aware of his reluctance to dance, Emery
would have returned to her seat, but it was too
late. The circle broke apart to include them
and one of her hands was grasped by a sweaty
young page while the other was taken by Lord
de Burgh himself.

Although Emery had known his touch before, there was something about his hand grasp-
ing hers, strong and sure, that was different.
The calloused palm was familiar, hard, yet soft,

the contact conveying a sense of companionship and, more, an intimacy that set her heart to
pounding. She imagined the fingers entwined
with hers moving elsewhere, to brush against
the turn of her wrist and long swathes of skin
that were hidden from view, secret places that
throbbed and pulsed at the thought.

Another sudden memory of Nicholas de
Burgh stripped to the waist and sliding soap
across his torso made Emery falter in her steps
and he reached out to steady her once more.
She looked up and in his eyes she saw her fevered yearnings magnified tenfold. For a long
moment, they stood, gazes locked, while the
hall and all of its revellers fell away, leaving
them in their own world, silent and aware only
of each other.

'Twas the jostling of their fellow dancers
and a few loud calls from the audience that finally broke the spell. Appalled at her own display, Emery would have fled immediately, but
Lord de Burgh made light of the laughter that
attended them as he led her away, ignoring a
few unsavoury shouts.

'Twas only when they reached his grinning
squire that Lord de Burgh made his displeasure
known. 'In case the wine has chased such con-

cerns from your head, I would remind you that we are trying not to attract attention,' he said in a low voice directed at Guy.

The knight's words were sobering and gave Emery even more reason to regret her behaviour. 'Twas one thing to enjoy the entertainment from their out-of-the-way position in the hall; 'twas quite another to participate, for all to see. Were they watched only by harmless gossips, which was bad enough, or someone more dangerous?

Emery shivered as what had been a lovely gathering took on sinister overtones. She glanced around her, especially at the people in the shadows, and wondered whether they were looking back. If Gwayne were here, would they recognise him without his Templar robes? And what of Lord de Burgh's suspicions of another pursuer?

Suddenly, the arrival of the minstrel group seemed ill timed and Emery eyed its members warily. But what did she expect to see? Although afraid to admit the answer, even to herself, when she stared into the faces of the strangers, she couldn't help searching for her brother's amongst them.

This night she had forgotten why she was

here, but those who murdered her uncle would not be distracted by merriment. Emery drew in a deep breath, her delight in the festivities gone. ''Tis late, and I should seek my chamber.'

Lord de Burgh nodded. 'I think 'tis an opportune moment for us all to retire.'

'I'll be along in a moment,' Guy said.

'No,' his master said firmly. 'We will stay together, for now, at least.'

Guy frowned, but Emery could see why Lord de Burgh might not trust the squire in his absence. Who knew what Guy would do or say, especially if he'd had too much to drink?

Emery was relieved to find that she felt better once she was moving and she longed to walk outside in the fresh air. But thoughts of their pursuers had shaken her and she did not mention her wish to Lord de Burgh, only following as he led the way to her chamber. When he paused to open the door, Emery glanced behind her, expecting to see the squire, only to find the narrow passage silent and empty.

'Where's Guy?' she asked as Lord de Burgh opened the door.

'Where's your attendant?' he said.

Emery looked inside and saw the tapers had been lit and a pleasant aroma filled the air, but there was no sign of Alda. And the perfume was not all that was out of the ordinary, for Emery spied wine and two cups. Had someone been here? She thought of the people below and wondered whether one of them had watched and waited for an opportunity. And should anyone have searched the room, they would have found some odd possessions for a young lady. Emery swung around abruptly, slamming into Lord de Burgh's solid form.

'What of the parcel?' she asked, alarmed.

''Tis well hidden,' he said, with his usual calm.

'But someone might have sent Alda away in order to look for it—or me,' Emery said.

Lord de Burgh lifted his dark brows. 'I hardly think anyone intent upon mayhem would leave the place so cosily arranged—unless a different sort of mayhem was intended.'

'So you think Alda did this earlier?'

'I'm certain of it,' he said. Obviously, he did not share her concerns about intruders, yet he still seemed ill pleased.

'What of Guy?' Emery asked. 'I thought he was to follow us. Do you think he has been waylaid, or is he with a maid, after all?'

'Oh, he's with a maid, all right,' Lord de Burgh answered. 'Your maid.'

Emery was confused.

'I suspect that we will find the good squire with your servant, though I'm sure he has more interest in her absence rather than her presence,' Lord de Burgh said.

Emery shook her head dizzily. Had the great knight consumed too much wine, too? But 'twas hard to imagine Lord de Burgh laid low by anything, even drink. And he looked the same as always. In fact, with the wine singing in her veins and her fears abating, Emery suddenly was aware of how close she was standing to him. She had only to lift her hand to touch his broad chest…

Swallowing hard, she tried to make sense of his speech. 'What are you saying?'

For once, he looked uncomfortable and glanced away, rather than meet her gaze. 'I realise you do not know my squire as well as I do, nor do you have a suspicious nature. But think upon his behaviour this day, from his efforts to closet us together in the solar to his insistence upon us dancing. And now, both he and your servant are missing, leaving you unattended and your bedchamber beckoning.'

He gestured behind her, drawing Emery's attention to the cosy setting, and she realised the circumstances could not be better for a tryst. If Lord de Burgh had not paused on the threshold, she would have followed him inside, her thoughts muddled by too many cups and the nearness of him. And then? Temptation, hot and heavy, settled within her, making her mouth dry and her pulse pound.

Aghast, Emery swung back towards him. 'But, my lord, I—I can't—' Her speech faltered and she paused to take a deep breath. Although she did not know why Guy would try to throw them together, she knew well enough not to encourage it in any way. Alternately hot and cold, light-headed and panicked, she managed to shake her head at last.

'I'm sorry, but 'tis impossible,' she said.

Instead of arguing with her, as Emery might have expected—or hoped—Lord de Burgh nodded, his expression rueful.

'Yes,' he said. ''Tis impossible.'

The muscle in Nicholas's jaw would not stop twitching, but that was better than overt violence, he decided as he stretched the fingers that had tightened into fists. Most of his brothers were more prone to bad temper than he. A lifetime of watching their misbehaviours had curbed his own. But right now Nicholas felt like throttling Guy within an inch of his life.

He was not sure what angered him the most, for the squire's conduct was appalling on so many counts, not the least of which was putting him in such an awkward situation with Emery. Worse yet was the fact that Guy had endangered her. Although Nicholas did not expect the attack that she appeared to fear, he had not liked leaving her alone while he went in search of his wayward squire.

Thankfully, she had barred the door, remaining safe until he returned with a tearful Alda in tow. At least the serving girl had been sober and none the worse for the experience. However, the same could not be said for Guy, who must have poured himself two cups of wine for every one he'd pushed on Emery. He was in no condition to protect himself or the secrets entrusted to him, let alone fight.

And Nicholas desperately wanted to fight, to release some of his pent-up emotions in a good brawl like the kind he'd had with his brothers years ago. Grabbing Guy by the neck of his tunic and lifting him a good foot off the ground had done little to calm the tempest raging inside.

Now, Nicholas watched as the youth finished emptying the contents of his stomach into a basin in the chamber they shared. And it only angered him further, for if he could not fight a drunk, then he could hardly fight a sick boy. All he could do was stalk the length of the room, tightening and flexing his fingers while his jaw muscle twitched.

'I'm sorry, my lord.'

Guy's pitiful whine had Nicholas rounding on him. 'Why? What on earth would prompt you to such nonsense?' Nicholas paused to draw a hand through his hair as he tried to gain control of his volatile mood.

''Twas only a bit of harmless matchmaking, my lord,' Guy said, in a tone that hinted Nicholas was responding with excessive spleen.

'Harmless? You would have me disregard my noble name and dishonour a young woman under my protection, an innocent who appears to be alone in the world?'

'No, my lord,' Guy said. 'I would have you realise, by fair means or foul, that Emery is the best thing that ever happened to you.'

Nicholas turned and stalked away, wonder-

ing when his private life had become a subject
of debate, but the past year had left few secrets between them. Still, his relationship with
Emery, with her bright blue eyes and soul-deep
gaze, felt private and precious, not something
to be manipulated by a drunken youth.

''Tis none of your concern,' Nicholas insisted.

''Tis more my concern than searching for
a man who does not want to be found,' Guy
retorted.

Nicholas rounded in surprise, for Guy seemed
too occupied with his matchmaking to contrib-
ute any useful insights. Yet the possibility that
Gerard might not want to be found had occurred
to Nicholas, as well. The Hospitaller had seemed
to disappear, perhaps by choice, when unable to
retrieve his parcel. And 'twas no wonder, considering the contents.

The golden statue was no small trinket and
Nicholas was not sure what aid he could provide, should Gerard prove to be a thief. However, 'twas Emery he had promised her brother
to help, though he had not known her identity
at the time. And helping Emery meant trying
to find her brother, a task that had appeared
simple at first. It had grown ever more compli-

cated until Nicholas wondered whether 'twould be best for all if Gerard was not found.

But then, what of Emery's future?

As if aware of his thoughts, Guy turned apologetic. 'I am only looking out for your welfare, my lord,' he said, a claim so ludicrous that Nicholas snorted in response.

''Tis more likely that you are amusing yourself at my expense,' Nicholas said. 'And I won't have it.'

'Amusing myself? You think it's easy to try to push you two together?' Guy said. 'For days I've watched you ogle each other and exchange fervent glances even when you thought her a boy! Yet now, when you have a bit of privacy, you shy away from each other, unwilling to take advantage of it. I was just giving you both a little nudge.'

A nudge that Nicholas did not need. He told himself that it was enough just to have met her, to enjoy her company for whatever length of time he might have, but 'twas only human to want more. And being human and a de Burgh, Nicholas was inclined to reach out and take what he wanted, to hold and to keep. The urge was there, simmering just beneath his calm exterior, and kept at bay by force of will.

'Into what?' Nicholas asked. 'A night of selfish pleasure that would ruin a young woman's good name?'

'No, my lord,' Guy said, shaking his head as if Nicholas made no sense. 'I had a more permanent arrangement in mind.'

Nicholas felt as though the wind had been knocked from him. ''Tis impossible, as well you know,' he said through gritted teeth.

'Why?' Guy said, unrepentant. ''Tis obvious how you both feel about each other. You'd be a fool to let her go—and the de Burghs are no fools.'

'You know why,' Nicholas said, ignoring Guy's outrageous claims. He could not believe they were having this conversation after all they had been through together. ''Tis too late,' he said, putting an end to it.

But Guy would not be deterred. 'Even you cannot know the future, my lord.'

Nicholas loosed a low breath, suddenly weary. 'Sometimes you have to accept what will be, rather than struggle against it.' Hadn't Guy descried his previous reckless behaviour? With acceptance came a kind of peace and a certain appreciation of unexpected pleasures, like Emery.

'The de Burghs don't give up,' Guy said, his expression fierce.

Nicholas shook his head. 'Sometimes it takes more courage to face the inevitable.'

Guy would have protested, but Nicholas held up a hand to stop him. His squire had pulled him back from the brink more than once and sometimes Nicholas had not been grateful for it. Now he had enough sense to appreciate Guy's dogged determination and devotion, however misguided.

But while the night's events would be forgiven and forgotten, there could be no real accord between them because Guy possessed something Nicholas no longer did: hope.

The next day a grim group gathered to resume reading. The young woman who had blossomed at Stokebrough now more resembled the quiet boy Nicholas had once thought her, ducking her head and refusing to meet his gaze. Guy was sulking like a child whose best-laid plans had been thwarted. Even the weather had taken a turn for the worse, and the solar that had been warm and sunny became dreary as rain lashed against the castle walls.

While Nicholas could ignore his squire's ill

mood, the change in Emery was harder to over-look. He had not realised how much she buoyed his own spirits, how he treasured her soft voice and rare laughter and the seeming bond between them. Had he imagined it? Desperate for a connection, had he forged one with a woman who did not share his feelings?

Although Guy's accusing glances and disgruntled frowns made it clear he blamed his master for the failure of his matchmaking, the squire had not been privy to the conversation between him and Emery that resulted. And Nicholas had no intention of enlightening him. Guy probably would roar with laughter to learn that the woman from whom Nicholas had vowed to keep his distance had refused him outright. And Nicholas had enough of his de Burgh pride left to find it wounded.

'Tis impossible, she'd said. And while Nicholas knew his own reasons well enough, he was left wondering just why Emery thought so. As he watched her bent head, he knew a sudden urge to take her by the shoulders and demand an explanation, a reckless action that only the remnants of his good sense prevented.

Instead, he threw himself into the manuscript, but with little interest, and the day dragged by, gloomy and tedious.

Dinner had passed mostly in silence, but Guy had managed to coax a smile from Emery with his recitation of various remedies they might pursue for their aching heads, all unpalatable, including fresh eel and bitter almonds.

Nicholas did not know which, if any, the squire had tried. But something seemed to have an adverse effect on the youth's digestion, because not long after the meal he turned green and raced from the solar.

'I'm sure it's no more than he deserves,' Nicholas said, when Emery appeared concerned. He studied her carefully, hoping that she had suffered no such ill effects from the wine. And then, suddenly, she caught him looking at her and he was aware that they were alone for the first time since last night.

'He means well,' Nicholas said, his voice huskier than usual.

'I know.'

The conclusion of the evening's events seemed to hang in the air between them and Nicholas realised now was his chance to ask why she had refused him. But how could he question her reasons when he was unwilling to reveal his own? He turned away, too wary to broach the subject and heard her heavy sigh.

''Tis hopeless,' she said, the soft words recapturing Nicholas's attention immediately. Would she speak openly of that which he could not? Nicholas steeled himself for anything since 'hopeless' sounded even worse than 'impossible'.

'Why?' he asked.

'I doubt that we shall ever discover anything about the object, here or anywhere,' she said, gesturing towards the manuscript.

Nicholas felt his sudden tension ease at the knowledge she was referring to their search, but his reprieve was brief.

'I fear that we waste our time, that *you* waste your time, and that I have asked too much of you, an important man with far more significant duties,' she said, the words coming out in a rush as she ducked her head. 'Perhaps 'tis time I released you from your vow.'

'My vow was to your brother, so you do not have the power to release me,' Nicholas answered, more sharply than he ought, but he felt a surge of anger, hurt, frustration and, yes, fear. Was this because of last night? If so, he would

gladly strangle his squire. Did she so dread his
attentions that she would flee them? Nicholas
did not care to think so, but she must realise
that whatever happened between them was the
least of her problems.

'And what of the parcel?' Nicholas asked, in
a gentler tone.

Emery blinked, as though flustered. 'You
may have it,' she said. 'I don't want it.'

'Nor do I,' Nicholas said. 'But there are
those who do and I doubt that they will take
our wishes into consideration.'

She paled.

'Would it make you feel better if I swore to
keep my distance?' he asked.

'What?' she asked in obvious surprise, and
a rosy glow was visible on her cheeks before
she ducked her head again. 'I can fault you for
nothing, my lord.'

Nicholas lifted his brows at the implication that he was blameless, for he had over-
stepped his bounds more than once. And he
could hardly be credited for good behaviour
last night when only the worst sort of rogue
would take advantage of a woman in her cups.
If Emery knew the strength of the desire that
he held at bay, she would not be so willing to

trust him. Indeed, she must harbour doubts, for her brow furrowed when she glanced up at him anxiously.

'But how long can I ask you to continue to aid me?'

At her words, denial rose in him with such force that it threatened to choke him. Nicholas no longer cared what her reasons were for offering him the chance to go; he only knew that he could not comply. He had no choice and he gave her none.

'I won't leave you,' he said, through a throat thick with emotion. Not now. Not yet. 'Twas no promise, but a declaration, and Nicholas did not know what he would do if she could not accept it. But in her bright blue eyes he saw a kind of wary relief and shuddered with the strength of his own response. His gaze met hers—there was no mistaking the bond between them. 'Twas no figment of his imagination and he wanted to hold on to it, just as he wanted to hold on to Emery.

But Guy chose that instant to return. His entrance was comical, for he strode in to find the two of them locked in silent communion and stood gaping, as if unsure whether to go or stay. But the moment was gone. 'Twas just as well.

'Guy's complexion is much improved,' Nicholas said, inclining his head towards his squire. 'Perhaps he can advise us as to our course.'

Guy eyed them cautiously. 'What course?'

'Our work here seems to have yielded little,' Nicholas said.

Guy perked up. 'Does that mean we can stop reading?'

'When we have finished,' Nicholas said, for they would soon be done.

'If you would find out more about the statue, let us go to Campion,' Guy said. 'Your father might even be able to identify it.'

'Campion is too far away and we are pressed for time,' Nicholas said. Although he did not elaborate, he did not have to. Guy knew what he meant.

'Your brother Geoffrey's manor is closer and would be a safe haven,' the squire said.

Nicholas shook his head. 'A safe haven will do us little good in the end, for there is no guarantee that interest in our parcel will wane while we hide ourselves away. And the de Burgh name is well known, so someone who is determined to seek me out would not have a difficult time of it.'

At his words, Emery blanched. 'I've brought

trouble on you and your family,' she said, looking dismayed.

But Guy dismissed her concerns with a snort. 'This business is hardly what the de Burghs would call a problem.'

Frowning at his squire, Nicholas turned to Emery. 'I'm sure Guy did not mean to make light of the danger you are in, only remind you that the de Burghs have vanquished far more powerful enemies.'

'Not that anyone is menacing the family now,' Guy said. 'Campion rules in peace, as do his sons.'

Did they? Nicholas wondered. The steward at Stokebrough might know if something had happened to his father, but his brothers could be facing threats that were not common knowledge. And Nicholas felt a twinge of shame and guilt that none could reach him, should they need him.

When the message from Reynold had been received two years past, they had all rallied to his aid, only to find he had prevailed without them. Still, there was nothing like riding with his brothers, certain of right and might and triumph. Nicholas felt a heady rush of pleasure at the memory, followed all too swiftly by regret.

'If not to your family's strongholds, then where?' his squire asked, breaking into his reverie.

Both Guy and Emery looked to him in question and Nicholas felt the lack of his brothers' counsel, if not their swords. He could use some fresh insight into this puzzle, for his quest for both Gerard and more information had been unsuccessful. Then, eyes narrowing, Nicholas wondered whether he'd been searching too far afield when he might simply turn around.

'First, let us see if our sojourn here has shaken off any who might follow,' he said. 'And, if not, perhaps we should look behind us for answers.'

Chapter Eleven

❧❧❧

Once she had dismissed Alda, Emery set aside the fine clothes she had borrowed and donned her brother's old garments. At least they were clean, even the hat, and though she had grown weary of them, they would serve her well for now. She would have no need of delicate shifts and elegant mantles on the road or the place she would eventually make her home.

Her days here at Stokebrough had been like an idyll, a fleeting glimpse into Lord de Burgh's world, where it seemed, for a moment, that she might join him. But reality had intruded upon that waking dream, reminding her that she was not a high-born lady fit for a handsome lord or an idle maid with time to spend in flirtation.

She had another life to which she soon must return.

But not yet. For now Emery would continue to search for Gerard and she was thankful that she did not have to do so alone. Despite all the trouble she had caused him and the sudden awkwardness between them, Lord de Burgh remained committed to her quest. And Emery felt a giddy pleasure at the memory, hugging his words to her. *I won't leave you.*

Grabbing up her pack, she left the luxurious chamber behind without a thought to join Guy in the passage. She stayed close as they made their exit as unobtrusively as possible, while Lord de Burgh met with the steward. He was giving out the story that Mistress Montbard had departed earlier, a flimsy lie meant only to satisfy the household.

But it would do little to deter any serious pursuer, as Emery was well aware. When they slipped through the great hall into the bailey, without the great knight's stolid form nearby, she felt especially vulnerable. Guy told her not to be conspicuous as they made their way to the stables, and she kept her head ducked. But she couldn't help eyeing everyone she passed, even those on seemingly innocuous errands, and wondering whether they were looking for her, waiting for an opportunity to strike.

Guy called for the horses, and, as Emery grew increasingly nervous, she realised that Lord de Burgh would be talking to her to keep her distracted. He had a way about him that was naturally steady that Guy, with his wild theories and schemes, sorely lacked.

However, there was one thing that the squire did possess, which Emery found difficult to obtain from his master, and that was private information. Since she rarely could speak with Guy alone, Emery seized her chance. She told herself a conversation would calm her, but there was no denying her eagerness to learn more about Lord de Burgh.

'Tell me something,' she said.

'If I can,' Guy said, warily. Perhaps he expected her to ask about his matchmaking, but Emery wanted to steer clear of that subject. She was more concerned with what his master was hiding than Guy's machinations.

'What ails Lord de Burgh?' she asked. Although the question was a personal one, Emery was not prepared for Guy's reaction. He swung round to gape at her, all colour draining from his face before it flushed bright red.

'Wh-what do you mean?' he asked, his voice a mere croak.

Emery faltered under his wide-eyed stare, but persisted. 'Has he fallen out with his family? Why does he roam so far from home, refusing to seek shelter with his brothers?'

To her surprise, Guy's dismay appeared to vanish and he even loosed a low sigh before shaking his head. 'You would have to ask him that.'

Although disappointed with his answer, Emery could not fault Guy for his loyalty. 'Yet from the way he talks about Campion, he cares deeply for it, as you do.'

'Yes,' Guy said, with a sigh. 'I long to go home—'twould be good for him, too.' He paused, as though fearful of saying too much, this young man who usually spoke his mind without hesitation. 'But I won't go without him.'

Emery felt a rush of respect for Guy, who often played the fool. But he was staunch and brave and caring, and she nearly gave him a hug before she realised just how odd that would look while dressed in her current guise. 'He is lucky to have you,' she said, softly.

Guy snorted, seemingly himself again. ''Tis not a view he often shares.'

Before Emery could protest, the subject of their speech arrived, so tall and handsome Emery thought surely all attention must be upon him. She realised then how hard it would be for him to hide away, even without his famous name. He was born and bred to greatness and it rested upon his shoulders in a way that others could only hope to emulate.

With Lord de Burgh's return, Emery gave no more thought to those who might be watching until they left the castle walls behind them. Then her unease returned, for instead of eluding trouble, Lord de Burgh wanted to court it. His plan was to head in the opposite direction from whence they had come only to circle back, catching unawares anyone who followed.

They kept to a narrow path, as usual, rather than the wider, more travelled road, and Emery tried not to glance behind her. Still, any sound made her flinch and she felt on edge, as though they might suddenly be attacked by a horde of pursuers. Yet when she did look back, she saw nothing, making her wonder whether this effort would yield as little as the manuscript search.

Eventually, Lord de Burgh veered off the

track, and they made their way along the edges
of fields and hedges towards the castle and the
path that had taken them away from it. They
hung back, unwilling to get too close, but even
then, they could see that it was deserted. Still,
they remained where they were, as out of sight
as possible, and waited, watching.

They dared not speak or make noise of any
kind, and Emery grew to appreciate the skills
required to maintain such vigilance. She began
to suspect that unless Gerard had changed, he
did not have the necessary patience for the task,
and she was not sure whether to be relieved or
alarmed at that realisation. For if not her brother,
then who? As much as she feared Gerard's in-
volvement, she would rather face him than
Gwayne or someone else...

Emery drew in a deep breath and shifted
restlessly in her saddle, as did Guy. But Lord
de Burgh remained still as stone, his dark eyes
alert, a formidable foe to any who dared approach. Emery found herself staring so hard
that the packed earth began to swim in front of
her eyes, yet nothing stirred, not even a shepherd or villein in the fields.

It seemed that time stopped, bringing everything to a halt around them, so when Lord

de Burgh finally moved, Emery jerked to attention. He lifted a hand to point to his right, away from the narrow path in the distance, and Emery turned her head, her heart in her throat. Afraid of what she might see, she held her breath, but there was nothing except the forest that served Stokebrough, providing venison for the Strongs' table.

Emery blinked in confusion and Guy looked just as puzzled. 'What is it, my lord?' he asked softly.

'A plume of smoke,' the great knight said.

Emery squinted and finally made out a faint line, barely visible in the sky above the trees, though she did not see its significance. 'But we have not been there,' she said.

'Yes, but 'tis a good vantage point from which to view all those entering and leaving the castle,' Lord de Burgh said.

'If someone was watching for us, they would have followed us when we left,' Guy argued, eyeing the woods warily.

'Twas a wariness that Emery shared, but that Lord de Burgh did not. Indeed, he lifted his dark brows and nodded towards the smoke. 'There's one way to find out,' he said, urging his mount forwards.

''Tis probably poachers,' Guy muttered, falling in behind.

'Or worse,' Emery said, exchanging a chary look with the squire.

But Lord de Burgh ignored their comments and they could do nothing except follow as he led them towards the forest. When they reached the outskirts, he gestured for them to fan out alongside him, an order that Emery obeyed with dismay. Did he think whoever had lit the fire was still there and would quickly surround a lone rider?

Although Lord de Burgh wasn't that far away and Guy was on the other side of her, within hailing distance, Emery felt the press of the trees and the darkness that came under their canopies. This was not the familiar copse near her home, but a strange place, where anyone could be hiding, before or behind or all around. And Emery listened intently, leery of every crack of twig or rustle of leaves.

Swallowing hard, she reached for her short sword and told herself that she was prepared for anything. But the rib that had bothered her little these past days suddenly ached, making her wonder how well she could acquit herself in a fight. Still, she had no choice but to heed

Lord de Burgh as he motioned for them to hang back while he headed forwards.

Every sound was loud in the silence, including the rapid thud of her heart, and once Lord de Burgh disappeared from sight, Emery found it hard to remain behind. Only the sight of Guy kept her still as they waited and she became more agitated with each passing moment. She told herself that if Lord de Burgh had stumbled across bandits, there would be some signs of a struggle. But what if the villains were aware of his arrival and surrounded him?

Although 'twas hard to imagine the knight being overcome by anyone or anything, Emery's concern for him began to outpace her own fears. Finally, she could bear it no more, and she slipped from her horse, determined to see for herself. Ignoring Guy's frantic signals to stay back, she crept as quietly as possible through the growth into the small clearing.

'Twas obvious that someone had made camp here, for the fire was still smouldering, sending up its slender waft of smoke. But the area appeared to be deserted now, except for Lord de Burgh and... At her first sight of the Templar's white robes, Emery choked back a cry. But the figure was lying on the ground, seemingly subdued, while Lord de Burgh kneeled over him.

Indeed, the Templar was unmoving, and Emery hurried forwards, eyeing Lord de Burgh with alarm. 'Did you kill him?' she asked, her voice a cracking whisper.

Lord de Burgh rose to his feet to face her. 'No, but someone did.' He looked down then and Emery followed his gaze. The Templar knight's neck was broken in much the same manner as her uncle's had been and on his back lay another card from the Moorish Game.

Emery sucked in a harsh breath as bile rose up in her throat, but she swallowed hard against it, for this was no place to fall ill. In fact, a sound from behind made her swing round, fearful that Gwayne's squire had appeared to avenge him. She blinked in relief as Guy made a noisy entrance, rushing forwards, only to halt as he reached the dead body.

The squire blanched, then glanced nervously at Lord de Burgh. 'But if Gwayne is not following us, then who is?'

Lord de Burgh frowned. 'The man who killed him.'

They made a hasty inspection of the clearing, but did not find any signs of the murderer.

In fact, Guy suggested that Gwayne's missing squire might be to blame, for it was not uncommon for villains to fight amongst themselves. But the presence of the card with its three ominous swords cast doubt upon that claim. Someone was sending a message, but who? And to whom?

Lord de Burgh found broken twigs and trodden earth that gave evidence of horses passing through, but the trail led towards the castle, disappearing on to well-travelled ground. And since they did not know who to look for, they soon abandoned the effort, automatically returning to the path they had taken this morning.

Guy, especially, was eager to be on their way, glancing behind him as though he expected the assassin to be on their heels. But they could not even be certain why Gwayne had been slain, let alone whether the guilty party was after them, as well.

'Perhaps the Templar didn't kill your uncle, but was just following us, while the real culprit was following him,' Guy said, with his usual penchant for convoluted theories.

'And who is this real culprit?' Emery asked, warily. ''Tis not Gerard!'

Guy shook his head. 'I doubt the Hospitaller is capable of such murders, unless he has gone completely mad.'

But Emery did not find the squire's words reassuring. Had her brother gone completely mad? She had only to remember Robert Blanchefort's ravings to imagine that possibility.

'It must be someone who has been in the Holy Land,' Guy said, as though privy to her thoughts. 'Else how would he have these pieces of the Moorish Game?' When no one replied, he turned to the great knight. 'Who do you think is responsible, my lord?'

Thus far, Lord de Burgh had been silent, but now his lips tightened into a firm line and he spoke with certainty. ''Tis the Saracen.'

Emery blinked in surprise, for that claim sounded as unbelievable as some of Guy's conjectures. Apparently, the squire thought so, too, for he quickly protested. 'But the man who menaced Robert Blanchefort would be even older than he is.'

'Not necessarily,' Lord de Burgh answered. 'And our man might well be the original Saracen's son or brother or someone who holds to his traditions.'

'But why reappear now? And to harry us?' Guy asked.

'Because the parcel has reappeared or he has finally determined its whereabouts,' Lord de Burgh said, with a shrug of impatience.

The gesture was unlike him and Emery wondered whether he was growing weary of the constant questions for which he had no answers. She knew his mail must weigh upon him in the heat, as would the strain of keeping them safe against unknown threats. He always seemed so strong and capable, 'twas easy to forget that he was subject to the same tensions as everyone else.

As if to prove her right, he drew in a deep breath. 'We can only speculate, unless we are able to ask him ourselves,' he said wearily.

'But how?' Guy asked. 'We've already circled back once, only to find a corpse.'

'Let us put some miles behind us and, when we find a likely spot, we will implement a new tactic, perhaps after we stop to eat the meal packed for us by the cook at Stokebrough.'

They travelled for some time until they found a place that suited Lord de Burgh. Obscured by bushes and undergrowth, they parcelled out bread and cheese and apples, though the great knight ate little. Again, Emery realised he felt the heat more than she in her thin boy's garb, for his face was flushed and he drank much of the water in his flask.

When they had packed their things away, Lord de Burgh explained his plan, which neither she nor Guy greeted with enthusiasm. Whether he was warm or weary or just frustrated, the great knight dismissed their objections, leaving Emery no choice but to swallow her misgivings. Soon, she and Guy were preparing to continue on with the great knight's destrier, but without its rider. Lord de Burgh remained behind, alone and on foot, in order to waylay any who might be following.

As soon as they rode away, Emery grew uneasy. She knew that she and Guy were more vulnerable without the great knight to protect them, but 'twas not fear for herself that dismayed her. She did not like to part with Lord de Burgh for a number of reasons, some of which she did not care to examine. Yet they could not explain the dread that filled her, as if of an ill portent. And she was not the one who was supposed to be prescient.

Finally, Emery suggested circling back, but

Guy shook his head. 'If someone is tracking us, rather than watching, it will take them longer to reach Lord de Burgh. And should we go back too soon, we risk revealing the ruse and losing our only chance to find out whether we are pursued.'

Guy spoke the truth and was obviously putting on a brave face while glancing about for any signs of danger. Yet Emery could not dismiss her increasing anxiety. 'Twas not that she doubted the great knight, who was both a warrior and a de Burgh, but she had come to realise that he was a man, as well. And while he was looking out for them, who was looking out for him?

'I'm concerned about him,' Emery said.

'Who?' Guy asked. His attention focused upon his surroundings, he was barely listening.

'Lord de Burgh,' Emery said. She steeled herself for the squire's derision, but when he turned towards her, he wore an odd expression. 'Why?'

Emery frowned. She felt foolish, for how could she explain her worries over a man experienced in battle, equipped with both weapons and wits? 'I think the mail is weighing heavily upon him,' she finally said. 'He seemed so hot and thirsty when we stopped.'

Emery expected Guy to laugh or snort as he dismissed her fears, but his reaction only fuelled them. Swearing under his breath, he urged his mount around and called for her to join him. Without waiting for her assent, he headed back the way they had come, even though they would run headlong into anyone following.

Although the path was too rugged for them to move very quickly, Guy kept a fast pace, all the while watching for signs of Lord de Burgh or any others. He slowed only when they neared the spot where they had stopped earlier, approaching the brush warily.

Now that they had reached the place where they had left him, Emery wondered about Lord de Burgh's reaction to their return. Would he be angry or insulted at her presumption? She was already considering how to explain why they had not followed his orders, destroying the trap he had been determined to set, but Lord de Burgh did not appear. Had he moved on?

To Emery's surprise, Guy gave up all pretence of secrecy and called out his master's name, but his shout roused nothing except a few birds. After they took to the sky the world was still and silent, the only sound the frantic beating of Emery's heart. Had Lord de Burgh discovered their pursuer and given chase? But why couldn't he see or hear them?

Panicking now, Emery followed as Guy veered off the path into the brush. She was not sure what he expected to find there—some sign of a struggle, perhaps, or a message left by his master. She only knew that she was unprepared for the sight that met her eyes.

Lord de Burgh was there, not far from where they had eaten, his tall form lying motionless upon the ground. And for one heart-stopping moment Emery thought he was dead, just like her uncle and the Templar, his neck broken and a colourful token left upon his corpse. Over her own stifled cry, she heard Guy's soft reassurance.

'He's all right,' the squire said, dismounting. 'At least I think so.'

'How can you know?' Emery asked. Without waiting for an answer, she rushed to join Guy, who was soon kneeling at his master's side. At least the knight was lying on his back, his throat unmarked. And when Emery saw it move, her heart resumed beating.

'I'm all right.'

The hoarse croak made Emery weak with relief, but still she examined his body for any wounds or signs of attack, while Guy leapt up to fetch water. Finding none, she sank back on her heels as Guy returned with a damp scrap of linen he applied to Lord de Burgh's face. When his lips twitched and his lashes fluttered, Emery swallowed a sob of gratitude.

He seemed to recover himself then, taking the cloth from Guy and sitting upright with little aid from his squire. But Guy's expression remained grim. 'If you can ride, let us return to Stokebrough,' he urged.

'Of course I can ride,' Lord de Burgh said, as though shrugging off whatever had laid him low. 'And we might draw unwanted attention by turning back.'

'But we aren't being followed,' Guy said, gesturing towards the empty path.

'Are you certain?' he asked, lifting his dark brows.

Guy paled then and looked over his shoulder nervously, as if the brush might conceal someone watching. Emery shivered, unsure what to think. Had Lord de Burgh's ambush attempt failed, or had he become the victim? He did not explain, but rose to his feet.

'We'll continue forwards, at least for today,' he said. 'Just give me a moment to catch my breath.'

But 'twas obvious he needed to do more than catch his breath and Guy seemed aware of that fact. 'My lord, we can not go on as we have before,' he said. 'We have Emery with us and the Templar idol and maybe even a murderer behind us.'

'All the more reason to go on,' Lord de Burgh insisted.

Emery studied him uncertainly, unwilling to question his decision, but concerned about his condition. 'Perhaps you should rid yourself of the mail, at least until the day grows cooler.'

Lord de Burgh shook his head. 'I'm fine.'

'But, my lord—' Guy started to protest, only to fall silent at a sharp glance from his master. Still unsure, Emery looked from one to the other. She knew that the weather alone could not fell such a strong man, but no purpose would be served by arguing, especially in the brush off a deserted road. For now, she held her tongue and prepared to follow, as always.

All talk of ambushes was abandoned and Emery was glad of it. She was still shaking when they set off again, her pulse pounding at

the fright she had received. She did not care to
dwell upon that heart-stopping moment when
she'd thought he was dead or the emotions that
came with it. Instead, she was thankful that he
was alive and able to ride, though she continued to worry.

She wasn't the only one. As the day dragged
on, Guy watched his master carefully while remaining more alert than ever before. Emery,
too, was vigilant, lest some infidel brandishing
a deadly, curved sword catch them unawares.

They travelled more slowly now, and when
Emery saw Lord de Burgh's wide shoulders
slump she feared he might fall, breaking his
neck without any help from the Saracen. She
could only wonder what had caused such a sudden change in the mighty knight.

Had he been overcome by some villain, who
knocked him out and took his purse, or had he
been overtaken by those he sought to trap? Was
he suffering some malady, or was an old injury
causing him distress? From what Emery had seen
of his body, Lord de Burgh had plenty of scars,
but none seemed capable of laying him low.

Whatever had happened, it was clear that he
did not intend to speak of it, not to his trusted

squire or to Emery. She felt a stab of disappointment at the knowledge, but how could she
expect more when she had no hold upon this
man?

Yet she had only to remember that heart-
stopping moment of terror to know that Lord
de Burgh had a hold upon her, far greater than
she had ever imagined.

Chapter Twelve

The manor in which they sought refuge was small and shabby, as though its owners had abandoned it, and indeed, they were said to be travelling, having left only the steward and a few servants behind. At least, that's the story Manfred, the steward, told.

Small and dark and shifty-eyed, he seemed ill disposed to invite them in until he realised 'twas a de Burgh seeking shelter. Then he fawned over the knight in a manner that Emery found repulsive, rubbing his hands together as though already counting a reward for services rendered.

Manfred claimed that they had arrived too late for supper, but he would see what the cook could provide for them. 'Twas just as well, for

Emery was eager for Lord de Burgh to get some rest, away from prying eyes. The chamber, like the steward who led them there, was small and dark and smelled musty. But it was better than making camp outside, and soon Guy had helped his master out of his mail and tunic, so that he could lie down.

'I'm going to see about some food,' Guy said. He opened the door to find Manfred on the other side with a bowl of water, making Emery wonder if there were any servants at all.

Although Guy thanked the steward, he took the vessel and closed the door, shutting the man out. Exchanging a look with Emery, Guy set the bowl on the floor, since there was no furniture besides the bed. He waited for Manfred to be gone before venturing out again and Emery followed, anxious to speak to him privately.

'I don't like the looks of this place,' she whispered. 'And I like the looks of our host even less. If the Saracen or anyone else is following, this steward will happily sell us out for a handful of coins.'

Guy nodded in agreement. 'I'll have a look around while fetching some food. Can you wash Lord de Burgh?'

The unexpected question flustered Emery so

much that for a moment all she could do was gape at the squire. When she finally recovered her wits, she stepped back, shaking her head in denial. 'Twas startling enough to view the man's bare chest. She could not remove the rest of his clothing or look upon his naked body or *touch* him…

'I'm not asking you to give him a bath,' Guy said, with annoyance. 'Just cool him down a bit. I'm sure he's…overheated.'

Immediately Emery regretted her refusal. Guy was not intent upon matchmaking any more, but concerned about his master's condition, as was she. She nodded her assent and, although the squire looked like he wanted to say more, he turned away.

Emery reached out to grasp his arm, whether to comfort him or herself, she wasn't sure. 'Be careful.'

Guy nodded. 'Bolt the door and open it only for me.'

Emery felt the blood drain from her face at the warning, but she did as Guy bid. Slumping against the worn wooden portal, she eyed Lord de Burgh's prone form and realised that without his strength and skills they would be hard pressed to protect themselves. And, if anything happened to Guy, she would be responsible for Lord de Burgh, should he be unable to defend himself.

Emery shook her head at the daunting prospect, but she had no other choice and vowed to do whatever she must in order to keep him safe. Straightening, she schooled her features to betray none of her thoughts and moved to the bed, intent upon the task Guy had assigned her.

But for a long moment all Emery could do was stare at him stretched out in all his golden glory. She had tended to her father and, less often, to Gerard, but she had never seen anyone like Lord de Burgh. Admiration and something new and dangerous shot through her, filling her with both a sense of urgency and a sweet languor. Despite her earlier qualms, all she wanted to do was reach out and touch him, to run her fingers over his skin, exploring each muscle and scar and throbbing pulse.

Emery shuddered, trying to gain control over her riotous emotions. Just as Guy had put aside his matchmaking, she needed to dismiss such thoughts and concentrate on giving this man the care he needed. For even though Lord de Burgh appeared little different from the last time she had seen him bared to the waist, his eyes were closed, his face was flushed and his breathing ragged.

The shock of these changes spurred Emery to action. Removing her kerchief, she dipped it into the water and dabbed at his forehead. As she pushed aside dark strands of his hair, the silky texture brought back memories of the other times she had touched him and she swallowed hard. Tentatively, she slid the cloth down his throat and over his wide shoulders, shivering when her fingers inadvertently brushed against him.

Gradually, Emery grew bolder and her ministrations became a labour of love. By the time she had washed his arms, one after the other, she was lingering over every inch of his sun-bronzed flesh until it was more familiar than her own. With each swipe of her kerchief she laid claim to more of him until she reached his flat stomach and hesitated. She was eyeing the shadowy indent of his navel and wondering just how far to go when her wrist was seized in a tight grip.

Gasping in surprise, Emery glanced up to find his dark gaze upon her, smouldering with more heat than the entire length of his body was giving off. Her heart skipped a beat before beginning a raucous rhythm.

'I'm not dead yet,' he whispered.

The words flustered her. Was he asking a question or making an accusation? Abruptly aware of the intimacy of her actions, she blushed and struggled for words. 'Of course not,' she said. 'You aren't dying.'

Releasing her wrist, Lord de Burgh frowned and turned his head away, as though disputing her words. 'Now you know.'

The stark look on his face gave her pause, but Emery spoke soothingly. ''Tis just a bit of heat,' she assured him. Although earlier she would have argued that hot weather could not fell such a man, now she was determined to believe it. Yet when he refused to look at her, Emery grew uneasy.

Although rarely at a loss for words, he seemed to be having difficulty and suddenly Emery did not want him to speak, for she was fearful of what he might say. She lifted a hand to put her fingers to his lips in an attempt to stop his speech. He needed rest, she told herself, and should remain quiet. But she was too late.

'I'm sick,' he muttered, his voice low. 'A

fever repeatedly assails me and, unlike any mortal foe, it does not fear a de Burgh. It cannot be vanquished by strength or skill or intelligence and, eventually, it will triumph.'

Emery felt dizzy, as though she wasn't getting enough air, and she sucked in several deep breaths. 'No,' she said, shaking her head in denial. How could he be well one moment and talk this way the next?

''Tis impossible,' Emery said, trying to remember everything she had ever heard about such ailments. She was no healer, but she had learned much when taking care of her father. And she knew those who suffered these kinds of fevers did not look like Lord de Burgh, hale and hearty and strong, for they had no time to recover before they were struck down again.

'Intermittent fevers come every few days and are far more...debilitating.' Emery swallowed hard, unable to finish.

''Twill get worse before it gets better,' he said softly. 'If it doesn't kill me this time.'

Emery looked shocked at such a sentiment. 'Don't say that. There must be something that can be done, some treatment—'

He cut her off. 'I have sought help more than once, to no avail. The first time, when

I recovered fully, I shrugged it off, but it returned, leaving me weaker. In between attacks, I struggled to regain some semblance of my old strength, but for what purpose? Slowly, it ate at me until I wondered if 'twould be better just to give in.'

He turned away again, as though ashamed of the admission, and Emery was so horrified she remained mute until he continued on. 'For a while I courted danger, eager for a violent end, for who would not prefer to go out fighting than lying abed, until all is sapped away?'

Emery stifled a cry of both pain and defiance. No matter what he might have done, it was not enough and she would not rest until she had tried every possibility more than once. Her myriad emotions coalesced into a single focus, hardened with determination: she would not let this happen. There must be someone, a learned monk at a hospital, a wise woman or…

Emery eyed him sharply. 'What does your father say?'

'He doesn't know.'

'What?' Emery faltered, unable to believe what she was hearing.

He turned his head to face her. 'I won't have my family see me laid low,' he said, with sudden ferocity. 'And I hoped that you would not see me this way, either.'

'What? Why?' Emery said. 'Do you think I only care for you because you are a great knight? Or that I would sink so low as to abandon you in your time of need?' Emery felt strengthened by her outrage, a sentiment far preferable to the grief that threatened to overwhelm her.

'You do a disservice to me and to your family,' she said. 'Is your pride so great that you would deprive yourself of the comforts and joys of home, of looking upon your loved ones, for the sake of…vanity?'

''Tis not vanity to spare them all the sorrow and disappointment and frustration that has been mine this past year,' he said, dark eyes flashing. 'Do you think I want my last memories of them to be those of pity and loss? Your scorn is easily given when you have no notion of what I've been through.'

He looked to say more, but he was interrupted by a knock upon the door. Eager to end the argument, Emery hastened to answer. If Guy had heard raised voices, he did not admit it, but brandished a paltry array of provisions: hard cheese, wrinkled apples and bread.

'He needs hearty broth and a tisane to bring down the fever,' Emery said, dismayed.

Guy shook his head. 'You will find little below.' They exchanged a wary look, unwilling to burden Lord de Burgh with more worries. But Guy was able to get a small fire going so that Emery could steep some herbs without creating too much heat. She only wished that she had more supplies and thought longingly of the stores she had once kept at Montbard.

But what little she had must have helped, for Lord de Burgh soon fell asleep, and Emery slumped down beside the bed in relief, the strain of the day threatening to overwhelm her. She would have eaten nothing herself, if not for Guy's insistence, and he waited patiently until she finished, much as he had watched over his master's meal.

'Are you a healer?' he asked, sounding both hopeful and desperate.

'Hardly,' Emery said, unwilling to mislead him. 'I know just a little, having learned some lore while tending my father.'

Guy's disappointment was obvious and Emery realised how pale and drawn he was. The seemingly frivolous squire had become solid and dependable these past few hours, and she was struck with a sudden fear that he, too, would fall ill. 'Do you...suffer, as well?' she asked, panic setting her heart to thudding.

Guy shook his head, then drew a deep breath. 'We were visiting his brother Reynold, whose manor sits along the coast. When turning towards home, we travelled a different route, north through low-lying marshy lands, where summer fevers are commonplace. He was stricken and I was not.'

Emery heard the guilt in the squire's tone, but knew 'twas no fault of his that only his master was affected. She would have said as much, but he continued on, as though eager to unburden himself.

'We were taken in by residents there, familiar with such ailments, and Lord de Burgh quickly recovered. But when it returned, again and again, he grew discouraged, claiming that a knight with the ague was...of no use to anyone.'

The catch in his voice made Emery's throat thicken and she struggled to dispute his words. 'I am no physician,' she said, 'but I do not think he has marsh fever or the ague, as you called it. That illness has a definite cycle, with only days between bouts that do not allow for recovery. And Lord de Burgh seemed perfectly well this past week.'

Guy nodded. 'He has been well now for some time, though not as strong as he used to be. And with every day that passed, I thought that perhaps it wouldn't come back. And then it does, suddenly, with no warning.'

Emery heard Guy's anguish and shared it. 'But he is a strong man who has fought it off before,' she protested. 'Surely he will do so again.'

Guy shrugged in abject misery. 'I don't know. He was always the best and the brightest of the de Burgh brothers, nearly as steady and clever as Geoffrey, yet more of a warrior than a scholar. But after the illness returned, he grew reckless, as if he cared little for his life and was intent upon losing it. And he refused to return home, though that is where he would be most likely to find aid.'

Emery swallowed hard as the enormity of what Lord de Burgh faced became apparent. And she had thought him free of troubles? She shook her head at her own folly. How had he carried on in such an easy manner with this hanging over his head, an ever-present threat of death?

Guy cleared his throat. 'When he met you, he seemed to put that recklessness behind him, and, for the first time in months, he spoke of his family. I had hopes that he had found something to live for—perhaps I erred in my efforts to see him happy...' There was no need for him to say more, for Emery already had forgiven him his matchmaking and she put an arm round his shoulders to confirm it.

But the comforting gesture seemed his undoing. 'I just want to go home,' he said, sounding as though he had reached the end of his resources. And Emery could not blame him, for he had shouldered this burden alone for nearly a year. 'The earl is so wise, I am certain he would be able to help his youngest son, but I can't convince Lord de Burgh,' he said.

Emery drew in a ragged breath. 'Maybe he wants to spare his father that responsibility,' she said, softly. She was ashamed now of her earlier outburst, for it seemed that the knight wanted to save his family from what she and Guy were experiencing.

'Twas a more noble reason than vanity, but, in the end, just as misguided.

Emery jerked awake, fighting against the bone-deep weariness that tempted her to sleep

again, for she had been roused by the sound
of her name. 'Twas spoken in a low voice, so
deep and urgent that there was no ignoring it,
and she braced herself to see a curved sword
swinging over her head.

In the darkness, her fingers closed over a
knife Lord de Burgh had given her. She prepared to roll over as she lifted it up, to fend off
the Saracen, the steward or any other assail-
ant, but when she opened her eyes, 'twas only
Guy bending over her, touching her shoulder.
Emery loosed a low breath, relieved that she
had not gutted him.

'He's calling for you,' Guy said.

In an instant, Emery was on her feet and
at Lord de Burgh's side. 'I'm here,' she said,
though her voice was unsteady.

He muttered something unintelligible in response and she lifted a hand to his forehead in
an effort to soothe him, but she was dismayed
by the heat that met her fingers.

'He's too warm,' she whispered.

Guy moved quickly in response, stirring
the fire to life and adding more water to their
makeshift pot. Still, it seemed to take far too
long before they could get him to drink the ti-

sane and settle down to sleep again. Even then, Emery felt no relief.

'I have few herbs with me,' she said. 'If I had access to proper stores, I could help his fever and any pain, as well. But I can't do it from here.'

Guy nodded. 'This is no place for him and he would not want to linger, if he were aware of the circumstances. The odd steward, the lack of supplies and servants... We can't be worrying about what is really going on here, while tending to a sick man.'

Emery could only agree, but what was the alternative? She said nothing and Guy sank into silence. When he finally lifted his head, he wore an expression that Emery had never seen upon his face. So often fearful or wary, now he looked both determined and relieved, as though he had made a momentous decision.

'If we can get him on a horse tomorrow, we will go,' he said.

Emery swallowed hard. She did not feel safe in the empty manor, with little they needed at hand and the shifty-eyed steward spying upon them. But the road was even more treacherous, and if Lord de Burgh should become sicker, how would she care for him? Where would they head? Lord de Burgh had always led them, but he was in no condition to do so and had not made his plans clear. Perhaps they should just remain where they were for the time being? Emery thought, though Guy's fierce look kept her from speaking.

'There are two of us now,' he said, as though to convince both her and himself. 'And two hold sway over one.'

Emery blinked, for the squire was bound to serve Lord de Burgh's wishes, not theirs. But Guy's resolve only seemed to harden. 'We'll knock him out or drug him, if we have to, in order to get him there,' the squire said.

Emery's eyes widened. 'Where?'

'Geoffrey de Burgh's.'

Nicholas counted himself lucky to get into the saddle. Whatever Emery had been forcing down his throat seemed to keep the fever at bay, but he ached as though he had been pummelled relentlessly by all six of his siblings. Unfortunately, it was a feeling he recognised too well.

This was what came of yearning for adventure, he thought. With all his brothers married and gone, he had felt restless, for they had all risen to challenges while he kicked his heels at Campion. His father had begun shifting more responsibility upon him, but the tasks were unstimulating ones that would stifle even Geoffrey, the most staid member of the family. Or at least that's what he'd told himself.

Nicholas had balked. He'd wanted to get out into the world and discover new experiences, just as his brothers had done, before settling down with stewards and account books. So he'd set out, ostensibly to visit, while hoping to see and do and learn and find something that he seemed to be missing.

What he'd found was a fever that had taken the de Burgh bluster out of him. Whether for good or ill, the brothers shared a sense of power and might designed to strike fear into their opponents. 'Twas not so much aggrandisement as a certainty that they would prevail, which usually served them well. And having seen his brothers triumph over more than one foe, Nicholas had believed there was nothing they couldn't do.

But the betrayal of his own body had proven him wrong, for he could not heal himself. And it seemed that no one could. Guy repeatedly pressed him to return home, but Nicholas had not wanted his family to remember him like this, barely able to think, weak and ailing.

Perhaps there was some pride involved, as Emery claimed, for he did not want to draw the pity of his healthy siblings, or, worse, remind his still-strong brothers that they were not invincible. He couldn't remember now all the reasons that had kept him from home or even the last time that they were together. He only felt an absurd longing for them that made his chest hurt. Or was that the fever?

He had gone through a host of emotions, shame and resentment and grief and denial, before finally reaching a point of acceptance. With the arrival of the Hospitaller, he had gained a purpose, and with the arrival of Emery, something more.

She had recalled to him all the joys of living. Her unstinting faith in her brother made him yearn for the family he'd left behind. She'd reminded him just what was important. This slender girl garbed as a boy had taught him that there was nothing more powerful—not force of arms or intellect or will—than the strength of love. And perhaps that knowledge was what he had been seeking all along.

Nicholas shook his head and felt himself

sway in the saddle. Arms tightened around him then, in an effort to keep him upright, and he felt her behind him, bolstering his strength, keeping him steady. He wondered how he could condemn a journey that had taken him here, into the embrace of the woman he loved.

Emery told herself that safety lay at the end of this day's travel, that Lord de Burgh would finally get the care he needed and they could all rest. Beyond that, she could not think. Her own troubles and even Gerard's disappearance faded in significance and she had no idea what she would do once Lord de Burgh was back with his family. For now, she simply concentrated on getting him there.

Guy was doing his best. Having only been to Geoffrey de Burgh's manor once, he had sought a more-travelled road, so that he could ask others for guidance, and Emery was grateful to be away from the deserted tracks, where she felt isolated and unprotected. Still, they remained wary when anyone approached, for fear that a cape or hood might conceal the Saracen or the Templar's squire or anyone else intent upon doing them harm.

Emery had her hands full trying to keep

Lord de Burgh upright. Finally, unable to summon the strength to handle his weight any longer, she traded places with Guy. They had loaded the riderless mount with their gear, including Lord de Burgh's mail coat, so Emery had the reins of that animal, as well. 'Twas a tiring and difficult journey made more so by her worries over the knight, who slumped further as the day wore on.

When afternoon came and went with still no sign of their destination, Emery felt the first stirrings of panic. She did not like the unfamiliar country with its tall cliffs and ashes marching into the distance. If not for the heather that covered the hills, she might have been in another land entirely.

The prospect of making camp somewhere off the road in this strange place filled her with dread and she urged Guy to ask again whether they were headed in the right direction. A man with a cart of goods was duly hailed, but when Guy asked about Ashyll Manor, the fellow shook his head, as though he'd never heard of the place. Emery felt her heart sink. Were they lost?

''Twas formerly known as Fitzhugh Manor,' Guy said. ''Tis home to Geoffrey de Burgh now.'

'Ah, the Fitzhughs' stronghold!' To Emery's relief, the grizzled old man nodded and pointed them on their way. They did not even stop for supper, but kept going, hoping to see the manor topping each new rise. But, finally, Guy, too, was struggling to keep his master from slipping from the saddle and they were forced to draw to a halt.

Emery dismounted and hurried towards the destrier, though she could do little to help from the ground. 'How much further is it?' she asked.

'Not far,' Guy said, but he avoided her gaze and Emery wondered whether he had any idea where they were. If he'd approached the de Burgh manor from a different route in the past, he would not recognise their location. Was he just placating her?

'I would rather hear the truth than a lie meant to comfort me,' Emery said.

'The man said Ashyll was not far,' Guy all but shouted, and Emery could see his patience was worn thin, as well. Perhaps he was clinging to a false promise, but she could not scold him for it. What else were they to do?

Slipping out from his position behind Lord de Burgh, Guy dismounted as best he could. 'We're going to have to lay him over the saddle.'

'Like a sack of grain?' Emery asked. She could hear her voice rising and tried to modulate it. 'But he's so sick!'

'And he will get sicker,' Guy said, turning on her. 'You think I don't know what will happen? It starts with the fever and the pains, then the rash on his legs and swelling and tenderness in…other parts…' His words trailed away, and Emery blinked back tears.

'Then we will do what we must,' she said when she could speak. Together they managed to lay the great knight across the saddle, a seemingly dead weight. But he breathed still and Emery clung to that fact. 'Twould not be much longer, she told herself. Safety, food and stores of herbs were nearly within reach, or so she hoped.

'We'll have to walk now,' the squire said.

Emery gaped at him, only to realise that they could hardly ride off with Lord de Burgh so precariously perched. But to walk alongside him would slow their pace to a crawl. No matter how far or near Geoffrey de Burgh's manor, they wouldn't reach it soon. Emery glanced at the sky, where the sun was on its downward trek, then looked at Guy. He met her gaze, unflinching, and they both knew that they had no choice.

And that's when they heard it: a rustling noise, faint but unmistakable. Emery glanced about warily, but she could not see anything except grass and leaves moving in the wind. And maybe that's all it was, yet she was reminded of the danger they were in, especially now, with the knight lying prone upon his war horse. They were in a hollow that obstructed their view of the road both ahead and behind, making them even more vulnerable to attack.

If the Saracen was out there, they probably would have little chance against him, Emery knew. She froze, listening to the ensuing silence, but she heard only Lord de Burgh's laboured breathing. The breeze had stopped and nothing stirred in the summer air while she and Guy waited, poised to move, if necessary.

And then a shout rang out. There was no time to look for cover or plan a defence. They would have to make a stand where they were, on either side of Lord de Burgh. Drawing her sword, Emery turned to face whoever advanced upon them.

But the shout was followed, not by a call to arms, but by the sound of…singing? Emery glanced at Guy, who shrugged, but remained at the ready, and she wondered if this were some bizarre battle tactic intended to catch them unawares.

Emery thought she heard the sound of hooves, as well as the creak of wheels, but it was hard to tell above the man's voice raised in a familiar tune. The words, however, were new to her and she flushed, shocked at the references to certain female attributes.

Still, she remained tense, holding her breath as something topped the hill and she saw the head of a horse. But 'twas no destrier, only a stout farm animal pulling a cart, and she soon recognised the conveyance, as well as the grizzled man who drove it. 'Twas the very same fellow who not long ago had pointed them in this direction. Had he been lying? 'Twas hard to imagine the friendly character in league with their enemies, but at this point, Emery suspected everyone.

The singing stopped when the fellow saw them and its cause was soon apparent. The man's face was a bit red and there was no mistaking the odour that clung to him when he drew to a halt.

'Hello there, fellow travellers! I took my rounds of cheese to my brother and he gave me some fine ale in return,' he said, patting one of the barrels that stood in the cart behind him. 'Of course, I had to sample it first,' he added, grinning broadly to reveal a missing tooth.

His brows furrowed, as if in vague recollection of their earlier encounter. 'Have you gone astray again? Where were you bound?'

'Fitzhugh Manor,' Guy answered. 'And we have yet to arrive, though our master is late. He has had a bit too much ale himself,' the squire added, inclining his head towards Lord de Burgh.

Emery blinked, startled by the squire's lie. She had not thought Guy capable of such quick thinking, but she could only admire it, for a drunk would not instil the fear that a sick man might. Indeed, the cart driver seemed amused by the news.

'Well, toss the poor lad back there with the casks, and, as long as he doesn't have a go at them, I'll take you there myself,' the man said, with an expansive gesture of welcome.

Although Emery was still wary, Guy gave her no opportunity to argue and they managed, between the two of them, to get Lord de Burgh situated in the cart. But Emery refused to leave his side, so Guy tied her horse behind the conveyance before mounting the destrier and taking the reins of the other.

Thankfully, the cart was littered with straw, so the ride would be far more comfortable for Lord de Burgh than the one they had planned. Emery put herself between him and the barrels and cradled his head in her lap, gently pushing the dark locks from his face. Although unwilling to trust their new acquaintance completely, she felt some of the tension leave her for the first time this day, yet just as she knew some ease, she heard it again, a faint rustling.

Heart pounding, Emery looked around her, but she saw nothing, and when the cart careened to life, the sounds of their movement obliterated all else.

Chapter Thirteen

The sun was near setting by the time they reached Ashyll, but Emery was so glad to see it rising from the green hills that she nearly wept with relief. Although it was home to a de Burgh, Ashyll was a manor, not a castle of the order of Campion or Stokebrough, yet it was larger than Montbard and boasted fortifications that would protect them well.

Although they saw no sentries at the outer walls that enclosed all who served the manor, at the inner bailey they were stopped and Guy moved forwards to speak over the drunken greeting of the cart driver. A sharp glance from the guard towards Lord de Burgh was enough to gain them entrance and someone must have hurried ahead, for when they reached the doors of the manor, a man already was rushing out to greet them.

He was so like Lord de Burgh that Emery looked from one to the other in amazement, but as he came closer she could see Geoffrey de Burgh was older and leaner, his features softer and his demeanour more serious.

Wondering whether they would share the same sort of bond that she had with his brother, Emery searched his face, waiting for his dark gaze to connect with hers. But when it did, she felt nothing, his brown eyes settling upon her as he whispered his thanks before moving on.

And suddenly Nicholas de Burgh was moving on, too, without her. Strong arms reached out to carry him, orders were shouted and servants surrounded him and his brother until Emery was shunted out of the way and left behind. She followed as best she could, but once inside the great hall they disappeared into the throng. Weak with weariness and emotion, she sagged against a wall and sank to the floor.

Emery shook with relief that they had managed to get the great knight here, where he could safely recover. She had been able to think of nothing else, but having accomplished her task, what now? As a strange woman in boy's garb, she had no claim on Lord de Burgh or his family. And although her problems had faded in significance, they had not disappeared and she must face them.

In that bleak moment, Emery wondered whether she ought to leave the way she had come, slipping into the gathering twilight to be on her way to the life that awaited her. She had no heart for farewells or explanations and would sooner avoid both, and yet…the thought of never seeing Lord de Burgh again made her bury her face in her hands.

Just as despair threatened, she became aware of a presence in front of her and a soft touch upon her shoulder. Lifting her head, Emery saw a beautiful woman kneeling in front of her. Dressed in the finest clothing, thick hair shot with fiery strands coiled at her neck, she leaned close. 'Emery?' she asked. 'Can you stand?'

Was she to be tossed out? Emery nodded.

'Come, then,' the woman said, her voice low and husky. 'You need some rest.'

Before Emery could protest, she was helped to her feet. The elegant woman was surprisingly strong and Emery blinked, gazing into unusual eyes the colour of amber.

She called herself Elene, and Emery wouldn't

even have known that she was Lady de Burgh
if not for the deference of the servants. Lacking
the regal airs one expected of a noblewoman,
she personally led Emery to a small chamber,
where a bed and tub waited, along with the
promise of food.

Emery felt spent, too tired to bathe or eat
or prepare herself for bed, but somehow this
lovely lady, who said little yet saw much, managed to get her to do all those things. And to
tell her tale, as well. Later, she would not remember Elene de Burgh asking any questions,
yet Emery willingly spoke of her frantic search
for Gerard, the parcel that he had sent her and
the murders it had precipitated.

And Elene listened. Although the lady was
not a nurturing sort, Emery somehow felt com-
forted, perhaps simply by the act of sharing
her troubles. And while Elene expressed no
dismay at her story and made few comments,
she suggested that Emery show the statue to
her husband.

'Geoff will know what it is. He knows everything,' Elene said, a smile of pride touching
her lips. Having said goodnight, she headed towards the door, but turned to speak once more.

'He can take care of almost anything, too. And if he can't, his father can.'

Hand upon the latch, the lady paused to eye Emery from across the room, as though urging her guest to heed her words. But Emery closed her eyes and feigned sleep, for she had not told Elene all. And she knew that there were some things even the Earl of Campion could not change.

Emery awoke late, to bright sunlight and the sound of children's laughter somewhere nearby. She blinked and settled back into the softness, and for once her heart did not hammer with panic at her surroundings. But all too soon her worries returned and she knew that instead of burrowing back into her bed she must face what lay ahead.

Emery had not known what to expect of Nicholas's family. In truth, she had thought of nothing except the importance of reaching them. But she would not have been surprised had they tossed her out upon her ear, a girl in boy's clothing, with nothing to her name.

Yet the de Burghs had welcomed her, without question or judgement, throwing open their home to her. Ashyll might not be as large and luxurious as Stokebrough, but it was clean and bright and filled with love. A haven in a dangerous world, 'twould be a lovely spot to linger, enveloped in the kindness and prosperity of the famous family.

But it was not her home or her haven. Long into the night, Emery had tossed and turned over her future, fear and duty and longing warring within her. But despite her determination and all the hopes and plans that she had clung to, she could come to just one conclusion.

This was the end of her quest.

Whatever Lord de Burgh had vowed to Gerard, Emery could not hold him to it. She only wanted him to rest and recover, to regain the strength to make new vows and take on new quests. But it would be too late for her.

Not that long ago, Emery had thought to continue the search for Gerard on her own, but the past two days had taught her the impossibility of that. Travelling even a short distance without the knight's protection and guidance would be difficult enough. She knew nothing of these lands or where to look, and if a de Burgh couldn't find her brother, how would she?

Returning home was out of the question. The distance was too great, her resources too limited and the dangers all too real. Even if she could manage to make her way there, how would she live? Where would she go? She knew what awaited her and 'twould be no welcome. Emery had abandoned her responsibilities to try to help Gerard, but she had failed and she could delay the inevitable no longer.

'Twas time to resume her duties and there was a safe haven not far away where she could do so, if allowed. Perhaps someone there might be persuaded to ask after her brother, and she would receive news of him some day, especially if he returned to the fold. She could only hope.

Emery choked back a surge of emotion she had thought spent during the night hours when the loss of both Gerard and her…companions had seemed too much to bear. Swallowing hard, she focused on the task ahead. As with anything painful, 'twas better done quickly, sooner rather than later, and without any tearful goodbyes that would give her away.

Although Emery had considered asking the de Burghs for an escort, she did not want anyone to know where she was bound. And, in truth, she felt uneasy about sharing her plans with her hostess, who might not approve. Although Elene had been nothing but gracious, there was something about her that hinted at banked fires and formidable will, and Emery did not care to test them.

She had already said too much, regretting her long talk with Elene the evening before. Leaving the comfort of her bed, Emery resolved to avoid the lady of the manor. Yet she could not find her brother's clothing and stood blinking in nothing but her shift until Elene appeared at her chamber door, with a cup of watered wine and female clothing, including a pair of slippers.

Emery started forwards in pleasure at the sight of the simple yet appealing linen kirtle. Unlike the bright hues she had worn at Stoke-brough, this was a subdued shade of green that could only flatter her colouring, but 'twas not the garb she needed in order to leave Ashyll unnoticed. When Emery asked for her brother's worn garments, she was informed that they had been whisked away for washing while she slept.

Disconcerted, Emery glanced at her hostess, but she could hardly ask for their return without rousing suspicion. Although Elene seemed unaware of her distress, Emery wondered just how much she had revealed, perhaps unintentionally, during last night's conversation. However, she had no choice but to dress in the garments generously provided, and soon she was seated upon a low trunk, being served a late dinner.

'Twould be no hardship to linger at Ashyll, but having worked up the nerve to leave, Emery was eager to get on with it, lest her courage fail her. She suspected that the longer she stayed, the more difficult it would be to go.

Deep in thought, she was unaware of attention upon her until she felt a tug upon her kirtle. A little boy, probably no more than two, stood beside her, staring up at her intently. With his mop of dark hair and huge brown eyes, he looked so much like Nicholas that Emery choked back a cry.

'Miles is just like his father, a friend to all,' Elene said, shaking her head, but she spoke so lovingly there was no doubt the boy was her son. Any hint of shadows in her amber eyes was banished as she watched him and Emery knew a moment's envy.

Another tug made Emery glance back at the child, who was now reaching up for a hug. Obliging, Emery caught him close, her heart squeezing at all the things she would never have. Then he was gone, heading towards his mother, his shyer, older sister not far behind.

Swallowing against a lump in her throat, Emery suddenly wanted nothing more than to see Lord de Burgh, as though a last look at him could ease all her aches. 'Twas foolishness, yet, when Elene suggested just such a visit, Emery hadn't the strength to refuse.

Guy met her at the door, having slept upon the floor, and Emery felt a stab of regret that she could not have stayed so close to Lord de Burgh. But she was not the great knight's squire, relative or healer, and she could make no claim to be here even now. Yet she walked past Guy and Geoffrey de Burgh towards the bed where Nicholas lay, sleeping peacefully.

Emery had known the day would come when they would part, but somehow she had pictured it differently, perhaps a reunion with Gerard making it less painful. Certainly, she had not imagined the knight ill and asleep, leaving her unable to say all that she might, but Emery told herself 'twas easier this way, though it did not feel so.

Leaning near, Emery looked upon his handsome face for long moments, committing each familiar feature to memory. Would he recall her so well when he recovered? 'Twould be better if he did not, she realised, with a pang. She hoped only that he would stay well this time and live a long, healthy life surrounded by those who loved him.

Blinking rapidly, Emery reached out to touch his forehead, relieved to feel the fever had eased. She smoothed away that dark hair near his closed eyes, lingering perhaps too long at her task. Then she deliberately drew her hand—and herself—away.

'The fever is gone,' Emery said, when she could speak.

'For now,' Guy said. 'And Lord de Burgh's brother has been searching through his accumulated lore for a new treatment.' The squire no longer looked pale and drawn, but rested and hopeful and glad to be amongst those who could help.

'The answer is more likely to be found at Campion, but I have sent a message to our father, who might have some knowledge of this illness,' Geoffrey said. He drew a deep breath, as though willing it to be so, before turning to Emery and thanking her for bringing his brother here.

''Twas Guy's doing,' Emery said.

'Yet he credits you,' Geoffrey said, with a smile, and before she could argue he continued, 'The de Burghs are in your debt. Should you have need of anything or a service of any kind, you have only to ask.'

His offer gave Emery pause and, for an instant, she wondered whether he had some special ability to divine her problems. But both Guy and Elene knew her tale and, no doubt, had discussed it with Geoffrey. Perhaps Guy had even suggested that Geoffrey assume his brother's vow of aid to the Montbards. But she had caused the de Burghs too much trouble already and Guy had done enough. Emery could ask no more. She said so, simply and politely.

Geoffrey de Burgh nodded gracefully. 'Nevertheless, I am at your service, should you ever have need of me, as is my family. And, in the meantime, I understand that you have an item you wish to show me?'

Since the onslaught of Nicholas's illness, Emery had nearly forgotten the parcel that had loomed so large in their lives. But now she glanced at Guy, who soon produced the worn pouch from Lord de Burgh's pack.

Although Emery knew well what was inside, none the less she held her breath as Geoffrey de Burgh unwrapped the old linen, revealing, bit by bit, the glitter of gold. To Emery's eyes, it seemed brighter than before, but perhaps that was because of the dimness of the chamber where Nicholas slept. Even so, the treasure seemed to inspire awe and, despite all the troubles it had caused, a hush fell over the room.

Geoffrey lifted the statue high and, for one dazzling moment, Emery thought it really might have some power shining forth, as Guy had claimed. If so, she wished 'twas the power to heal and cure the man who lay before them, oblivious to its presence. But if the gleaming figure worked some kind of Moorish magic, 'twas not apparent and Nicholas slept on.

As though sharing her thoughts, Guy broke the silence with a nervous mutter. 'Is it possessed of some force unbeknownst to us?'

'I suppose that depends on your way of thinking,' Geoffrey said, his own tone pragmatic. 'It has witnessed the movement of armies, the deaths of rulers and the conquering of the world. Is it a talisman or simply one of the trappings of he who held it?'

Emery blinked, uncertain, and Geoffrey turned towards them, statue in hand. 'This, my friends, is the mace of one of the finest warriors and empire-builders who ever lived. He was once King of Macedon, but you know him as Alexander the Great.'

Flashing a grin much like his brother's, Geoffrey led them to the solar, where an astounding number of manuscripts were kept, the bulk of them on astrology and medicine and subjects Emery didn't understand, along with histories of the ancient world. 'Twas one of these Geoffrey opened, pointing to a large, detailed illustration of a king upon his throne.

Leaning close, Emery saw that the king held an intricately carved staff that rested upon the ground and reached past his shoulders. The top gleamed golden and was crafted in the shape of a man, naked but for the wrapping round his waist and his tall hat.

'That's it,' Guy breathed. 'That's the idol!'

'The mace,' Geoffrey said. 'It must have once been part of Alexander's own, probably created after he went to Egypt. 'Tis said that while there, he travelled alone to a remote temple devoted to the sun god. As the new ruler of Egypt, he sought confirmation of his own divine power. And though there is no record of what occurred, perhaps he returned with this, a statue of the god he claimed as his ancestor.'

'But how did it get here?' Guy asked, dumb-founded.

'How do all things come from the east? With those who have been in the Holy Land,' Geoffrey said. 'I can only speculate, of course, but from what I've pieced together of your tale, I would guess that Robert Blanchefort and another man, perhaps more, came across the prize while serving there with the Templars. After Robert returned, somehow it fell into other hands, perhaps several, before reaching Gerard Montbard.'

'It might even have resided in a Templar preceptory as a relic or one of the spoils of war for a while,' Emery said, ignoring Guy's surprised glance.

Geoffrey nodded slowly. ''Tis certainly possible, for some years have passed since Robert Blanchefort's return. And 'tis possible that some, if not all, of those who are aware of its existence know only that it is gold and therefore precious, but do not realise its true significance.'

Silence descended then, as they mused over that implication, for even Emery realised that any king or general or soldier going to war would covet such a talisman. Some might even claim it was the source of Alexander's great power and try to use it to create their own empire.

'I think at least one person knows,' Guy said, lowering his voice as though someone outside the thick walls of Ashyll might overhear him. 'And he wants it back.'

Emery lay awake again, her thoughts unsettled by the day's revelations. Guy had several theories about what to do with Alexander's mace and vacillated between schemes to present it to King Edward or to the Templars, who he thought might come after it anyway.

Geoffrey had said little, watching Emery with those de Burgh eyes that seemed, if not prescient, then more knowledgeable than most. But Emery remained silent. Now that they had identified the statue, she remembered her conversation with Father Faramond and suspected that it did not belong to the Templars or anyone else from this country.

Yet she had no idea how to return the sun god to its rightful owner. In a weak moment, she was tempted to ask Geoffrey de Burgh to fulfil his promise to aid her, but the mace was not his responsibility. And he had a wife and

family who would not want him endangered
over a contested piece of gold.

Emery sighed. Despite Nicholas's vow to
Gerard and his tireless efforts on her behalf,
the task did not fall to the de Burghs. The parcel had been sent to her and she would have to
muster the courage to do what was right, if she
could just work out how...

Coming as it did in the midst of such dire
thoughts, the low knock on the door made
Emery stifle a cry of fright. But even the Saracen could not manage to infiltrate the fortified
manor house and find her chamber. Could he?

The sound of Guy's soft voice soothed
Emery's fears and she loosed a sigh of relief
until she realised that the squire would not
disturb her at this time of night without good
cause. Donning the robe that Elene had given
her, Emery hurried to open the door. In the
darkness, she could see little of Guy, but his
voice cracked as he spoke.

'He's asking for you.'

Emery did not need to wonder who and, as
she followed, Guy told her the great knight had
taken a turn for the worse. Nothing seemed to
be able to ease his fever, not Emery's tisane or
anything Geoffrey de Burgh had tried. Sud-

denly, things looked bleak and Emery's hopes for his permanent recovery premature.

'But I thought this bout might be his last,' she said.

They halted before the great knight's chamber and Guy turned to give her a grim look. 'It might well be.'

Emery's heart nearly stopped at his words and all that they entailed, but somehow she stepped inside. Barely aware of the door shutting behind her, she realised that there was no one else in attendance. She had been given a private audience with Lord de Burgh. Was it in order to say her last goodbyes? At the thought, a sob rose to her lips.

'Emery?' His deep voice was so raspy that she nearly didn't recognise it, but she straightened and moved forwards. By the time she reached his side she had regained some semblance of composure.

'I'm here,' she said, taking his big hand in hers. It felt warm, too warm, but she clung to it.

'They keep giving me something to make me sleep, but I must…speak,' he muttered.

Emery was tempted to urge him to silence, yet she had been with her father in the end and she knew that sometimes there were no more opportunities to talk. So she listened, though she cringed at the effort it cost him.

'I was wrong...about us,' he whispered. 'We must seize the day, grab hold of life...take what we can while we can. Love is too precious to throw away.' His gaze found her own then and he squeezed her hand. 'Nothing *is impossible*, if we but make it so.'

He took a long, rattling breath and closed his eyes, while Emery blinked against the pressure behind her own. 'I was wrong, too,' she said, 'to hide the truth.' She cleared her throat, thick with emotion, and forced herself to go on.

'When my father was ill, my uncle convinced him to sign over his wealth and lands to the Hospitallers, who were to provide for my brother and myself. Although 'tis not an unusual arrangement for widows or young children, it was not what I would have wished for us. And after my father died and we were both accepted into the commandery, 'twas revealed that we were to take orders. My brother was happy to do so, while I was not...'

Emery hesitated, but there was no point in delaying the inevitable, which is what she had thought at the time, as well. 'I was grieving and

upset and was pressured by others to abide by
my father's wishes. So I took the vows.'

There. 'Twas out in the open now, the secret
that she had kept for so long, first out of a desire to protect herself and later out of a desire
to protect the man whose hand she held.

'When you found me, I was living apart. Although I understand that women are allowed
at some commanderies, the priest at Clerkwell
wanted to send me to Buckland, a female house
far from my home.' Emery's voice broke. 'I
balked and we settled into a compromise of
sorts.'

'Twas a compromise that she had violated
when she fled without leave, which is why she
planned to go directly to Buckland now. Perhaps the women there would treat her offence
more leniently, though she would pay for her
actions the rest of her life...

Emery ducked her head at that admission.
'When I took those vows, I didn't see any other
choice. Nothing in my narrow world gave me
hope for a different future. I didn't dream that
some day a knight errant would come into my
life and tempt me to all that I could no longer
do and make me want all I could not have.'

Emery drew a deep breath. 'I couldn't imagine…you.' She lifted her gaze to him, but he was so still that for one terrifying moment she thought he'd left her. Only the slow rise and fall of his great chest told her that he carried on, and in that instant, she was forced to acknowledge the one final secret that she had kept even from herself.

She loved this man.

Her heart constricted so that she struggled for air and it took her some time to speak. 'But you came into my life and made me wish to follow you anywhere,' Emery admitted, her voice breaking as she eyed his prone form. 'Please don't go where I can't follow. You promised never to leave me.'

But he gave no sign of having heard her and, finally, Emery slumped forwards on the bed, silently giving vent to her grief.

Emery must have slept, for the next thing she knew, she heard voices, low and urgent, and someone was opening the shutters. Guy had returned, along with a bleary-eyed Geoffrey de Burgh and an older woman who carried a bowl of water. Aware that she was still in her nightclothes, Emery mumbled an apology and slipped away while they attended to him.

Outside his chamber, a servant asked her if she wanted something to eat, but Emery's stomach churned at the thought and she shook her head. Returning to her room, she slumped against the door wearily. The bed was as she had left it, hours ago, as though awaiting her return. But she knew she would find no rest there.

Stepping forwards, Emery automatically reached out to straighten the blankets, yet something made her pause. She sucked in a sharp breath, unable to believe her eyes at the sight of a brightly coloured design upon her pillow. With trembling fingers, she reached for it, only to draw away in shock and horror.

'Twas a piece of the Moorish Game.

Choking back a cry, Emery would have called for Guy or raced to his side, but as she stared at the four curved swords depicted there, she noticed something different. Like the other one left upon her bed, there was writing upon this card. Had Gerard left her another message?

Shaking, Emery snatched up the heavy parchment, only to realise 'twas not her brother's hand. Nor were the Latin words any he would write. Swaying upon her feet, she let the paper slip from her grasp as she realised the significance of what was written there.

To heal him, return what you hold.

Emery blinked numbly down at the fallen card with its violent image and vile missive. Her first instinct was to step away, for its promise was likely false, a desperate bid to obtain the statue. Yet, who other than the Saracen would even possess such a thing? Only Gerard, Emery thought bleakly, but her brother would not offer such a bargain, no matter what state he was in. And even if the Moorish Game was known to others, this card clearly was part of a set, with its four swords so similar.

Emery shook her head. Whether the Saracen or someone else, how had that person gained entry to her chamber in the darkness? She shivered at the thought that she had been tucked in bed, seemingly safe, earlier in the night, vulnerable to any attack. Had the villain hoped to find the mace and leave her for dead as he had her uncle?

Emery's hand flew to her throat in a protective gesture, her heart pounding. She even glanced around the room, as though someone might, even now, be waiting in the shadows.

But there was no place to hide and she released a low sigh of relief.

Perhaps she was letting her imagination and fear get the better of her. It could be that someone from the manor had overheard her story and, lured by gold, had concocted this ruse. But when Emery stared down at the card at her feet, she knew differently. Despite the temptation to dismiss it or ignore it or rid herself of it, she felt certain the message had come from the Saracen.

And he had left it for her, not Lord de Burgh and not Guy. Perhaps he knew somehow that the prize was hers to give or that she had been mulling over this very predicament earlier. Well, now she had her answer, for here was the opportunity she had desired. She could return the mace to its rightful owner, as well as aid the great knight.

If she didn't get killed in the bargain.

Chapter Fourteen

Dressed once again in her brother's clothes, Emery sent for Guy and Geoffrey de Burgh to come to her chamber, rather than meet them at Nicholas's bedside. To their credit, they did not question the summons, though they both looked dismayed by her garb. But before either could comment, Emery held out the card.

Guy gasped and stepped back at the sight, while Geoffrey took it gingerly, examining the parchment from all sides. 'Is this one like the others?'

'Yes,' Emery said, with a grim nod.

'"*To heal him, return what you hold*",' Geoffrey read aloud, eliciting another gasp from Guy. 'And do you believe it?'

Again, Emery nodded.

Sighing, Geoffrey reached up to rub his eyes with his palms and she wondered how long it had been since he'd slept. 'How would this person, the one you call the Saracen, know of my brother's sickness?'

'He collapsed the day before we arrived here, which would be evident to anyone watching us. And the last day of our journey, 'twas obvious that he was unwell,' Emery said. She glanced at Guy. 'At one point we were forced to lay him across his destrier and we were...discussing the situation loudly enough for someone nearby to hear.'

'That only proves he knows of the illness, not that he will help Lord de Burgh,' Guy protested. 'He's more likely to break my lord's neck!'

Geoffrey frowned. ''Tis true that he might be playing upon our fears, but there is no denying that those in the east have access to ancient texts and curatives that we do not have here.'

Guy snorted. ''Tis a trap to steal the statue!'

'Which might well belong to him,' Emery said, softly.

Guy ignored her. 'He cannot be trusted,' the squire said. 'He is a murderer who will stop at nothing to get what he wants.'

Since Guy's opinion was clear, Emery looked to Geoffrey de Burgh. When she met his gaze, she sensed a kindred spirit. If any chance to save Nicholas existed, however slim, they must take advantage of it. 'Then we will give him what he wants,' she said.

Geoffrey nodded slowly. 'I will treat with him, on my brother's behalf.'

But Emery shook her head. 'The message was left for me. I'm the one who has the mace and I am the one who must return it.'

'The message was left for you because he would rather face a woman, or someone he deems a scrawny lad, rather than a de Burgh,' Guy said, his voice shrill with a mixture of outrage and fear.

'Then we shall see she is well protected,' Geoffrey said. 'I have several knights here and a couple of excellent archers, who can be well placed to shoot a man from the heights.'

Emery shook her head. 'He is too clever to walk into a trap. He is like a phantom, slipping in and out of your own manor, without notice, and would surely see anyone, even those hidden, intent upon harm.'

Once again, Geoffrey de Burgh loosed a weary sigh and rubbed his eyes. 'Then I can't let you do it,' he said and Guy grunted his approval.

Emery had expected as much, but she knew they could not stop her. Instead of arguing, she faced Geoffrey, gazing directly into the dark eyes so much like his brother's, and stated her case. 'You must know that I would do anything to aid him.'

Geoffrey appeared torn between hope for Nicholas and concern for her. 'But this man might accept the statue and give you no remedy in return. He might even kill you for your trouble.'

Emery did not look away. ''Tis a chance I am willing to take.'

'It's not a chance that Lord de Burgh would be willing to take,' Guy said, turning to appeal to Geoffrey. 'My lord, you sent a message to the earl. Surely he will have an answer that will help Lord de Burgh, without endangering Emery for no good cause. Let us wait until we hear from him.'

But Geoffrey shook his head, his expression bleak, and gave voice to what Emery was thinking. 'We dare not wait.'

Emery did not delay, pausing only to shoulder the worn pouch with its heavy burden and to don her short sword. The weapon would be little help against the Saracen, who had killed a Templar knight, as well as her uncle. But she would rather be armed, especially if the Saracen didn't know she was a woman.

Although Guy wondered aloud where she was to find him, Emery suspected that he would find her. He was unlikely to approach her within the manor walls, where he might be seen or trapped or marked by an archer, as Geoffrey de Burgh had suggested, so Emery had her mount readied and soon was headed out of the bailey.

She had not allowed herself time to indulge her fears, but as she left the protection of the de Burghs, she felt a chill at what lay ahead. Earlier, she had been too set upon her course to dwell upon its consequences, but now they became all too clear. 'Twas one thing to face threats with Lord de Burgh and Guy at her side and quite another to ride out alone to confront a killer. She drew in a sharp breath, trying to bolster her nerve, only to freeze at the sound of her name.

'Emery!'

Turning, she was surprised to see Guy riding towards her. Had she forgotten something, or had he some last-minute message from Geoffrey? For an instant, she had the horrifying thought that Nicholas no longer had need of a remedy and she stifled a cry. But the squire did not look grief-stricken, only fearful, and Emery loosed a sigh of relief.

Yet her relief did not last long. She glanced about her, worried that Guy's sudden appearance might make the Saracen wary. Although she could see nothing, she knew their pursuer was out there, watching and waiting, and she shivered.

When Guy reached her, he was red-faced and Emery let him catch his breath. Obviously, he was here to tell her something important, but when he spoke, his words were not what she expected. 'I'm coming with you,' he said.

Emery blinked in surprise, but before she could respond, he rushed on. 'It's been the three of us through all of this and I won't have you go alone now to meet…' His words trailed off, as though he were unable to finish, though 'your doom' or 'your death' both seemed likely.

He held up a hand to stop her protest in the manner of Lord de Burgh. 'You saved my life once and I would do what I can to save yours.'

Emery shook her head. 'You don't owe me

anything,' she said. 'You and Lord de Burgh gave me back…myself, which is more than enough.' Suddenly she felt the prick of tears, as though this was the farewell she had hoped to avoid. She swallowed hard. 'You might scare away our quarry.'

Guy snorted. 'He's always seen us in each other's company, so if we aren't, he might think I'm hanging back, planning an attack.'

Emery realised the squire might be right. He must have sensed her capitulation, because his expression grew more resolute. 'The three of us have banded together and it's going to take more than the Saracen to separate us.'

If only he knew, Emery thought. She had not shared the truth with anyone except Lord de Burgh and now was not the time to speak of the future. She could only concentrate on the present and, despite her misgivings, she was heartened by the squire's presence.

She knew that Guy was no great knight and her own skills were few, yet the terror that had gripped her when she was alone was gone. Now this journey seemed little different from the others they had taken together, except for the absence of the man to whom they both were devoted.

Thoughts of Nicholas reminded Emery why she had accepted this task, yet she hardly dared hope that her purpose would be served. She suspected the Saracen of offering what she most desired in order to gain his prize, whether he could deliver or not. For even if those in the Holy Land knew more of healing, 'twas unlikely that this man possessed such wisdom.

Yet, as long as the possibility existed, Emery had to pursue it, and so she rode on, looking for any signs of company. When the road dipped, she grew even more alert. Soon she heard something, though 'twas not the telltale rustling she associated with the man who had long pursued them. 'Twas an odd whistle, as though of some foreign bird, and its very strangeness made her glance at Guy, who nodded, his face grim.

Heading in the direction of the sound, they turned into the tall grass that marked the edge of field, moving towards the remains of some old structure, now overgrown. Like a shadow or a wraith, a figure seemed to appear out of nowhere, though perhaps that was simply a product of his stealth. Yet, with no noise beyond the flutter of the breeze, he was suddenly there before them, astride a tall grey horse that stood so still beneath him that only its eyes moved.

From the fantastic beast, Emery's gaze shifted to the man who rode it. Somehow she had expected him to wear flowing robes and head coverings like those in illustrations of the Holy Land, but she realised that he could hardly disappear into the shadows in such garb.

Indeed, he looked like anyone else, except perhaps for his bearing, tall and as commanding as any knight. Only the darker tint to his face hinted that he had not been born here and his voice, though silky, showed that Latin was not his usual tongue.

'You have it?' he asked.

'Alexander's mace,' Emery said, with a nod. After coming this far, she suddenly hesitated to give away such a powerful weapon to one considered the enemy. 'And what shall you do with it?'

'I shall return it to him,' the man said and Emery's eyes widened. For a moment she wondered whether they dealt with a madman, but he must have guessed her thoughts, for he spoke again. ''Twas stolen from his tomb.'

'But I thought no one knows where he is buried,' Emery said.

The Saracen smiled, a gesture that conveyed the extent of his knowledge, as well as his contempt for the conversation that Emery saw no point in continuing. Drawing a deep breath, she took up the pouch and opened it. As she grasped the worn linen inside, she realised this was the first time she had touched the statue and gripped it tightly, holding it up so that the Saracen could see. The gold seemed to catch the rays of the sun and throw them back, gilding everything around it in a warm glow.

'Bring it here,' the man said.

'I'll do it,' Guy muttered, but the Saracen kept his attention upon her and Emery knew it was her responsibility. She had accepted this task. Now she must see it through.

Somehow the mace seemed to give her strength and she did not hesitate as she neared the stranger, reaching out to hand the figure to him. He took the heavy object as though it weighed nothing and slipped it away, though Emery could not see where. In fact, she wondered whether he was some kind of conjurer, for now that the mace had passed out of her grasp, it seemed as though she had never even held the thing.

His head lifted and Emery sensed his piercing gaze upon her. 'And now for my part of our bargain.'

Emery steeled herself for a knife through the heart or some kind of blow to the neck that would twist her head like her uncle's, and she heard Guy's horse move forwards. But when the Saracen reached inside his tunic, 'twas to produce an innocent-looking packet. He held it out to her and Emery took it with trembling fingers. Did he truly intend to honour his promise?

'It goes by many names, originally hermodactyl when described by Alexander of Tralles, but you call it saffron. Like the mace, it was stolen from our land and brought here, but you may make good use of it. Collect it now, while you can, and dry it for use throughout the year. He will need to take some every day.'

'For how long?' Emery asked.

'For ever.'

The blunt response stirred Guy to speech. 'How do you know this will help when you haven't even seen him?'

'I have seen him, from a distance, but, more important, you told me what ailed him.'

Although Guy did not reply, Emery nodded, for 'twas on this very road that Guy had de-

scribed the course of Nicholas's recurring illness loud enough for anyone to hear.

'I have something else for you,' the Saracen
said and Emery wondered whether the herbs
had been but a taunt to make them let down
their guard.

This is where it ends, she thought. Although
she heard Guy surge forwards, Emery did not
reach for her weapon. It would be no match for
the curved sword depicted upon the cards and,
when the Saracen reached down, she expected
to see the flash of that huge blade. But instead
of a weapon, he lifted up a piece of rope.

'You may take this with you, as well,' he
said, tossing the end to her.

Emery did not know what it could possibly
be tethered to—an extra mount, perhaps? She
tugged upon it, but nothing moved, and when
she would have raised the question she looked
up to find the Saracen gone. She blinked stupidly, wondering again if he was some kind
of mystic, for who else could disappear so
quickly?

'What is it?' Guy asked, inclining his head
towards the knot in her hand.

Emery shook her head, baffled, then urged
her mount forwards.

'Don't follow it,' Guy said. 'It might take us to a bog or a cleverly disguised hole, leaving none to tell the tale of our encounter with the murdering bastard.'

Emery frowned at his words, for the Saracen hadn't seemed such a villain. Perhaps Gwayne and Harold had provoked him into killing them, though there had been no signs of struggle. Absently, Emery tugged again on the rope, only to start when it tugged back.

With a gasp, she followed the line, ignoring Guy's increasingly frantic warnings. Eventually, it led her to the remains of a cot, overgrown with weeds. And when she reached a fallen timber, she could finally spy what lay at the end.

'Twas no trap or bog that greeted her, but the tied and battered body of the Templar's squire. Bruised and barely breathing, he served as a reminder that the Saracen was far more dangerous than he seemed—and that they were lucky to have escaped with their lives.

Guy was convinced that the Saracen's remedy was poison. Although Emery once might have thought otherwise, the condition of Gwayne's squire gave her pause. Ultimately, 'twas Geoffrey's decision and he obtained other saffron from the manor stores to dose his brother.

There was little they could do after that except wait and hope, so Emery was grateful when Geoffrey suggested a visit to their unexpected guest. He led her and Guy to the vaulted cellar, where Gwayne's squire had been sequestered in a small room. Though the chamber was no prison, it was watched by one of the manor's knights, who made their beds in the open area adjacent.

Emery was grateful for the precautions, for she did not trust the young man who had been thrust into her charge, despite his condition. Indeed, he looked much better already, having been washed and tended. Apparently, he suffered from no real wounds, only the ill treatment he had received from his captor.

'He probably abandoned his master as soon as he saw the Saracen coming,' Guy muttered and Emery was of a mind to agree. However, it fell to the lord of the manor to decide his fate, so she said nothing as they followed Geoffrey inside.

The young man was at the mercy of those he had once fought, but he spoke readily enough, giving his name as Mauger. He said he had been fetching water and fled upon finding his master dead, only to be hunted down himself.

None disputed his claim. In fact, Geoffrey nodded, encouraging him to speak further. For a moment, Emery worried that Nicholas's brother might be too kind and trusting, but she realised that behind his gentle demeanour, his scrutiny was sharp and his mind sharper. Nothing would get past this man.

But Mauger was not clever enough to notice and, with his tongue loosened by ale, he soon spilled his tale. Or at least his version of it. Although he little looked the part, he painted himself as an innocent, assigned to serve the Templar knight Gwayne in fighting the infidel. But Gwayne had been given a task that his squire only discovered later: that of returning a precious object to the Holy Land.

Although she made no comment, Emery suspected that events occurred a bit differently. When Mauger claimed that Robert Blanchefort and at least one other Templar knight wandered foreign lands and had stumbled across a tomb, Emery wondered if the two Templars had deserted and gone grave robbing. But whatever the real story, they found some treasures, including the mace. And whether stricken by his conscience or fear of the Saracen, Blanchefort brought it back with him to Temple Roode.

There it was kept hidden as a relic, though Emery thought plunder the more likely description. But after years of failures in the Holy Land, including the recent fall of Margat, the brethren decided their find might better serve the cause if returned there, perhaps even to be wielded in battle, and so Gwayne was given the task.

But once he had the mace in his possession, the Templar was loath to deliver it. While Mauger claimed he was shocked and dismayed over this turn of events, he did nothing to prevent his master from trying to sell the treasure, an act that drew unwanted attention and forced them to flee back to England.

'But he followed us,' Mauger said. 'Somehow, when we got off the ship, he was there.' He shook his head and licked his cracked lips. 'Gwayne slipped the mace into the Hospitaller's pack and we tried to keep track of him, while avoiding the foreigner. 'Twas only to be for a short time, but it took longer than we expected.'

No doubt the delay caused Gerard to discover what weighed him down, Emery thought. Uncertain what to do with such a thing, he had sent it on to her for safekeeping. At least, that's what Emery told herself, for she refused to believe that her brother had succumbed to the lure of gold, too.

'We finally found him at an inn, but when I went through his things, it wasn't there,' Mauger muttered. 'That's when the other knight attacked us.'

'Lord de Burgh did not attack you,' Guy said, his voice sharp. 'Your master engaged him in combat and, while he was fighting, you sneaked up from behind and struck him down.'

Mauger shook his head, unprepared to admit to such a deed in front of his victim's brother. 'We didn't know who the knight was,' he protested. 'We thought he was after the mace. In fact, Gwayne was convinced he had taken it from the Hospitaller, so that's why we followed him later—all the way to Stokebrough Castle.'

Guy might have argued, but a barely visible gesture from Geoffrey stopped him and Mauger continued on in a more subdued manner. 'That's where the Saracen found us,' he said, shuddering as though none too eager to relive that part of his journey.

'Why did he capture you, instead of killing you as he had the others?' Geoffrey asked.

Mauger took a big gulp of ale and wiped his mouth with the back of his hand. 'He told me he would keep me alive as long as I was useful to him,' he said in a low voice. 'He'd found out we were following a de Burgh and wanted to know all about the family. But I didn't know much.'

No doubt he pretended to know more in order to retain his life, Emery thought. But she did not argue. There was only one part of his account that interested her.

'What of the Hospitaller?' she asked.

Mauger eyed her with some surprise, then shrugged. 'I don't know what became of him.'

'You asked at Clerkwell for him and then went to Montbard Manor in search of him,' Emery said.

'Yes, but he wasn't there and we soon had our hands full with you lot.'

Emery saw Geoffrey's nearly imperceptible reaction to his brother's company referred to as 'you lot' and she suspected Mauger would soon be turned out upon his ear. He should be thankful for it—he was lucky to have his life, as were any who had dealings with the Saracen.

But of those, what of Gerard? Did he still live?

Nicholas was aware of a heavy weight upon his arm. Had he fallen asleep with the limb tucked under him? He opened his eyes to find himself looking at the hangings above the bed at Ashyll. How long had he been here? He turned his head, still thick with sleep or sickness, and saw a spill of dark hair across his arm, like fine silk.

He smiled.

Although loath to disturb her, Nicholas lifted his free hand to touch the thick strands, rubbing them between his fingers, then stroking the length. He was alive and awake and Emery was by his side. And in that instant, he could ask for nothing more.

The last time he'd recovered from a bout of fever, he'd wondered whether it would have been better if he had succumbed, but now he clung to this moment and whatever moments lay ahead as far more precious than any gold. No matter what happened this time, he wasn't going to let the fever stop him from living.

He had Emery to thank for that change of heart. She had reminded him that while strength and power were fleeting, love endured, the love that bound him to his friends, to his family…and to her. Nicholas loosed a ragged sigh of pleasure and she nestled closer, as if burrowing against him.

Savouring the sensation, he envisioned waking with her beside him for the rest of his existence, however long or short that might be. Indeed, he would have been content to continue on as he was, but she stirred, lifting her head to regard him sleepily. She blinked in confusion before her eyes opened wide in surprise.

'Nicholas!'

The sound of his name on her lips was bliss. 'How long have I been asleep?' he asked, his throat dry, his speech a raspy whisper.

For a long moment, she simply stared at him, her beautiful face registering shock and joy and concern in quick succession. 'Twould be difficult for her to hide anything from him, Nicholas decided, for it was all there for him to see.

'Long enough to get well,' she said, her voice cracking. He reached out to squeeze her hand, to thank her for waiting for him, and

she squeezed it back, her eyes bright with un-
shed tears.

'You are going to be fine now,' she said.
'This time, you're going to be fine.'

Nicholas groaned as he lifted his arm, then
turned to step out of the way as the heavy
weapon swung close to his body, narrowly
missing his gut. The clang of metal against
metal was followed by a sharp knock and Nicholas froze, along with his brother. When another knock rang out, he handed over his sword
and returned to bed, pulling a thin blanket over
the braies he had donned.

Closing his eyes, Nicholas affected sleep as
Geoff put away the dulled blades and went to
the door, but 'twas only Guy bearing a trencher
of food ostensibly for the lord of the manor. Instead, the squire presented it to Nicholas, who
sat up and dug into the meal, far more hearty
than the bread and broth he'd been receiving.

Guy sat down on the trunk to study him with
a frown. 'You're pushing yourself too hard,'
he said.

'I need to be ready to travel,' Nicholas answered between bites.

'Emery's not going anywhere,' Geoff as-

sured him. 'Between Guy, Elene, the servants
and the children, someone is watching her at
all times.'

Nicholas did not bother to argue, for he knew
that despite Geoff's precautions, it was not a
question of *if*, but *when* Mistress Montbard
made her escape, an event he hoped to delay
by pretending to be still abed. Hopefully, she
would not leave him while he was recovering,
but he could not count on that much longer.

When he said nothing, Geoff shifted uneas-
ily. 'Elene does not approve of this deception.'

Nicholas eyed his brother askance. 'Elene is
a master of deception,' he said.

For a moment, Geoff looked like he might
take offence, but then he grinned and they
shared the look of de Burgh males who were
proud of their mates. These women were not
easily won, Nicholas well knew, and Emery was
proving to be just as difficult as his brothers'
brides, for she would never consider marriage
while things stood as they did.

However, Nicholas was determined, and the
sooner, the better, as far as he was concerned.
Although Geoff had high hopes for the new
treatment the Saracen had recommended, Nicholas wasn't so sure. He'd recovered before, only

to be felled again and again, so it was difficult to believe that this time would be any different. Yet he felt differently.

Instead of throwing away whatever time he had left, he would make a future for himself. He savoured every moment and each simple pleasure, revelling in the warmth of home and family, but he wanted more. He wanted his own. Unfortunately, the object of his affection was avoiding him and he suspected she had all intentions of fleeing.

Although this might have proved daunting to someone else, Nicholas had gone through too much to give up now. And he had a vague recollection of a certain conversation, which he had shared with his brother as soon as he was able.

'Emery's not stupid,' Guy protested. 'She's not going to go off by herself.'

'She's definitely not stupid,' Nicholas said, 'but she feels she has no choice and sometimes that makes people do stupid things.' And Nicholas knew that Emery had already done so once before.

'I am no expert in ecclesiastical law, but contracts such as her father's can be annulled and women returned to the world, if no vows were taken,' Geoff said. 'In fact, in some cases, the contracts stipulate that the women are not to be forced to take vows.'

Nicholas frowned. 'It sounds like her father's stipulated just the opposite, or at least that's what she was told,' he said. 'I think her uncle wished to be rid of his brother's heirs, and the commandery's priest, wanting the lands, did as he was bid.'

This time, 'twas Geoff who frowned. 'Although there have been cases of women arguing that they took their vows under coercion, rarely are they granted their freedom.'

Nicholas remained undaunted. 'Yet, with Harold dead, there's no reason for the Hospitallers to be plagued with a recalcitrant female of questionable commitment, is there?' he asked, lifting his brows.

Geoff nodded his agreement, a smile touching his lips. 'Especially when the Earl of Campion can take the case all the way to the Pope himself.'

Chapter Fifteen

Emery looked over her shoulder again. She
had barely left Ashyll, yet she felt as though
someone were following. Holding her breath,
she listened to the sound of the wind in the
grass and wondered whether she heard the familiar rustling of the Saracen. But she knew the
foreigner must be long gone, taking the mace
with him back to its resting place. She needn't
fear him or Gwayne or even Gwayne's squire,
who still resided at Ashyll.

There was none who would follow her, so
she had only to be wary of the usual villains
who would prey upon a young man riding
alone. But she intended to take to the main
roads, where she might fall in with a group of
pilgrims and make her way to Buckland.

Emery told herself that the difficult part was already over. Travelling alone was frightening, but 'twas the leaving that had taken all of her courage. She had even avoided visiting Nicholas, for fear she might give away her plans or break down and weep at their parting.

Only the vows she had taken kept her from remaining by his side, for when he woke from his fever, it was all too easy to imagine staying with him in whatever manner he would have her. But she cringed at such cowardice and self-ishness, for she would seize her happiness at what cost? She could not repay the kindness of the de Burghs by bringing trouble to their family and shame to their name.

Emery blinked against the sudden pressure behind her eyes and tried to focus. Had something stirred in the tall grass? She barely had time to put her hand to the hilt of her sword when a rider came bounding out of nowhere to halt in front of her. Surely she was not being harried by robbers this close to Ashyll?

Her heart pounding, Emery blinked again, uncertain, for this was no ordinary horse and no ordinary villain. Few who robbed travellers would possess a destrier and this one reminded her of Nicholas's mount. At that realisation,

Emery's attention flew to the man astride it, tall, broad-shouldered and dark-haired.

For a moment she thought Geoffrey de Burgh had gone out riding, only to stumble upon her, or perhaps this was another de Burgh brother arriving to see Nicholas. 'Twas only when the horse came closer that Emery began to doubt her own eyes. Yet there was no mistaking the rider's handsome face and the gaze that soon locked with hers.

'I hope you don't plan on engaging me in battle because I am in a weakened state,' Nicholas said, inclining his head towards her sword arm.

Emery looked stupidly down at the weapon that she did not remember drawing and then at the man she loved. Her rush of euphoria at the sight of him was tempered by dismay that he was upon a horse so soon after his near-fatal illness. 'You should be in bed!' she said.

'Indeed, I should.'

Something about the silken purr of his deep voice made Emery feel as weak as he claimed to be. Sucking in a sharp breath, she sheathed her sword and tried to gather her composure.

'You should not be here,' she said, fearful that he would fall from his mount, though he looked suspiciously fit. Her eyes narrowed. 'What are you doing?'

'I am fulfilling a vow I made to a Hospitaller,' he said. 'I swore to aid his sister, and, in turn, to help her find him.'

'But I must—' Emery began to protest, only to be cut off.

'We are bound for Clerkwell, where we will sort out your situation, and, hopefully, find news of your brother,' Nicholas said.

He spoke with such calm certainty that Emery found it difficult to resist. Hadn't she wished to follow him anywhere? She swallowed hard, for she knew she had no business spending any more time with this man or on the search for Gerard. But love for them both made her waver.

And Emery had the suspicion that should she refuse, she would find herself well and truly followed. Nicholas was no bully, but he was… unyielding and she did not care to test the de Burgh will. But if the famous name should carry any weight with the Hospitallers, then perhaps she could at least return to her place in the old gatehouse.

Ignoring the sharp stab of pain that came with thoughts of her future, Emery straightened and nodded, although she knew she was only delaying the inevitable parting once again. 'Twould be a bittersweet journey…

Nicholas smiled his approval, then whistled, and to Emery's surprise Guy rode up to join them. The squire flashed her a grin and Emery felt a rush of affection for him when he spoke.

'You didn't think to go on adventures without me, did you?' he asked.

Nicholas was becoming frustrated. Despite travelling together for several days and nights, he had rarely spent more than a moment alone with Emery. It had taken him a while to realise, with some surprise, that she didn't trust him. Or perhaps she didn't trust herself. Initially, he had been amused by her antics: avoiding his attempts to bathe, taking to her pallet instead of a bed and sticking so close to Guy that she seemed the squire's shadow.

And Guy, who had once thrown them together eagerly, now seemed determined to protect Emery's virtue with his life. Had Geoff given him that duty? Or Elene? The Saracen? Nicholas shook his head. He resorted to ploys in order to separate them, but Guy saw right through his efforts and seemed to take delight in thwarting them. Perhaps this was some kind of revenge for his earlier reaction to the squire's matchmaking?

But with illness and recovery behind him, Nicholas was becoming increasingly aware of how long it had been since he had held Emery in his arms, kissed her, touched her… Yet every time he reached for her, she slipped away, disarmingly skittish, which only made her more desirable.

The night before he had tossed and turned and thrown off the thin blanket, tormented by the knowledge that she was lying only a few feet away. And this morning, seeing the gentle sway of her hips as she hastened to follow Guy from the chamber, he fell back upon the bed with a groan.

But instead of rushing away, she turned towards him with an expression of concern. And though Nicholas had intended no ruse, he remained right where he was as she leaned over him, her breasts in their boy's clothing tantalisingly close. His breath left him then and he shut his eyes, revelling in her scent and the touch of her fingers against his temple. He could grow accustomed to such treatment…

'Do you feel warm?' she asked, her tone anxious.

'Yes,' Nicholas answered truthfully. And in an instant, he had rolled her beneath him, feeling the give of her softness against the bed. It had been too long. Far too long.

'My lord!'

'Nicholas,' he whispered, his face bare inches from her own.

'Nicholas,' she echoed, flushing deliciously. Bright blue eyes widened under lashes so thick and lush, how could he ever have thought her a boy? Yet there was something about her guise that made his body respond and he longed to remove the male garments to reveal the female beneath. Tugging at her cap, he tossed it aside, loosing her hair to spill forth like silk.

'You are not ill,' she said, though the accusation carried little bite.

'I ache,' he answered in all honesty. Then he dipped his head and brushed her cheek with his lips. Here. There. And there. He heard her soft intake of breath and found the pulse at her neck.

'Nicholas,' she warned.

He drew back, but she would not look at him. 'Just one kiss,' he said.

'I cannot,' she said. 'And you know why not.'

'Ah, but I might not be long for this world,' he said. 'Won't you give a dying man a boon?'

'Don't say such things,' Emery said, putting up a hand to stop his speech. But before she could scold him further, he took her finger into his mouth, sucking gently. Her gaze flew to his and the playful moment changed into something else, as fierce need, long denied, seized them both.

He lowered his mouth and took hers, open, wanting, taking, and she responded in kind, rising up to meet him. He felt her fingers entwine in his hair, tugging his head down to hers, and soon they were rolling around amongst the bedclothes, trying desperately to assuage the hunger that had been building between them.

Nicholas gasped as he pressed himself against the juncture of her thighs and he heard Emery's breathless cry, urging him on. He had only to pull down her men's braies to get inside her, to give them both what they wanted, and his heart thundered at the thought, his blood rushing at dizzying speed.

But 'twas not what they both wanted.

Emery had made her wishes clear, and in the heat of the moment Nicholas had forgotten

his oft-deliberated plan to remove each piece
of her clothing, slowly and surely. When they
came together, he would not have it be a hurried affair conducted in the bed of a strange
manor, with the chamber door standing open.

So he lifted his head and took a deep breath
and rolled away from that greatest of all temp-
tations. He waited while Emery's bright blue
eyes lost the dazed look of passion, only to
focus on him with no little alarm. And if he
saw a bit of regret in them, too, Nicholas soon
hoped to remedy that.

He sat up and helped her to her feet just as
Guy appeared in the doorway to frown at them.
'Are you coming, or do you intend to dally here
all the day?'

Emery's euphoria at being reunited with her
companions had faded once she realised that
things had changed between them. No longer
was Nicholas restrained by the scruples that
had kept him from standing too close, lingering too long or reaching out to touch her. Each
day, his gaze became more heated, as though
fuelled by the recovery of his strength, and
each night, Emery both feared and hoped that
he would join her.

For her own desire was growing, as well, until she hungered for him as she would food or drink. But she no longer trusted herself to stop at just one taste and her fears had proven well founded. Emery could not think about that morning on the bed without blaming herself, for she had succumbed immediately, without thought to the consequences.

Even now, she wondered what would have happened. And a part of her longed to take that experience with her wherever she went, to cherish in the bleak years ahead. But she was glad she did not have anything worse upon her conscience and knew the Hospitallers would not be pleased if she returned with child, no matter who the father.

Emery had been right about one thing: the trip was bittersweet, for the three of them had fallen into the same habits as before. Although this journey was not fraught with tension over her burden and fear of murderous pursuers, each day her heart grew heavier as they drew closer to their destination. Her eventual parting loomed before her like the coming of night. And, though Nicholas seemed undaunted by the prospect, Emery was hard pressed to keep her composure by the time they reached Clerkwell.

* * *

When they approached the entrance, she tried to hang back, for she did not look forward to a confrontation with Udo, the commandery's priest, who had little love for her. She suspected he did not like to be reminded of his perfidy and that, rather than the prospect of a mixed house, was behind his attempts to send her away.

Yet when the doors swung open, 'twas not Udo, but a brother she did not recognise who welcomed them warmly—far more warmly than any reception she had ever received there. In fact, he appeared to know they were coming, greeting Nicholas by his title and smiling upon Emery as though she were a beloved member of his flock, not an errant one soon to be banished—or worse.

He introduced himself as Grimbald, the new head of the commandery, which caused Emery even more confusion. 'What happened to Udo?' she asked.

'He was recalled by his superiors and I am delighted to take his place here at Clerkwell amongst the good brethren. 'Tis a lovely place, as you well know.'

Emery nodded, numbly. Udo had been replaced?

'I believe there is something here you would like to see,' he said, his face crinkling with a gentle smile as he led the three of them to one of the small sleeping chambers. Emery tried to suppress the suspicion that once inside, she would be locked in there for ever. But still she trailed behind until he flung the door open to reveal someone sitting up in the narrow bed.

'Gerard!' Emery rushed forwards, heedless of the others, and threw herself into her brother's arms. He was thinner than when she had last seen him and more pale, and she leaned back to eye him with concern.

'Are you ill?'

He shook his head. 'I am well now, Em,' he said with a smile. 'And I understand you are, too.' He sent a knowing look over her shoulder and she began to suspect that Nicholas had guessed her brother was here. Emery didn't know whether to be indignant or angry at being kept in the dark, but she was so relieved to see Gerard alive and well that she hugged him again.

When she introduced her companions, they all gathered round to hear her brother's tale, the last piece of the puzzle that had consumed them for so long. He began with his trip home to England, though he could not recall much of his time aboard ship, having been unwell. Indeed, he was uncertain what had transpired, especially when he discovered the mace in his possession.

Unwilling to carry such a valuable object in his condition, he sent it on to Emery for safe-keeping, at least until he could discover more about it and recover his strength. After his squire left to deliver the parcel, Gerard made his way more slowly, stopping frequently to rest. Finally, in need of decent food and a bed, he sought shelter at the inn, where he was attacked by Gwayne.

His expression turned bleak and he spoke haltingly. 'Upon fleeing the Templar, I stumbled across my squire, dead, with something from the Holy Land left upon his body as though as a token.' Panicking, Gerard hid the youth's body under some brush, but kept the card as he hurried onwards, barely making it to the gatehouse before collapsing.

When he woke up in Emery's bed, Gerard could not remember anything except the importance of finding the mace, though he did not know whether it had even been delivered. And he didn't know who to trust, having been assaulted by a Templar knight, who claimed a deadly Saracen was hunting for him, as well.

'I'm afraid it all got tangled up together in my mind until I suspected everyone, even members of my order and my own uncle,' he said, ruefully.

Emery exchanged a glance with Nicholas, acknowledging Gerard was probably right in his suspicions of Harold. But that discussion could come later.

'I remember leaving Montbard, despairing of ever finding the thing again, and, to be honest, by that point, it all seemed like a dream. Or a nightmare,' Gerard said. He ended up collapsing in one of the once-disputed fields, where he was found by his brethren. Taken to Clerkwell, he finally received the care he needed.

'When I regained my senses, I couldn't recall much of what had happened, but I was told that you had disappeared,' Gerard said, turning to Emery. 'I was frantic, especially since I was responsible for putting you in danger. And when they told me Harold had been murdered…' He trailed off, unable to go on.

''Twas only when I arrived with news that his sister was safe that he began his full recovery, at last.'

Emery glanced up in surprise to see it was
Grimbald who had spoken. He was standing in
the doorway, eyeing them benignly.

'But how did you know?' Emery asked.

'The Earl of Campion's man spoke to my
superior and I was charged with passing along
the good tidings. I also have some news for you
that I suspect will prove welcome,' he said, ad-
dressing Emery.

'As the earl's emissary pointed out, there was
some confusion over your father's wishes and
your status as donat is restored, leaving you
free of any commitment to the order. In fact, I
am authorised to restore your property, as well,
should you care to receive it.'

Stunned, Emery turned to her brother, who
shook his head. 'I am content to serve the Hospitallers in any way I can, though my leg may
prevent any further fighting. I have no need
of the manor house, but you are welcome to
it, Emery.'

Blinking at the astonishing turn of events,
Emery looked to Nicholas, who was smiling
down at her. When his gaze met hers, she knew
the answer. 'I doubt I will have need of it,' she
said, her voice cracking with emotion.

'Well, I will let you think upon the matter,'

Grimbald said. 'And if I can be of any service to you, please let me know.'

'There is one more thing,' Nicholas said, his gaze still locked with Emery's.

'Certainly, my lord.'

'Can you marry us?'

Emery stood at Nicholas's side, accepting the well wishes of his family even as she tried to remember exactly who was who. But with six siblings and their wives and children to identify, Emery knew it would take some time. And even though Nicholas still worried that his fever would return, Emery was convinced it would not, which gave her all the time in the world.

Out of the corner of her eye, she caught sight of Guy talking earnestly to the daughter of the steward. No doubt he was making much of his adventures, but he had been so happy to return that he had kissed the ground, swearing never to leave again. And who could blame him?

Emery immediately had fallen in love with her new home, despite being a bit awestruck by its splendour and beauty. Embraced by Nicholas's family as one of their own, she did not think her happiness could grow any bigger. Yet when she glanced at her new little nieces and nephews, she thought perhaps there was one thing that might accomplish that feat.

And considering that her husband insisted on making the most of every moment, there had been more than enough opportunities for her to get with child. She put a hand over her belly, wondering how soon she might know, only to find the earl's gaze upon her. Was he really prescient? He smiled gently before turning away, as if to survey the great hall, teaming with life and love.

The Earl of Campion was, indeed, surveying the throng, his heart as full as the castle. Fawke was old enough that he was grateful whenever his children and grandchildren could gather together. And he was thankful that the last of his sons was settled. He had been worried when they'd received no word of Nicholas for so long, but now he had faith that all would be well.

The youngest de Burgh embodied a bit of all of his siblings: Dunstan's leadership, Simon's battle skills, Geoffrey's scholarship, Stephen's easy charm, Robin's sense of humour and Reynold's tenacity, along with his own sharp insight.

But each were admirable in their own way.

A few had more difficult challenges than the others, Stephen with his drinking and Reynold with his bad leg, and all were stubborn and had a tendency towards arrogance. Yet they had managed to find wives who made them better men, just as Fawke had done. And he sent up a prayer of thanks not only for Joy, who stood beside him now, but to the two women who had preceded her in his life.

Look what you have wrought, he thought silently, knowing that they would be just as proud as he of the legacy they had left behind. And it would continue long after he had gone, living on in all those who bore the name de Burgh.

* * * * *

A sneaky peek at next month...

HISTORICAL

IGNITE YOUR IMAGINATION, STEP INTO THE PAST...

My wish list for next month's titles...

In stores from 1st March 2013:

❏ The Accidental Prince — Michelle Willingham

❏ The Rake to Ruin Her — Julia Justiss

❏ The Outrageous Belle Marchmain — Lucy Ashford

❏ Taken by the Border Rebel — Blythe Gifford

❏ Unmasking Miss Lacey — Isabelle Goddard

❏ Inheriting a Bride — Lauri Robinson

Available at WHSmith, Tesco, Asda, Eason, Amazon and Apple

Just can't wait?

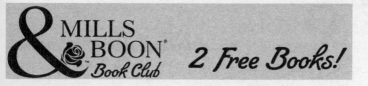

MILLS & BOON® Book Club   *2 Free Books!*

Get your free books now at
www.millsandboon.co.uk/freebookoffer

Or fill in the form below and post it back to us

THE MILLS & BOON® BOOK CLUB™—HERE'S HOW IT WORKS: Accepting your free books places you under no obligation to buy anything. You may keep the books and return the despatch note marked 'Cancel'. If we do not hear from you, about a month later we'll send you 4 brand-new stories from the Historical series priced at £4.49* each. There is no extra charge for post and packaging. You may cancel at any time, otherwise we will send you 4 stories a month which you may purchase or return to us—the choice is yours. *Terms and prices subject to change without notice. Offer valid in UK only. Applicants must be 18 or over. Offer expires 31st July 2013. **For full terms and conditions, please go to www.millsandboon.co.uk/freebookoffer**

Mrs/Miss/Ms/Mr (please circle)
_____

First Name
_____

Surname
_____

Address
_____

_____

Postcode
_____

E-mail
_____

Send this completed page to: Mills & Boon Book Club, Free Book Offer, FREEPOST NAT 10298, Richmond, Surrey, TW9 1BR

Find out more at
www.millsandboon.co.uk/freebookoffer

Visit us Online

0113/H3XEb